2/17/09

It All Started with a Dog

Leigh Somerville McMillan

For Claire,
Thanks for going
to such lengths to
get a copy of this book,
Hope you'll think it very
worth the trouble!

iUniverse, Inc.
New York   Bloomington

It All Started with a Dog

iUniverse books may be ordered through booksellers or by contacting:

iUniverse
1663 Liberty Drive
Bloomington, IN 47403
www.iuniverse.com
1-800-Authors (1-800-288-4677)

ISBN: 978-0-595-53288-9 (pbk)
ISBN: 978-0-595-63343-2 (ebk)

Printed in the United States of America

This book is dedicated to my mother.

Years later, Rachel remembered the scene. The body of a baby bird lay at the base of a tall tree where a flock of birds sat in the branches, screaming at the cat below. Finally, all but one bird left, and Rachel listened to the lone mother bird scream until she, too, flew away. And there was silence.

Chapter 1

Ralph was the dirtiest, skinniest, most morose looking creature Rachel had ever seen – and being a divorce lawyer, she had seen her share of rejects.

The dog found her one evening as she walked home from her office in Georgetown. Deadlines loomed and she dictated answers to interrogatories until almost eight o'clock. After 25 questions and answers and a take-out Chinese dinner, she turned off the lights and locked the door behind her.

As Rachel stood on the corner of M and 33rd Streets to hail a cab, watching the tourists watching each other, she heard a whining in the alley behind her.

She set her briefcase down on the sidewalk and stooped to the dog's level, ignoring the voice in the back of her head that told her he might bite, might have fleas, might have rabies . . . or worse.

Hesitant at first, Ralph seemed to sense the strange woman was not to be feared and slowly inched his way out of the black toward where she crouched.

Rachel wasn't a dog person, but something about Ralph touched something about Rachel Springer.

Convincing the cab driver to allow him in the backseat was a different story. Nothing about the cabbie was touched, but a $20 tip persuaded him that Ralph could make the short ride to Rachel's house on O Street.

The veterinarian Rachel found the next day hadn't held out much hope for Ralph, diagnosing severe malnourishment, assorted worms, advanced mange and a couple of other medical conditions which he and his owner soon forgot as his health improved.

1

Five years later, Ralph is a poster dog for the healing power of love. He sports a shining thick coat of black fur, clear eyes and perky tail that at one time looked like it was permanently stuck between his legs.

Sometimes Rachel takes him to work, where he sits on a window seat with a view of 32nd Street. Passersby who know him look up to see if his familiar silhouette frames the upstairs window of Springer & Associates.

Rachel doesn't have any associates. Once, years ago, right after she left the large law firm where she began her career, she agreed to associate herself with another attorney, but that didn't last long. Some folks play best alone.

Today, she and Georgia Payne make a great team.

Georgia is about five years younger than her boss. She could have easily earned as many degrees as Rachel, but didn't. Instead, she has focused on her family. Married for 25 years to the same man, she has two grown sons and four grandsons. She has worked for Rachel as long as the office has been open, running the show in more ways than one.

People with problems love her, and it is not unusual for Rachel to walk up to Georgia's desk and find a bouquet of fresh flowers from an appreciative client. Georgia keeps a box of tissues near her in-box and a willing ear ready to hear the parts of the story they are reluctant to share with Rachel at $300 an hour. Georgia always makes time, even as her work pile grows higher and higher.

The outer office is decorated to create a relaxed mood with lots of African violets in the window sill, Good Housekeeping on the coffee table, rocking chairs and an overstuffed sofa covered with a faded flowered slipcover. Hooked rugs complete the grandmother's parlor décor.

Behind the closed door that separates the reception area from Rachel's office is another world.

Once clients have filled out the intake form, Georgia chats them up with a cup of coffee and one of her homemade chocolate chip cookies, and then they're ready to get down to business on the other side of the door.

Rachel's office is streamlined for business. The top of her huge antique mahogany desk is uncluttered, except for the bare necessities. Clients see a simple black phone – no bells and whistles – a small green banker's lamp and a blank yellow legal pad with two sharp pencils lying ready beside it.

Rachel Springer, 62, sits tiny behind the desk, in front of a towering backdrop of legal reference books. Her diplomas from the University of Virginia and the Georgetown Law School are framed modestly in a corner.

The heavy braid that hangs halfway down her back is steel-wool gray and tied at its coiled end with baling twine – two orange ceramic beads secured at each tip. Rachel found the beads at the flea market outside Santa Fe on the first trip she made to New Mexico and wears them as a reminder of the "returning home" feeling she experienced out west.

Her eyes are heavily lashed and almost lilac. Strangers sometimes stop her in the street to ask if she wears tinted contact lenses. She's known they are her best feature for years – perhaps even when she was a baby and the doctor in the delivery room remarked that he had never seen a child with eyes the color of spring.

Now, as her other physical attributes begin to sag, begin to mottle, begin to dimple and crinkle, the clear pools still sparkle and, even edged in wrinkles and cornered by crows feet, they often attract the kindness of strangers. Rachel figures everything else can be covered.

She's not one to go in for cosmetic surgery – face lifts, botox, tummy tucks – or spend a lot of time exercising to beat her body into submission. She eats right without being obsessive but admits to a chocolate craving. Rachel especially loves Almond Joy bars.

And Ralph.

*   *   *

Rachel lives on O Street in the Dupont Circle neighborhood in a three-story brownstone within walking distance of the Dupont Circle metro station.

She found the house despite herself. Actually, a friend found it for her.

While Rachel meditated one day, the phone rang. Usually, she let it ring, aware of the sound, letting it jangle on the outer edge of her consciousness, not judging whether she should answer or not, just letting it be and hoping whoever was calling would leave a message.

This time, she decided she had sat still long enough and got up from her zafu cushion and caught the phone on its last ring before it rolled over to the answering service.

Her friend Susan was on the other end of the line. In her usual fashion, she launched into the purpose of her call with no preliminary chitchat.

"Rachel, I've found your house," Susan said.

Rachel sat down in the rocker she kept beside the kitchen phone and took a deep breath, preparing herself for yet another one of her friend's Rachel-improvement schemes.

After a few seconds of silence, Susan said, "Rachel, are you there?"

"Yes, I'm here."

"Well, why didn't you say something? I've found your house."

"I'm not looking for a house."

"I know, but this is definitely the house you *should* be looking for, honey, and it's right across the street from *me*. Please promise me you'll come look at it."

"You mean the Mason house?"

"Yes. They've been transferred to the west coast and they want to sell it in a hurry. You'd get it for a song, honey – less than a song, in fact."

Susan spoke in the honeyed tones of the deep South, something that had irritated Rachel when they first met at the University of Virginia 40 years ago. But, over the years, she had learned that underneath the sickening sweetness that came out of Susan's mouth was a true green pea goodness.

Rachel lived comfortably across Key Bridge in Crystal City in a small condominium. On a clear day, she easily made the walk to work in Georgetown.

Susan insisted she needed more space for a garden, maybe a pet, more room to entertain – all things Rachel wasn't sure she wanted. She knew she didn't want the hassle of moving. The thought of packing her hundreds of books alone gave her a headache.

"Isn't that house three stories?" Rachel asked.

"Well, yes."

"What do I need all that room for, Susan?"

"Maybe you could rent out some of the rooms, honey. In fact – yes, I'm sure of it – there's a tiny little basement apartment in the back. The Masons used it to sleep overnight guests, but you could fix it up and use it as a rental unit. Get some nice young man in there who knows how to fix things so when . . ."

"Susan, I don't want to move."

"Just look at it, honey. Just promise me you'll look at it."

And so Rachel allowed Susan to make an appointment for her to see the house a week later – finally giving in to her friend's constant nagging – and made an offer on the house for the asking price within an hour of returning home.

The cherub fountain in the back courtyard had charmed her right out of Crystal City.

The courtyard was enclosed by a six-foot tall brick wall and was laid with cobblestones. She first saw it in the spring when the azaleas bloomed in several shades of pink under the towering oak trees. Daffodils peeked out from several corners.

But the focal point was the fountain. The sound of water dropping from the cherub's cupped hands reminded Rachel of trips to her grandmother's house in Fredricksburg, Virginia, where the same cherub held court in the backyard near the boxwood bushes.

Rachel toured the house – the English basement apartment the Realtor assured her she could easily rent for $1,000 month; the living room to the left of the entrance foyer on the main floor, library on the right – both with working fireplaces and the eat-in kitchen and dining room across the back of the house, looking out onto a small wooden deck and the courtyard.

The second floor held the master bedroom and bath – also overlooking the courtyard – two guestrooms and the bath they shared.

The third floor featured one big room – a garret with floor-to-ceiling windows perfect for the artist who originally built the house.

Rachel left it empty of furniture and used it for a meditation room – one lone cushion sat in the middle of the floor. She loves to sit there in the spotlight of a full moon and practice the stillness she is convinced helps her practice the law that is her livelihood.

She started her Buddhist meditation practice in her 20's and found that the daily ritual not only created a stillness in the hectic life inside her head, but an acceptance of what went on outside it.

Rachel also likes to piece together quilts. What thrills her most is finding the fabrics. Scavenging in antique shops and yard sales – even traveling some distance out into the countryside to an estate sale advertised in *The Washington Post*. It's all an adventure and once she gets the scraps of material home, she has great fun imagining what they were used for and by whom.

Rachel is a creative cook and doesn't mind eating alone. Her mother died when she was eight years old, leaving her father to parent her and her little brother, Edward.

John Springer hired a woman to come in to help with the cleaning and to do the laundry once a week, but he figured he and Rachel could manage to scrape together a meal.

Even at eight, Rachel's cooking was imaginative – much to her little brother's horror. Not many six-year-old boys take a liking to mint showing up in unlikely places. But Edward's complaints didn't discourage Rachel, and her father just smiled at her culinary surprises.

She never follows a recipe, so sometimes her concoctions turn out well, and sometimes they don't. She loves to entertain, and her friends always know they're in for a treat when they're invited to join in one of her last minute dinner parties.

The dining room table only seats six, but it's not unusual for her to spread her guests throughout the house if she starts out fixing a pot of soup and ends up with enough for an army.

When Rachel moved into the house across the street, Susan figured she would benefit from her friend's love of cooking. Not only was the food tasty and pretty to look at – often garnished with juicy oranges and lemons, fresh green parsley or purple violets in bloom in her garden – but Rachel served her meals on a collection of mismatched china and crystal she had collected in her years of traveling.

No cup matched its saucer. No plate was the same size or shape as the one next to it. The only thing on the table that was a complete set was the monogrammed sterling silver she inherited from her maternal grandmother – a 24-serving set of heavy and very ornate Georgian flatware that was probably worth as much as the house.

When the family lost all its money in the Depression, they managed to hang on to the silver, and Rachel loves to polish it and use it when she entertains.

She plays a guitar – badly, but with great gusto. Her instrument is an old beat-up acoustic guitar given to her by a high school sweetheart when she went away to college.

She learned to play "Stewball was a Racehorse" over and over and drove her college roommate crazy. Her repertoire doesn't include too many more tunes 40 years later, but she loves to take the guitar out into her back courtyard in the late evenings and play.

The neighbors never complain.

Sometimes, she remembers Joe, the boy who gave it to her and wonders where he is as she sits near Dupont Circle strumming "Stewball."

They had kissed many times in the back seat of Joe's father's Pontiac, but not much more than a kiss. Not with Joe or any of the boys who followed him into her arms.

And there had been many men who had been attracted to Rachel over the years. She enjoyed sharing a movie in high school and college, and she loved to dance, but that was about it.

As her friends began to announce their engagements, got married, had babies, she thought she might follow that path, but after she hit 30 and had never had a serious romance, she began to believe that living alone would be her lot in life.

She never felt lonely – a state of being she was convinced drove many of her friends into unhappy marriages.

She certainly saw plenty of disastrous relationships walk through her office doors during her law career.

And perhaps what influenced her the most to remain single was the fact that her father had been one of the happiest people she had ever known, and he lived alone until the day he died of a heart attack at 75 years old.

Rachel knew he missed her mother, but she also saw him accept her death. After Agnes Springer fell from a horse and broke her neck, he found happiness alone, surrounded by animals, his children and a few friends.

Rachel learned by his example.

*   *   *

Rachel had absolutely no intention of offering her basement apartment for rent. Occasionally, she used it for out-of-town guests, and she certainly didn't need the income it might generate. Having the extra space was a luxury she could afford.

When Susan called to suggest that she rent it to a man who needed a temporary home while he was in town working as a consultant, her immediate reaction was to say "no."

But in her typical way, Susan refused to give up.

"Just meet him, honey. Jim and I had him over for dinner last night, and he's very charming. He practically drooled all over himself when he saw your house over there across the street. Ralph was peeping out your front window, and that did the trick.

"He loves dogs," was her parting shot.

"But I don't want a tenant," Rachel insisted.

"Just meet him. He's leaving to go back to New York tomorrow. I'll bring him over tomorrow night after supper."

"But Susan, I don't . . ." was all Rachel was able to get out before Susan hung up the phone.

The next evening around 7:30 Rachel was on her way out the back door to water her impatiens plants when the doorbell rang. She wiped her hands on her apron and walked toward the front of the house, wondering who could be coming to see her unannounced at that hour. Ralph hadn't barked, so it must be someone he knows, she thought.

It was only when she opened the door that she remembered the phone call from Susan the day before.

"Honey, this is John Turner, the friend of Jim's I told you about," Susan chirped as she grabbed the embarrassed-looking man by the arm and almost pushed him through the door at Rachel.

"I hope we're not interrupting your dinner, Mrs. Springer," the man said. "It's so nice of you to offer to show me your apartment."

"Well, I haven't," Rachel was tempted to say when Susan interrupted her with, "Oh, I see you have your gardening gloves on. Rachel has the most lovely courtyard in the back, John. John is an expert gardener, himself, Rachel. He's created the most lovely rooftop deck at his apartment in the Village. I've seen the pictures.'

And with that, Susan pushed on through the foyer, dragging Rachel and John behind her like a magnet, Rachel all the while thinking that if Susan hadn't pushed her, she wouldn't be in this house. It wouldn't hurt to show the poor soul the apartment. He might not even like it.

And Ralph was wagging his tail and looking at the man adoringly.

Tall – at least six feet – lanky – almost skinny – slightly stoop-shouldered – a full head of curly slightly fading red hair – freckles and green eyes with a devilish twinkle that made him seem younger than the rest of his body hinted he might be.

"Would you like a cup of tea before we go downstairs," Rachel softened.

"Actually, I'm very anxious to see the apartment," John said. "I lived in this neighborhood many years ago, and I'd love to call it home again – even for a short time."

"Exactly how long will you be needing the place?"

"At least six months – maybe longer."

Well, that shouldn't be too bad, Rachel thought. She could share the house for six months – maybe longer – without a problem. It wasn't a long-term commitment. Just a short arrangement to help this man out.

So they went around to the side of the house, and Rachel dug around behind some ceramic pots and found the key to the basement door.

"You'll have to forgive the smell. It hasn't been used in at least six months – since my brother and his family came from Arkansas. I'm sure it's terribly musty."

She switched on the overhead light to reveal a small living room and kitchen area with exposed brick walls and a long window at street level.

"The bedroom is through the kitchen," she said.

"It's perfect," John beamed. "Reminds me of the place I rented in Adams Morgan the summer after my senior year in college. How much do you want for it?"

"A thousand dollars a month, all utilities included," Susan announced without missing a beat.

John looked at Rachel and smiled. "Is that right?"

"I guess so," Rachel laughed. "Susan's the boss."

The three walked around to the back so John could admire the impatiens and say good-bye to Ralph, who was whining because he had been left behind.

"When do you want to move in?"

"Next week, if you don't mind. I need to go home to get a few more things, but when I get back to D.C., I'd like to think I'll be coming home rather than to the Jefferson Hotel."

"I'll draw up a simple lease and send it by Susan to your office tomorrow."

Rachel and John shook hands, and she noticed the twinkle was even brighter as he smiled down at her.

"Good night, Mrs. Springer, and thank you for sharing this with me. It's perfect."

"You're quite welcome, but it's 'Ms.' not 'Mrs.' And you can call me Rachel."

Chapter 2

"What is *this*?" Georgia asked Rachel the next morning, dropping a freshly typed one-page lease on her boss's desk.

"A lease," Rachel said, hiding behind the arts section of *The Washington Post*.

"I can see it's a lease. I just spent the last 10 minutes typing it, but who is John Turner, and why are you renting your apartment to him? You've lived in that house for the past five years, and you've never so much as mentioned wanting to have a tenant, much less moving one in for six months."

"Well, Susan thought it was a good idea."

"Who is John Turner?" Georgia demanded as she reached across the desk and lowered the *Post* so she could see Rachel's eyes.

"I don't really know."

Georgia stood in silence, letting that bit of information sink in.

"You mean to tell me you've rented an apartment *in your house* to a man you don't know? I don't believe you."

"Well, I know he's an engineering consultant working with Susan's husband on a big hospital project. I know he lives in New York in the East Village and that he has a rooftop garden. And Ralph likes him."

"Oh, great. Ralph likes him. No need to check references then. The dog likes him. That's enough for me. ARE YOU OUT OF YOUR MIND? Surely, you are going to do a background check on this man before you give him a key to your house. Just because he's fit to work with Jim Sawyer's company on a mega-million dollar construction project doesn't mean you want to live with him. Just because . . ."

Rachel interrupted Georgia in mid-sentence with "Now, wait a minute. Who said anything about living with him? That apartment does not in any way connect with my home. We've got separate doors with separate keys, and, unless he's planning to come through the heat ducts, there's no way he can get into my upstairs any easier than Mr. Moser next door. What's the problem?"

"Well, this is just so sudden, Rachel – so not like you. You *love* living alone."

"I am still going to be living alone, Georgia. Relax. Don't worry. All is well."

"It's my job to worry," Georgia said as she walked back to her desk. She stopped and turned around. "What does he look like?"

"Why, Georgia, what an interesting question. This has nothing to do with what John Turner looks like. This man needs a place to live for six months. I've got an empty apartment. Period."

"And Ralph likes him, right?"

"And Ralph likes him."

Georgia seemed to be satisfied – or at least somewhat soothed – and was on her way back to her desk when Rachel poked her head around the door.

"He has curly red hair and freckles."

Georgia looked up and smiled.

"Freckles?"

"Sort of faded freckles."

"How nice. Certainly no need for a background check on a man with freckles, is there?"

"Absolutely none."

*   *   *

Rachel woke around two o'clock the next morning with second thoughts. Bug-eyed, she climbed the stairs to her third floor and took her seat on the meditation cushion. No full moon lit the room, but Mr. Moser's back spotlight cast a dim glow across the wood floor at her feet.

Ralph had followed her upstairs.

"Ralph, what have we done?" she asked the dog. He nudged her with his black nose and then left her side to curl up near the windows, as if to say, "Not 'we' – 'you'."

Doubts began to flood her mind as she sat cross-legged, eyes closed, hands grounding her knees. As each doubt surfaced, she acknowledged it and let it go – or tried to.

Suppose he likes music and plays his stereo too loud, late at night. Or worse yet, suppose he plays a trumpet loudly, late at night.

Let it go.

Suppose he smokes, and I can smell his cigarettes. Worse yet, cigars. Coming through the vents. I should have put a clause in the lease about no smoking.

Let it go.

Suppose he wants to entertain. Suppose he wants to have parties in the back courtyard. Suppose he gets a pet, and the pet fights with Ralph.

Let it go. Let it go.

Suppose he meets a woman and moves her in, and I can hear them . . .

Rachel couldn't let it go.

She got up and moved down two flights of stairs to the kitchen to brew herself some jasmine tea. Something warm in her grandmother's Blue Willow china teacup never failed to relax her – to reassure her that, in fact, all was well.

As she took the first sip, the phone rang, startling her so that she spilled hot tea on her nightgown.

"Hello," she said, glancing at the clock on the kitchen wall. Three o'clock. Who could be calling?

"Honey, what are you doing over there?"

"Susan, what are you doing up?"

"Hot flashes. Saw your lights on and just wanted to check to make sure you're okay. You know how I worry about you living alone."

"Well, it looks like you've taken care of that."

"Yes, isn't it just the most wonderful turn of events," Susan bubbled. "This time next week, John will be right downstairs, and you can just go 'yoo-hoo,' and he'll come right up those stairs and . . . well, who knows."

"I don't know, Susan. That's why I'm up at three o'clock in the morning instead of sleeping. I don't know if this is such a good idea after all. Georgia is worried."

"Oh, Georgia is a worry wart. Jim says John is a great guy – quite considerate – a real sweetheart. You'll enjoy him."

"Does he smoke?"

"No."

"Does he play a trumpet?"

"What kind of question is that, 'Does he play the trumpet?' My goodness, honey, you worry too much. Go back to sleep."

"I guess I could buy earplugs."

"Yes, you could buy earplugs. Better yet, maybe you could learn to like the trumpet," Susan said and hung up.

*   *   *

The next day, Rachel called a cleaning service to make arrangements to have the apartment cleaned. After all, she reasoned, it hadn't had a good going over since she moved into the house. Who knows what her nephews might have dropped down in the sofa cushions, she thought to herself.

Then she called the cable company to have cable hooked up.

"You sure are going to a lot of trouble for this man," Georgia said when she hung up the phone after her conversation with the exterminator.

"Well, I want him to be comfortable. After all, I am charging him $1,000 a month, and that's a lot of money to pay and not be able to watch more than a couple of local television stations."

"Why don't you just invite him upstairs to watch television with you? That, after all, would be the neighborly thing to do."

Rachel ignored Georgia and pretended to be reading a file. Actually, she was wondering if perhaps she *had* gone overboard. Too late now. The only thing left to do was wait for move-in day.

*   *   *

John Turner retired from his full-time job working for an engineering firm in New York City a couple of years ago and traveled across country for three months.

He enjoyed traveling alone, stopping whenever he wanted to check out a junk shop, eat in an appetizing looking roadside cafe or take some pictures of something he didn't want to forget. He traveled a lot in his job, but deadlines never allowed him the luxury of stopping as much as he would like.

His three-month hiatus had been like sitting down to a banana split with all the toppings. He visited some friends in several cities along his route, but more often, he preferred to check into a motel where he didn't feel obligated to anyone.

The older he got, John realized more and more how much of a loner he was.

After his wife died five years ago, his son and daughter encouraged him to date, and, after about a year, he had. In fact, there had been one rather serious involvement with a woman in his office, but they both agreed that they made better friends than lovers.

About a year ago, he took up ballroom dancing and enjoyed the lessons but didn't meet anyone he wanted to see off the dance floor.

Several of his partners' wives tried to fix him up with single women of "appropriate" ages, but they never held his interest past one or two dates.

It wasn't that the women couldn't compete with his wife. Most marriages would have ended in divorce if they suffered the problems his had.

Annie was an alcoholic when he met her in college. John grew up in an alcoholic family and fell right into the familiar patterns without recognizing them.

Her drinking was so different from what had been the routine with his parents. They mixed their five o'clock martinis every night, fought and passed out. Annie was a quiet, closet wino.

Toward the end of their marriage, most nights when John came home from the office – later and later as the years passed, and he and Annie grew farther apart – she was "asleep" on the sofa with the television blaring.

Because Annie wasn't a violent drunk, John didn't recognize the warning signs until it was too late, but as the hangovers took longer to recover from and the occasional blackouts resulted in lost car keys – and once the car itself – John began to make a connection between his childhood home and the one in which he raised his own children.

It wasn't until their children were grown and had their own families that Annie hit her bottom.

A trip to the doctor to check on abdominal pain and bloating revealed cirrhosis of the liver – too late. Annie died within a few months of the diagnosis.

Growing up with alcoholic parents equipped John with well-used tools of detachment. The grieving period after Annie's death was short. In fact, he was back at work the day after the funeral. Her closets were emptied within a week and, by all appearances, John Turner was going on with his life.

There was so little of Annie's spirit left by the time she died, that there was little of her to miss. He got in the habit of leaving the television on when he went to work so that when he came home, not much had changed. The body wasn't on the sofa, but in some ways coming home to nobody was easier than coming home to an unconscious wife.

The past five years as a bachelor had been the happiest years of John Turner's life.

*   *   *

John looked forward to moving into Rachel Springer's apartment.

Washington, D.C. had always intrigued him. In fact, as a child he visited it several times with his family and school groups. He loved the

Natural Science Museum with its huge mastodon, the Wright Brothers airplane and the space flight exhibits.

Knowing that he would have six months to revisit the exhibits on his own –without an adult rushing him through the museum and on to another attraction – made it easier for him to pack.

Trying to decide what to take for six months was a challenge, and he was glad he had something to look forward to helping him over the hurdle.

The new project was somewhat intimidating – not the engineering aspect as much as working with people he didn't know. Launching into a career as a consultant and working in a group of new faces every few months was still uncomfortably difficult for him after working in the same office for 20 years.

Leaving New York, where he had a couple of good friends, and moving to a city where he had none wasn't an idea he relished.

But probably what John dreaded most was the idea of not seeing Ben, his five-year-old grandson, the only child of his only son, William.

John never felt the intensity of his love for Ben with anyone else. It took him some time after the child's birth to drop the barrier he had always built up with other people all his life. Not being one to go nuts over babies, he didn't react much at all to his grandson the first two or three years of the boy's life. He sent the obligatory birthday and Christmas gifts and always asked William how Ben was doing when they spoke.

William and his wife Lucille lived in Hoboken, New Jersey, and John saw them about once a month for those first few years after Ben's birth, but as his relationship with Ben began to deepen, he had doubled his efforts to see the boy.

It occurred to him that he felt a love for Ben he never experienced with his own son. He wondered if William realized it.

Once when Ben spent the night with his grandfather so his parents could enjoy an evening in the city, John woke up to find a little figure standing beside his bed.

"Granddaddy, I'm sad," Ben whispered in the dark.

Forcing himself awake, John said, "What's wrong, Ben?"

"I'm sad," Ben repeated, as if the simple statement needed no further explanation.

Rain pattered outside the windows of John's eighteenth floor apartment. On the street below, cabs still honked at two a.m. The lights of the city illuminated the big brown eyes peering at him through the dark.

"Well, Ben, why don't you just jump under the covers with me and see if that helps."

Suddenly, Ben's face lit up and he burrowed in beside his grandfather. Before John could get himself comfortable again, the breathing next to him settled into the sound of sleep.

John lay, watching the rise and fall of the little chest and marveled at how much Ben looked like William. He couldn't remember ever sleeping with his own son and spent the rest of the night feeling grateful that he had been given a second chance.

He would miss Ben – miss building towers with Legos, miss ice cream cones, walks in Central Park, bus rides just for the heck of it.

Missing Ben would be the biggest down-side of the move. He had promised the boy – and himself – that Ben would visit at least once while he was in Washington and they would see the mastodon and the Wright Brothers airplane together.

Surprisingly, the image of Rachel Springer kept popping into his mind every time some regret slowed his packing.

She reminded him more of his grandmother – albeit a younger version of the picture he remembered as a boy – than any of the women he had dated.

It wasn't her age that created the comparison as much as something in her eyes and the way Rachel carried herself that reminded John of the grandmother he had adored.

As he packed his assorted collection of Gold Toe socks, he thought about what exactly that "something" was and decided it was a combination of gentleness and self-confidence lying deep within their eyes. Both women were tiny but held themselves so erect as to appear tall. Both had a way of looking down their noses that convinced people they were in fact much taller than their five feet.

John told himself not to mention to Rachel that she reminded him of his grandmother. If she were like most women her age, she probably would not appreciate it as a compliment.

Chapter 3

When Rachel answered the phone on the fourth ring, Susan launched right into a conversation, mid-sentence.

After five years of living across the street and seeing or talking to Susan almost every day, Rachel didn't need for her best friend to identify herself, but diving into the middle of a thought without any preamble at eight o'clock on a Saturday morning was a stretch.

She asked Susan to repeat what she had just said.

"Honey, I've had the most fabulous idea and don't try to discourage me just get your clothes on I know you're still in your robe I just saw you let Ralph out," Susan said in one breath.

"Wait a minute," Rachel interrupted before her friend could say another word. "I'm waiting for the cleaning crew to arrive to do the work downstairs. John moves in Monday, remember?"

"Well, leave them the key and a note. I need you."

Rachel sat down in the chair beside the kitchen wall phone and took a sip of coffee.

Susan rushed on. "I've had a great idea, and I need you to go with me. I've rented a booth at the European Market, and I'm going to write poems for $5 a piece."

Rachel sat stunned for several minutes before she said, "Poems?"

"Poems. I've been reading the best little book by a dear woman who said that's what she did for the longest time and that people just loved them and she had just the best time doing it."

"But, Susan, you don't write poetry, do you?"

"Well, I did write some verse in college, and it was published in the campus literary journal," Susan said, sounding like her feelings had been hurt. "My professors thought I was quite good, actually."

"Susan, I don't mean to be a wet blanket, but that was more than 40 years ago. Whatever makes you think you can just sit down at the European Market and write on demand?"

"Rachel Springer, you are the most pessimistic woman alive. My Daddy taught me I could do anything I set my mind to, and today I'm going to get on the metro, ride to the Market, set up my folding chair, and I'm going to write poetry and sell it for $5 a piece. Do you want to come or not?"

Rachel took a final gulp of cold coffee and glanced outside. The morning was gorgeous, and she really didn't want to spend it inside. The European Market was a colorful adventure on a Saturday morning, and Susan needed her.

"I'll be ready in 10 minutes," she said and hung up.

*   *   *

When Rachel answered the door eight minutes later, her friend stood on the stoop grinning. She carried two forest-green folding chairs, wore a huge straw sun hat, hot pink and white polka dotted Capri pants, a royal blue tank top, and very large, very dark sunglasses. At her feet sat a picnic basket and cooler.

"You can carry those," Susan nodded in the direction of her feet, turned and marched down the sidewalk.

As Rachel locked the door, she marveled at the blessing – or bane, depending on her mood at the time – of having two such bossy women in her life – Georgia at work and Susan at home. For someone who grew up with no mother, she certainly had made up for that lack of maternal nurturing in her later life.

"Are you sure you want to do this?" Rachel asked as she trudged behind her friend the couple of blocks to the Dupont Circle metro station.

Susan nodded emphatically.

Finding a place to sit on the subway car with room for all their paraphernalia was a challenge. Susan convinced a couple of teen-aged boys to give up their seats at the rear of the car, and the two women spread out for the short ride.

The car was full of Saturday shoppers, who got off at Metro Central, and tourists who left at the Mall. By the time the train stopped near Capitol Hill, it was almost empty.

Susan and Rachel gave up their seats to an elderly couple, grateful to have so much room. They thanked them profusely.

"Now, isn't that nice to see older folks out so early in the morning, heading out for an adventure," Susan chirped when they got off the train.

"Susan, those people weren't much older than we are."

"There you go again, Rachel – being pessimistic. Thank god, you've got me, that's all I can say."

"Thank god," Rachel echoed as she followed her friend up the escalator into the carnival atmosphere of the Market.

"Where is your booth?" Rachel asked as they stood looking at the rows of vegetable stands, tables piled high with handcrafted Mexican rugs and beaded jewelry, racks of Indian saris and embroidered peasant dresses. The wind blew the colorful fabrics like kites against the brilliant blue sky.

Susan's hot pink fit in much better than Rachel's uniform of black linen top and beige cotton pants. She was glad she had remembered the turquoise bracelet and necklace her brother had brought back from a recent trip out west.

Susan consulted a map for a few minutes and then took off toward the far end of a row of baked goods. An empty card table stood next to a woman frying funnel cakes.

Susan looked at Rachel and smiled. "Well, at least we won't get hungry," she said.

Efficiently, she began to set herself up to work. She yanked her chair out of its cover, snapping it into place and propping up a tiny umbrella to protect her against the rising sun. Out of an old canvas bag on which UVA could barely be read, she took several well-sharpened pencils and a brand-new spiral-bound notebook. Last, she pulled out a paperback version of Webster's dictionary and plopped herself down to wait for business.

Rachel watched all this in awe. Almost afraid to ask, she timidly broached the question. "Susan, how are people supposed to know what you're doing – that you're here to write poems?"

"Oh my goodness, I almost forgot," Susan said and dug around in her bag again to retrieve a small sign that she propped up against the cooler. "Original Poems Written for You for $5" was printed in bold black letters.

She sat back down with a sigh of satisfaction.

"Now, honey, you don't need to feel like you have to sit here with me all the time. Go on off and see what's happening and come back and tell me all about it. I'll be fine."

"Are you sure? I thought you said you needed me."

"I did need you. I needed you to get me going. I'm fine now."

"Well, I would like to get a cup of coffee. Can I bring you one?"

"No, I think I'm coffee'ed out right now," Susan said as she tapped the end of her No. 2 yellow pencil on the pad in her lap.

As Rachel walked away, she noticed the funnel cake vendor, a very large black woman with dreadlocks and African robes, staring at Susan like she was an alien from outer space.

*   *   *

Rachel found a wizened old man brewing Turkish coffee not too far from the entrance to the metro and decided to be daring and order a cup. If Susan could bare her soul, surely she could venture from her instant Maxwell House lifestyle for one morning.

The man didn't appear to know more English than "two dollar" so Rachel didn't linger after she took the tiny jigger of hot syrupy black liquid and headed back to Susan, taking the scenic, longer return route.

As she choked on the first gulp, she heard a laugh over her left shoulder, and then her back was patted none too gently.

When she recovered, she opened her eyes to see her neighbor, Mr. Moser, smiling at her.

"Pretty strong stuff, isn't it," he laughed.

"Good grief. It could kill you. I had no idea."

"It's definitely an acquired taste. What are you doing here so early in the morning?"

Rachel told him about Susan's scheme, and they laughed together about their friend's latest adventure.

"I couldn't help but notice the cleaning company van at your house as I left," Mr. Moser said. "Are you expecting company?"

"Actually, that's another one of Susan's hair-brained plots. She's talked me into renting my downstairs apartment for six months to a consultant who's in town working with Jim."

"That should be interesting – having someone new in the neighborhood. Doesn't by any chance play chess, does he?"

"I don't know. Actually, I know very little about him other than Jim and Ralph both think he's nice to have around."

"Ralph?"

"My dog."

"Of course – that Ralph," Mr. Moser laughed. "Well, good luck. And let me know about the chess. You know, Sylvia is a good wife, but she's a lousy chess player. We've been playing going on 50 years now, and I don't think the woman's won one game yet."

"Well, you've got to admire her for continuing to play."

"She just doesn't seem to care whether she wins or loses. In fact, maybe that's the problem."

"Or the solution," Rachel said as a parting shot. "Got to get back and check on Susan and her poetry. Stop by and get a poem before you leave."

"Why would I want a poem?" Mr. Moser asked, looking shocked by the suggestion.

"Ask her," Rachel yelled back at him as she disappeared into the thickening crowd.

*   *   *

When she finally made her way back to Susan, following the sweet smell of funnel cakes to relocate her tiny table, she was surprised to see a little girl sitting in the chair next to her friend, waiting patiently for a poem. Her mother stood nearby smiling.

When the woman noticed Rachel, she walked over and spoke.

"Isn't this great? That lady is making a poem for Christy. I had the hardest time convincing her to come with me this morning – terrible time. That child threw a fit getting out of bed, threw a fit eating her cereal, threw a fit all the way here on the train – and now look at her. It's like that lady has put a magic spell on my child. She just heard that word "poem," and her eyes lit up, and she said she had to have one."

"Sounds like magic to me," Rachel agreed as she watched while Susan tore a page out of her notebook and handed it to the little girl, who looked like she had just been crowned Queen for the Day.

The child danced over to her mother and asked that she read her the poem.

They walked off before Rachel heard the words, but the message was clear enough – art heals.

"Wow, that was powerful," Rachel said.

Sharpening another pencil to replace the one she had already worn to a nub, Susan smiled up at her.

"I told you so," she said. "You've got to learn to listen to me, Rachel. I've written 10 poems since you've been gone. People love it, and I'm having a blast."

"I'm amazed. I'll admit I had my doubts you could pull this off. How do you do it?"

"It's not about *how*. It's about *doing*."

"Right."

"Remember that when John Turner arrives Monday," Susan said as another customer sat down beside her to buy a poem.

Chapter 4

Monday arrived, but it didn't pan out at all the way Rachel had planned.

Friday afternoon during her end-of-the week planning session with Georgia, Rachel had decided not to schedule any Monday afternoon appointments so that she could be at home to welcome her new tenant. When she and Georgia got to work Monday morning, Rachel double-checked both their calendars to make sure nobody had slipped something in on the day's date since then. All was clear.

But when she got back to her desk after the morning calendar call and lunch with a new female lawyer in town, a woman sat in the outer office with Georgia, waiting.

Rachel smiled as she walked through to her office. "Georgia, may I see you in my office, please."

Georgia had barely gotten the door shut before she launched into an explanation.

"I'm sorry, Rachel. I know you asked me to keep the afternoon free, but I was sure you'd want to see this woman."

"But what about John Turner? He's depending on me to be there to let him in his apartment."

"I'll go over and let him in," Georgia said, ready with what seemed like a logical solution.

"That doesn't seem very welcoming of me," Rachel countered, doubtfully. "What's so special about this woman's situation that it can't wait until tomorrow?"

"It's not so much the situation as the woman, herself," Georgia said – Georgia of the compassionate chocolate chip cookies.

"Give me the shortened version," Rachel said, knowing that Georgia had probably spent many minutes listening to every detail already.

"Her husband left her last week and this past weekend he took the children to the zoo but he didn't being them home," Georgia said in one breath.

"Well, why couldn't that wait until tomorrow?"

"She's afraid he's going to take them out of the country – to Mexico."

"Show her in."

Georgia ushered the woman in and made sure she was comfortable before she shut the door. When Rachel looked at her potential client, she felt like they were separated by a world rather than a desk.

The tiny woman's feet barely reached the floor as she perched on the edge of the straight-backed chair. In her lap she clutched a battered purse that reminded Rachel of one her own grandmother carried. It had several compartments on each side, and Rachel knew that if she were to open it, she would find a few more well-organized zippered pouches there, as well.

Mrs. Lopez wore a neat navy-blue polyester pants suit, a lacy white blouse and doll-sized white canvas Keds.

"Mrs. Lopez, my assistant tells me you are concerned about your children," Rachel prodded her, glancing down at her wristwatch in what she hoped was a subtle way.

"I am much afraid."

"Have you tried to contact your husband to find out why he didn't bring your children home?"

"Yes, but no answer, ma'am. And no answer at his work."

"Where does your husband work?"

"He work at Dean & Delucca. He stock boy."

"And what do you do, Mrs. Lopez?"

"I clean house."

"Did you and Mr. Lopez have any kind of separation agreement that stipulated custody of the children?"

Mrs. Lopez responded as though Rachel were speaking a foreign language. She looked blank.

"He leave."

"He left without any kind of warning?"

"Yes, ma'am. He leave. He come back to see kids. Now they leave too." Mrs. Lopez seemed to crumple – to grow smaller even than before, and it took every ounce of professionalism Rachel had learned over the years to keep her on the opposite side of her desk. She pulled a box of tissues out of her bottom drawer and pushed it across the desk.

"Take your time, Mrs. Lopez. I know this is hard." She waited.

When Mrs. Lopez regained her composure, Rachel continued.

"Do you have any family here?"

"No family."

"Who takes care of your children while you and your husband work?"

Rachel was able to piece together that the couple had worked alternate shifts so that while one worked, the other watched the children. After her husband left, Mrs. Lopez had been taking the children to stay with a friend during her shift.

"Why did your husband leave?"

Mrs. Lopez said she didn't know. She had been shocked even more when he didn't bring the children home as he said he would.

"Not like him. He family man. Good man. Always bring home paycheck. No drink. No drug."

And then Rachel asked the hard question. "Another woman perhaps?"

"NO. NO woman," Mrs. Lopez said, and Rachel believed her.

"Obviously, the first thing we have to do is find your husband. Has he been at work today?"

"Today his day off," Mrs. Lopez said and began once again to dab at her eyes with the balled-up Kleenex. Rachel pulled out a fresh tissue and passed it to her.

"Have you tried to find him?"

Mrs. Lopez said she had no idea where he was staying and that, as far as she knew, he had no friends. He was a "family man," she said. Any time he wasn't working, he was at home. He was devoted to his children and was very good about helping around the little apartment they had found in Adams Morgan.

"Have you called his employer to see if they know where he's living?"

Mrs. Lopez said she didn't have a telephone and had been embarrassed to tell her friend about what had happened. She hadn't called the police either, for the same reason.

Rachel asked her why she had decided to tell her.

"Your dog. I see you with such nice dog. I see your sign. You lawyer. You help."

Rachel picked up her pencil and pretended to take a few notes so her client couldn't see her eyes. She didn't want Mrs. Lopez to be able to read her mind as she thought about how Ralph had once again opened a can of worms she probably didn't want to have opened. Maybe she should just get rid of the dog. For now, she looked up at Mrs. Lopez and smiled.

"We'll try."

"How much?" Mrs. Lopez asked as she took out an envelope of money.

"Let's wait and see what we're going to have to do first, and then we'll talk about my fee," Rachel said as she walked out to Georgia's desk to get an intake form. "Maybe this won't take much work. In fact, maybe they'll be waiting for you when you get home."

Mrs. Lopez nodded her head hopefully as she bent over the form, carefully printing her name and address. When she got to the question, "How did you hear about our firm?" she looked at Rachel for help.

"Just put 'Ralph'," Rachel laughed.

*   *   *

After Mrs. Lopez left, Rachel placed a call to a private investigator and left a message for him to call her at home that evening. As she was going out of the office and locking the door, the mailman arrived. She stopped long enough to accept the stack of bills and magazines and sort through them before she left.

Finally, she closed the door and started her walk home.

It was one of those early April days when Washington is at its finest. Even traffic smells are pleasant.

The cherry trees were in full bloom. Not restricted to the area around the Potomac that makes them famous as a tourist attraction, they bloomed in several yards along Rachel's route home, giving the brick townhouses in Georgetown a natural beauty.

Daffodils, tulips and forsythia bloomed as accent pieces in many of the yards, behind wrought iron and the occasional picket fence.

Ralph seemed to rush the walk, as if he knew there was a reason to get home fast.

By the time they turned the corner onto O Street, both he and Rachel were out of breath. Georgia and John Turner stood at the top of the stairs leading down into the basement apartment.

"I see you two have met," Rachel said by way of greeting.

"Yes. Thank you so much for sparing your assistant. I know you appreciate her. She's been a great help to me already," John said.

Georgia laughed. "I'd better get back to the office now. Welcome to Washington, Mr. Turner. I hope you'll be very happy here."

"I'm sure I will. And thanks again."

Rachel couldn't help but smile to herself as she watched the interaction between her friend and the tenant she had doubted. Georgia seemed totally won over in such a short time.

"Thanks, Georgia. I'll see you tomorrow. The mail is on your desk."

"What about Mrs. Lopez?" Georgia turned at the last minute to ask.

"I've left a message for Stan Berninger to call me at home tonight."

Georgia nodded and set off down the street. John asked Rachel if she'd like to come downstairs and have a glass of water to cool off after her walk, and she said she would.

"How was your trip down?" she asked after they settled themselves on the futon in the living area. She noticed several personal touches he had already added to the room. A bright red and black Mexican blanket spread across the back of the futon caught her eye immediately.

"Uneventful. I hope you don't mind the minivan parked in your driveway. I know it takes up more space than you'd probably like, but I'll be trading it for a rental car tomorrow."

"You're fine. Don't worry about it. I don't even own a car. Got rid of mine the first year I moved into this house. Too many headaches owning a car in this city, and I don't really need one."

Rachel went on to tell John about the places to grocery shop and eat that were all within walking distance. Book stores, theaters, galleries – so many attractions so close.

"And when I travel, I just rent something," she finished.

"You're a smart lady."

"Some folks say so. I just do what's easiest and, in this case, that means not owning a car. No worrying about rising gas prices, no checking the oil, no getting tags and inspection renewed. No parking tickets. And you'll find that cab drivers and the people you meet on the metro are great companions."

"I look forward to it."

"Well, I'll let you get to work unpacking," Rachel said and got up off the sofa to leave. "Actually, it looks like you've already started. Where did you get the blanket on the back of the futon?"

"Got that my last trip to New Mexico."

"New Mexico is one of my favorite trips. Where?"

"Taos. Ever been?"

"As often as I can. I've found a great little bed and breakfast right in the middle of town. It's been my escape at least twice a year for the past five years."

"La Dona Luz?"

"You know it?"

"Never stayed there, but a friend told me about it, and it sounds like my kind of place."

"Well, it sure is mine. In fact, looking at your blanket reminds me that I'm due for a visit."

"Taos is magical, but you've got some magic of your own going on right here. I'm not sure I'd ever want to leave," John said.

"Well, I do leave occasionally, but I'm glad you like it so well," Rachel said on her way to the door. "Let me know if you need anything."

"Thanks."

"Oh, did Georgia show you where your breaker box is?"

"Yes, she did."

"How could I have doubted her?" Rachel laughed and said goodnight.

*   *   *

As Rachel walked through her front door, she noticed the message light on her cordless phone blinking. She retrieved one message, from Stan Berninger, the private investigator.

She poured some fresh water in Ralph's bowl beside the kitchen refrigerator and sat down in her rocking chair to return his call.

Stan answered on the first ring.

"Hey, Rachel. Whassup?"

"Thanks for getting back to me so quickly, Stan. You're a good man."

"No problem. Things have been kinda slow around here. I had just left to go to my granddaughter's ballet recital when you called."

Rachel smiled at the image of the ruddy-faced, barrel-chested, gum-chewing PI surrounded by Junior League mothers and little girls in pink tutus. When Stan wasn't talking about cases, he talked about five-year-old Lillian – "Lily" as he called her.

"How was it?" Rachel asked politely, knowing that the question was expected, if not required, and that no business could be conducted until the latest Lily story was shared.

"Actually, Rachel, I was a little disappointed," Stan started out.

Rachel opened the refrigerator to get out a Diet Pepsi with lime. She knew this might take a while. Disappointments relating to Lilly usually did.

"I'm sorry to hear that, Stan. What happened?"

"I just don't think that ballet teacher lady sees how talented Lily is."

Pause.

"Oh, really?"

"No, not really."

Pause.

"So, what happened?"

"Well, they did this ballet thing about some little girl tending her garden and she made Lily a petunia."

Pause.

"A petunia?"

"A pink petunia."

Pause.

"And you thought she should have been the gardener?"

"Well, of course not, Rachel," Stan shot back. "My god, she's only five years old, she can't play the star, but she ain't no petunia, neither."

"What other role did you think she should have been given?"

"A sunflower, at least. Rachel, you should have seen them. Tall, yeller, waving across the stage. My little Lily would have been a super sunflower. But, no, there that poor little girl stood, squoze into that puny little petunia outfit. Hell, Rachel, there was even a part where the gardener comes over and deadheads her. Not just a petunia, but a deadheaded petunia."

Pause.

"I'm so sorry, Stan," Rachel said, relieved he couldn't see her face.

"I think Stan, Junior should take her out of the class, don't you?"

"Well, that's a little drastic, Stan. I don't know. Maybe you should sleep on it overnight and see how you feel tomorrow. And Stan, the reason for my call . . ."

"Oh, yeah. Whassup?"

"I had a mother stop by the office today whose husband has disappeared with her children."

"My god, that's worse than my petunia story."

"Yes, I suppose it is, Stan," Rachel said and then proceeded to give him the details.

Stan promised he would put the petunia problem on the back burner while he focused on locating Mr. Lopez and the two children.

Chapter 5

As Rachel lay in her bed on the second floor of the house, she strained to hear any noises wafting up from the basement. Nothing.

She had heard John leave his apartment sometime around 9:30 p.m. and saw him sitting in the back courtyard in the moonlight. She thought that was a good sign – a man who could just sit, doing nothing. In fact, he sat there for a good while, doing nothing, and Rachel finally took her jasmine tea and went up to bed to read, comforted by his presence beneath her bedroom window.

But no sign of him since. No cigar smoke. No trumpet.

No midnight callers – yet.

Rachel fell asleep with a smile on her face.

*   *   *

"So, how are things at home?" Georgia asked the next morning. "Mr. Turner have any wild housewarming parties last night?"

Rachel sailed on by her into the inner office, ignoring the jab.

"Thanks for your help yesterday, Georgia. Everything is working out fine so far."

After a few minutes, she walked back out and stood at the front desk.

"What did you think?"

"About what?"

"About my new tenant?"

"I suppose it's too soon to tell much, really, but he certainly seemed nice enough to me. He didn't bring much with him, that's for sure."

"I know, but did you see that wonderful Mexican blanket? He's been to Taos."

"So?"

"Well, don't you think that's some indication of something? Something good, I mean."

"Maybe he's got family in Taos, and he just went to visit them and hated the town."

"I suppose that's possible," Rachel agreed half-heartedly, picking up Georgia's box of paperclips and turning them over and over from one hand to the other. "Maybe that's it."

"Or maybe he loves it like you do," Georgia conceded.

Rachel looked up and beamed like a child who's just been promised a new pony.

"You think so?"

"I don't know, Rachel, but maybe. Right now, you've got an appointment across town with Mr. Gilbert. Did you forget?"

"Oh, damn. Is that this morning?"

Georgia assured her that it was and began packing her briefcase with the files she would need.

Horace Gilbert had been a longstanding client Rachel had seen through several company mergers, pre-nuptial agreements, divorces and a fight with siblings over his parents' estate. Her current assignment was a revision of his Will to exclude one child and set up a trust fund for another.

"Don't forget to talk to him again about the healthcare power of attorney," Georgia reminded her.

"Right. Although Horace has no intention of ever needing one, you know, so it's probably a waste of time even mentioning it."

Horace Gilbert was a man in control, which was why he always insisted that Rachel meet in his office rather than hers. He was more than willing to pay her extra for her travel time to and from their places of business and always insisted she have lunch with him at the Mayflower Hotel near his office after they met.

"Shall I call you a cab?" Georgia asked.

"No, that's all right. I'm sure I can hail one at the corner."

"I'll make sure Ralph gets his walk while you're gone."

"I can't believe you didn't notice. Ralph stayed home this morning with John. He said he was going to work from the apartment and would welcome the company. I left them sitting out back enjoying the birds."

"Moving kind of fast, aren't you?" Georgia asked, closing the briefcase with a snap. "You hardly know the man."

"Ralph seemed fine with it, so why shouldn't I?"

"Time will tell."

*   *   *

Rachel's cellphone rang on her way across town to meet her client. The caller ID showed that Susan was on the other end, and she was tempted not to answer, thereby avoiding the 20 questions Susan was sure to have about John.

But she couldn't turn off the part of her brain that was always on alert for problems and finally said, "Good morning, Susan" on the third ring.

"What's Ralph doing at home this morning?"

"He's spending the day with John."

"Well, now isn't that just the sweetest thing you've ever heard. Didn't I tell you this man is a blessing? Didn't I?"

"Susan, I really can't talk right now. I'm in a cab on my way to Farragut North. Talk to you later. Bye," and she hung up, relieved that her friend wasn't calling to report a crisis across the street.

She tipped the cab driver, got out at the corner of 19th Street and Connecticut Avenue and walked to Horace's office. She climbed the stairs to his fourth floor suite, thinking she would have worn more comfortable shoes if she had remembered the appointment.

Rachel refused to join a gym, despite Susan's persistent nagging, but she was committed to exercise as a way of life. She always chose the stairs, laughing at women who rode the elevator and yet sweated at the gym's stairmasters. Her daily walks kept her short legs sturdy, and she liked to believe they were better looking than some of her friends who paid trainers to whip them into shape.

She had to admit that she was a little winded when Horace's receptionist greeted her.

"Good morning, Ms. Springer. Mr. Gilbert just called to say he would be about five minutes late. Can I get you a cup of coffee?"

"Something cold would be nice. Do you have any orange juice?"

The bouncy little redhead – one in a long string of pretty faces who had adorned Horace's front office over the 10 years Rachel had known him – looked horrified to have to tell her that she didn't have the juice.

"Water will be fine," Rachel said as she pulled the day's issue of the *Post* out of her briefcase. Georgia – knowing Horace used being late as another way to control – packed it for her so she could entertain herself with the crossword puzzle.

"Would you like a pencil?" Red asked.

Rachel looked up, puzzled.

"To do the puzzle with – a pencil?"

"Oh, no, thank you."

"Wow. You do puzzles in ink?"

"It's a trick I learned years ago – a confidence game. Pretend like I know what I'm doing, and then maybe I will."

"Sort of like being a lawyer," Red said with an angelic smile that assured Rachel she didn't realize the insult.

"Sort of," Rachel chuckled, relieved to hear Horace's voice echoing down the hall.

"Mornin, ma'am," he boomed, slapping her on the back with a huge paw. "Sorry to be late. Got stuck in the morning traffic coming across Key Bridge."

Horace Gilbert lived in Roslyn, a short way from his office, and Rachel failed to see how rush hour traffic could possibly prevent him from being late for a ten o'clock appointment. Still, she said nothing.

"You look great this morning, Barbara," he said on his way past the front desk. "Got some coffee?"

Rachel followed her client into his inner office and set her briefcase on the round conference table in the corner, overlooking Connecticut Avenue. Cherry blossoms lay in a canopy in the courtyard below.

Horace plopped his huge bulk into a chair beside her and banged his beefy fist on the table.

"So, what you got for me, little lady?"

"Let's start with you healthcare power of attorney," Rachel said with a wicked grin.

*   *   *

Lunch at the Mayflower wasn't something Rachel subjected herself to any time other than after her meetings with Horace. The hotel felt like an alien world compared to her simple life. Her favorite lunch for years had been a liverwurst sandwich on rye bread with lettuce and lots of mayonnaise. Sometimes, if she felt like splurging, she added Ripples potato chips.

She had yet to find liverwurst on the Mayflower menu, and Tuesday was no exception.

"What can I get for you today, Madam?" the young waiter asked. Packaged in his starched white linen jacket with the hotel emblem on its pocket and creased black pants, he looked like he might faint if she suggested liverwurst. He actually pursed his lips, prune-like, as he waited for her answer.

"What's your special today?" Horace chimed in, giving the young man his cue to launch into a long list of exotic dishes.

Rachel was always impressed by waiters who could memorize a new menu of specials each day.

Despite the wide variety of appetizing dishes listed by the waiter, Horace ordered his usual house salad with ranch dressing, a hamburger, well done, and steak fries. Rachel ordered the Maryland crab cakes and a glass of iced tea.

"Hear you've got a new tenant," Horace announced after the waiter had left to take their orders to the kitchen.

"Boy, news travels fast in this city. How did you know?"

"When I called to make our appointment, Georgia said you had left for the afternoon – something to do with a fellow moving in."

Rachel filled him in on John Turner – or at least what she knew about him. Over the course of their business relationship, she had grown to respect Horace Gilbert's opinion and was interested in hearing his reaction to her decision to become a landlord.

"You let me know if you have any trouble with that fellow," he said. "I've got stories you wouldn't believe about tenants."

And he reeled out landlord/tenant stories that took them through dessert.

*   *   *

When Rachel got back to her office, a pink message slip lay on her desk with Stan Berninger's name and phone number on it. Thinking he might have some good news about Mr. Lopez and the missing children, she sat down and picked up the phone to call him even before she unpacked her briefcase.

"Stan Berninger," the PI barked.

"Stan, it's Rachel. Sorry I wasn't here when you called."

"Not a problem. Just thought you'd want to know that Lily has a new ballet teacher."

Rachel took a sip of cold coffee left over from the morning, giving herself time to cover her disappointment. She knew her old friend expected something better from her.

"Stan, that's great news. Happy to hear it."

"It all worked out, and I didn't even have to do nothing. Her old teacher is moving to California with her husband, and Stan Junior has found a new class already."

"That's wonderful, Stan. Thanks for letting me know."

Rachel waited a few seconds to see if he would bring up her client, and when he didn't, she asked if there were any news on that front.

"Nothing yet. Gotta be patient, Rachel. You know that."

"Of course. I just thought maybe you'd have something I could tell Mrs. Lopez if she finds a way to call today."

"Tell her we're working on it. The folks at Dean & Delucca say he asked for a few days off. The only address they have for him is a post office box. Don't know how he got by with that. I'm still trying to trace where he lives. This thing with Lily has slowed me down a little. You understand."

Rachel assured him she did and that she had every confidence in the world that he would find Mr. Lopez – hopefully, within the next few days.

*   *   *

Rachel heard Georgia laughing even before she walked through the front door. When she poked her head around the corner to see what was amusing her assistant, she found her leafing through a fistful of photographs.

"What've you got there?" Rachel asked.

"Will Junior sent pictures of the twins," Georgia answered, passing Rachel the envelope of pictures of her two-year-old grandsons. "They've just gotten back from a vacation at Virginia Beach."

Georgia sat down beside her boss on the lobby sofa, pointing out Adam in the sand, only his head peaking out as his father and brother Aaron covered him. The mother lay sleeping under an umbrella in the background.

"Poor Cynthia. How she keeps up with those two is beyond me. I think I would have slit my wrists if I had twins. Their father was a handful, as it was."

One would have been more than I could have managed, Rachel thought to herself. She had helped raise her brother Edward, but that was the extent of her experience with mothering. As far as she knew, there had been no biological clock installed in her system. She had never reacted the way other young women did, cooing and cuddling babies. She had shown only a mild interest and saw no need to marry in order to have children.

As though she could read her boss's mind, Georgia asked, "Ever wished you had children?"

The same question came up every few years, and Rachel wondered when Georgia would accept that she really didn't.

"No, Georgia, but I sure admire those of you who have them. Which reminds me, have we heard from Mrs. Lopez today?"

"Yes, she called while you were with Mr. Gilbert. I told her we still don't know anything."

"How did she sound?"

"Better than yesterday, but this is mighty hard on her, Rachel. What is Stan doing about finding her husband?"

"He's working on it but says we need to be patient."

"Has she gone to the police yet?"

"I think she's saving that as a last resort. Let's hope we can find them first."

Rachel rose from the sofa and handed the pictures back to Georgia. "Thanks for sharing these. They're beautiful boys. You're lucky."

And suddenly Rachel was surprised to feel the faintest tick of maybe a very tiny, very slow, very retarded biological clock.

*   *   *

Walking home from work that evening, Rachel wondered about the strange shift she experienced earlier in the day. Sixty-two years was too old to be entertaining the warm cuddly thoughts she had off and on for the rest of the afternoon, she said to herself.

But she had to admit that every time she went out to get a file, her eyes were drawn to the framed family pictures on Georgia's desk. Christmas shots of the twins with Santa Claus; an anniversary picture of Georgia and her husband, Will, taken on a cruise to the Bahamas; Will Junior's wedding portrait.

Her own office was bare of any personal photos. Plenty of diplomas and certificates hung on the walls. Snapshots documented various trips around the world, but there were no smiling faces to offset the law books that lined one wall.

As Rachel walked, she looked down at Ralph and laughed. "What's happening to me, Ralph? I'm supposed to be withering on the vine by now, not thinking about sending out new shoots."

As she turned the corner to walk down O Street, she smelled the curry. The closer she got to her front door, the more confident she became that the smell was coming from her house – curry powder and some other spice she couldn't identify.

As she started up her front steps, John Turner poked his head out of the basement stairwell and called up to her.

"I've made chicken curry. Hungry? There's plenty here for an army. I've never learned to cook for just one."

Rachel hesitated for just a minute or two, trying to think of an excuse. She never had felt very comfortable accepting last-minute invitations. She really liked eating alone at the end of the day – especially on a day when she'd been forced to lunch with Horace Gilbert.

"Tell you what," John said. "Why don't you relax for a while and come on down around seven. That'll give you a chance to rest before we eat."

"Thanks, John. Can I bring anything?"

"Ralph, if he wants to come."

"We'll look forward to it," Rachel said and went inside. Checking her watch, she saw that she had an hour to check her phone messages, read the mail and soak the city off her body in a cool bath. Perfect, she thought.

She found a message from Mr. Moser, telling her about the next book club meeting, and one from Susan, asking her to call. The mail included a couple of bills and a postcard from a cousin traveling through Europe. Rachel was always curious to see what obscure place Virginia Springer had found on her latest gig as a travel writer.

The bathtub beckoned even more than usual. The garden tub nestled in an alcove overlooking the courtyard. Surrounded by potted plants and hanging ferns, Rachel thought to herself that she'd have to remember to close the shutters before she undressed now that John was downstairs.

As she looked down at her body, she tried to imagine someone else seeing it for the first time. It had been a faithful companion to her for so many years, and she didn't see many of the things a stranger might – the appendix scar that slashed across one side, another where an ovarian cyst had been removed. Her breasts were small and perky and her stomach muscles still firm. Not having children certainly paid off in some ways, she thought as she sank into the bubble bath, inhaling the soothing lavender aromatherapy.

But knees were another matter. No matter how much she walked nor how slender her legs, the skin from her thighs did have a way of drooping down over her kneecaps. She dipped them under the water, laid her head back against the inflatable bath cushion and sighed.

Ralph licked her hand, as if he knew she needed comforting.

*   *   *

After dinner, John suggested they take their French apple pie outside to enjoy the fresh air. The apartment was cozy, but after a while it began to feel cramped, they both agreed. The moon was waning, but the stars were bright enough to light the small area where they sat, comfortable in the Adirondack chairs Rachel had bought recently at an estate sale.

"Are you getting settled in at work?" Rachel asked.

"Pretty well. Things are coming together nicely, and I sure like the people I'm working with. That makes such a difference when you're away from home like this."

"Have you met anyone outside work yet?"

"Actually, Mr. Moser caught me as I was leaving this morning and asked me if I liked to play chess."

"And do you?"

"Since I was a child. We've got a game scheduled for this weekend at his house. He seems like a good guy to have as a neighbor. I got the feeling he was interested in more than just chess. I suspect he wants to check me out and make sure you're safe with me in your basement. He's very fond of you, you know."

Rachel smiled and looked toward the second-story windows of her old friend's house on the other side of the brick wall. A couple of years ago, she had a gate cut in the brick so they could walk back and forth without having to go through their houses and down the sidewalk out front.

She took a sip of her tea and looked at the man sitting next to her. His freckles were almost indiscernible in the dark, but she thought she noticed a silver hair amid the red. He had his eyes closed, so she took the opportunity to study his face while he wasn't looking.

The silence was stabbed by the ringing of Rachel's phone inside the house.

"Do you need to get that?" John asked.

"No, I'll let the machine answer it."

A police car careened past the house, siren wailing. Ralph howled in sympathy. A dog down the street joined in on the chorus.

"So much for peace and quiet," Rachel laughed. "It took me a while to get used to city noise, growing up on a farm the way I did. But I guess that's not a problem for you, moving here from New York."

"No, the only problem I'm having is missing my grandson. Ben and I are pretty tight. Saw each other about once a week. I'm already going through withdrawal, and it's not even time for our regular visit yet. I may need treatment by the end of the weekend."

"Will you be going back to New York some to see your family?"

"Some, but not much. The project is on a very tight schedule, and I'll be working pretty much every day – at least part of every day. I'll probably get home once a month."

"Will Ben come to see you here?"

"I hope so. In fact, he may come by himself in a couple of weeks. His parents are hoping to get a vacation and I'm the only person he'll stay with."

"Well, if you need an extra bed, I've got plenty of room upstairs."

"Thanks. That's mighty kind of you," John said and reached over to pat her hand.

His touch was cool and dry in the humid night air, and Rachel was surprised by how much she enjoyed even such a fleeting gesture.

"Well," she said, using her arms to push herself up and out of the depths of her chair, "Ralph and I very much appreciate your sharing the evening with us, John. Dinner was delicious. Thanks."

John leaned down to rub Ralph behind his ears. When he straightened back up, his face was in the shadows, but Rachel could hear the smile in his voice. "Thank you, Rachel – for everything."

* * *

Rachel looked across the street to see whether lights were still on at Susan's house and when they were, decided to return her friend's earlier call.

"So, how was dinner?" Susan asked by way of greeting.

"How did you know?"

"I saw John Turner shopping at Lee's Market, and he told me he was going to invite you. So how was it?"

"He's a good cook. A little heavy on the curry, maybe."

"I was right about him, wasn't I?"

"What do you mean?"

"He's got potential."

"Potential for what, Susan?" They had this conversation before, and Rachel admired her friend for not giving up on her crusade to pair her old maid neighbor up with some eligible bachelor.

"He's smart, handsome, financially secure . . ."

"You've seen his financial statement?"

"No, but Jim says he's done very well. Jim knows."

"Susan, I'm not interested in a romance with John Turner. You're right. He's a pleasant man, and I'm sure I'll enjoy having him as a neighbor for the next six months. Thanks for making it happen. Satisfied?"

"Jim and I have a couple of extra tickets to a lawn concert at Wolf Trap this weekend. Want to see if he can join us?"

"Susan, you're pushing it. Back off."

"Well, he's probably lonely."

"I doubt it. Now, go to bed."

Chapter 6

The next morning, on her way to the office, Rachel walked across the street and rang Susan's doorbell.

Susan opened it, wearing her pink babydoll pajamas and silver tap shoes.

"What in the name of God are you up to now?" Rachel asked.

"I'm dancing. Come on in and have a cup of coffee. I'm almost finished."

Rachel followed her friend down a long cluttered hall to the back of the house where the large eat-in kitchen looked out over a lushly overgrown vegetable garden.

"Didn't I tell you about reading that magazine article while I was waiting to see Dr. Horner the other day. The writer suggested starting your day by dancing to get your endorphins charged up."

"How's it going? You look a little flushed."

"I love it. I'm so glad I saved these tap shoes. Remember my taking tap dancing lessons last year? I knew they'd come in handy some day later."

Rachel looked over at the small black and white television set on Susan's counter and was amused to find the scene from the musical, *Chicago,* in which the women on death row are lined up behind bars, doing their energetic song and dance about murdering their husbands.

"I hope Jim doesn't get nervous when he sees the theme song you've chosen to dance to," Rachel laughed.

"That's just for this morning. I went to the library and checked out a different musical for each day. Tomorrow I'll be dancing to *Oklahoma.*"

Rachel laughed as she poured herself a cup of coffee and sat down at her friend's table. It was cluttered, as usual, with bills, recipes and several magazines and books. One corner was kept clean so Susan and Jim could crouch there to eat.

"Can't stay long," Rachel said. "I've got a new client coming in at nine, but I just wanted to stop by for a minute."

"Any second thoughts on Wolf Trap?"

"Not really, but I'll give it some thought. You can always invite another woman to be John's date, you know."

"I suppose I could, at that. How about the Market Saturday morning? Want to go back with me?"

"Are you really going to keep that up?"

"Of course. I had a great time, didn't you?"

"Yes, I suppose so. I'm just not sure I want to do it again."

"Don't feel like you have to, but if you do decide to go, I'm planning to leave a little earlier this time. Sally wants another poem, and her mother's taking her to the zoo and wants to get her there early. You know how it stinks as the day heats up."

Rachel said she did, gulped down the last of her coffee, kissed her friend on the top of her head and made her way to the front of the house.

As she walked down the front walk to the street, she heard the music crank up again, and found herself matching her steps to the beat.

*   *   *

John smiled as he watched Rachel through his living room window. He wondered what Susan had said that inspired the bounce in his landlady's step, her briefcase swinging at her side.

He liked the woman's style. The long silver braid always swung like a child's when she walked. That morning it waved wildly with each bounce. He guessed that she was going to meet a client since she was more formally dressed than what he had seen before.

When he had met her, she said she was having a "dressed down day." He chuckled to himself at this morning's "business attire" of long cotton skirt and loose blouse, topped by a baggy linen jacket.

He wondered what Rachel looked like under all that cotton and linen and remembered the way his fingers had felt the night before when he touched her hand – like they had been poked in an electrical socket.

John fast-forwarded last night's scene in the courtyard to his little bedroom cave. He wondered what loving such an independent woman would be like. Every female he had been involved with had been neurotically dependant – needy whiners who drove him off as quickly as they sucked him in.

The very thought pushed him away from the window just as Ralph noticed him staring and gave a joyful bark of greeting. Rachel looked up and their eyes met. She hesitated mid-step, then waved and walked on.

*   *   *

Rachel heard several high-pitched squeals as she approached her office. Ralph, ever on the alert, dashed forward and leaped up at the front door knob, trying to turn it.

She hurried forward and pushed open the door.

In the lobby, eating chocolate chip cookies, sat Mrs. Lopez and two children.

"Rachel, these are Mrs. Lopez's daughter and son, Maria and Juan," Georgia announced before Rachel was even able to close the door. She dropped her briefcase and had to pick it up again in order to get the door closed.

Mrs. Lopez stood up and smiled. The children rose and huddled next to her like little chickens.

"My husband, he home."

Rachel kneeled down to speak to the children, faces covered with cookie crumbs. They grinned chocolate grins.

"Why don't you kids stay here and talk to Mrs. Payne while I speak to your mother for a few minutes," Rachel said as she ushered Mrs. Lopez into her office and asked her to take a seat. She unpacked her briefcase, giving herself a few minutes to organize her thoughts as she tried to decide how best to handle the surprising turn of events.

Mrs. Lopez sat, smiling at her.

"How much?" she asked finally.

"Excuse me?"

"Money. How much I owe?"

"Well, how do you wish to proceed with this?"

"Ma'am?"

"Your husband disappeared for a period of time, abandoning the family. Then he took your children and didn't return them to your home as he promised. Don't you want to take some sort of action against him?"

Mrs. Lopez broke into agitated Spanish that escalated in volume and pitch for several minutes, soaring around Rachel's head like a stunt plane, up and down and around, until her voice lost volume and plummeted to the earth, landing with an emphatic English, "No."

"But, Mrs. Lopez, what's to prevent him from doing this again?"

"He stay home. He promise. How much?"

"I didn't really do anything for you, Mrs. Lopez. How about I send you the private investigator's bill when I get it, and you just pay that. It shouldn't be much."

Mrs. Lopez thanked her, stood and leaned over the desk to shake her hand.

When Rachel walked with her out to the front, the two children sat on the floor, coloring with Georgia. They both jumped up and rushed to their mother, grabbing her around her knees.

"Gracias," Mrs. Lopez said to Georgia.

When Rachel opened the front door for her client, she noticed the battered blue Ford pick-up truck across the street, a handsome young Mexican at the wheel. Mrs. Lopez and her two children piled into the front seat beside him. He waved to Rachel as they drove away.

Rachel turned back and saw her secretary still sitting cross-legged on the floor with the Scribble Pad and 24 Crayola markers.

"Want to play? It's fun," Georgia asked.

"Might as well," Rachel laughed. "Things seem to have a way of working out without me."

*   *   *

Later, she called Stan to pull him off the Lopez investigation. He didn't seem surprised to hear the news that Mr. Lopez had returned to the fold.

"Nevertheless, I'll keep the file," he said. "Never know when a wild hair will crop up again."

"Thanks, Stan. And how is Lily getting along with her new ballet class?"

"What?"

"You told me Lily's teacher moved and Stan Junior had found her a new class."

"Oh, that. Didn't work out, Rachel. She's decided to play soccer instead."

Rachel wondered if there was something in the air. Twice in one morning the road had taken a dramatic twist. She felt dizzy.

"That's great, Stan. Hope she enjoys it," Rachel said and went back out to Gerogia's desk to borrow the Scribble Pad and Crayolas.

*   *   *

Rachel embraced rituals. Friday afternoons, before walking home, she made a habit of walking down to the Watergate Hotel to enjoy a glass of white wine at a table overlooking the Potomac River.

She left the office a little earlier than usual since the day felt like it was going downhill after the Lopez visit.

Rachel was not much of a shopper, but she did enjoy looking at all the storefront windows along the streets in Georgetown as she strolled toward K Street. And almost as interesting as the art galleries, dress shops, antique stores and tourist traps were the people who crowded the streets, doing what she was doing – people watching.

Washington D.C. had always been a favorite destination for family vacationers and honeymooners. Rachel, unlike some natives, enjoyed sharing her hometown with visitors. Her sometimes-flagging energy was often revitalized by their enthusiastic reaction to the capitol city.

Seeing elderly couples stop to give a street beggar a dollar increased Rachel's tolerance for their growing numbers. Hearing a child squeal with delight at the pigeons in the parks made her more inclined to ignore their droppings.

Over the years, her attitude about living in D.C. alternated between feeling like she too was on a year-round vacation to resentment that everyone else was playing except her.

Friday, she basked in the eternal holiday glow.

The hostess at the Watergate greeted her by name and guided her to her favorite window seat.

"Your regular, Ms. Springer?"

"No, I think I'll try something different today, Cindy. What do you suggest that is icy cold, sweet and pretty?"

"I've got just what you need," the pretty blond sang and sashayed over to the bartender. Minutes later, she was back and, with great ceremony, placed a tall slender frosted glass in front of Rachel. Perched on its rim was an orange slice and a red cherry pierced by a tiny Japanese parasol.

"A Harvey Walbanger," she announced proudly. "Vodka, orange juice and grenadine. Try it. I guarantee you'll like it."

Rachel took a tentative sip and was surprised that a dry white wine lover like herself would indeed like the syrupy drink. She had asked for sweet, and what she got tasted like it was almost pure sugar – with a buzz.

"Thanks, it's perfect."

Sailboats skittered across the Potomac; several motorboats cruised carefully among them. A few yachts anchored at a nearby pier, their owners doing what Rachel was doing – enjoying the end of a clearly perfect day.

Rachel took a deep breath and let it out slowly. She liked to come there to review the week behind her and clear her mind of all unfinished business before going home.

Focused on a mental review of the Lopez case, she was startled to hear her name called from across the room.

Horace Gilbert strode toward her table, beaming.

"Rachel, Rachel, Rachel," he boomed. "So good to see you. Mind if I join you a minute?" he asked as he crashed down in the seat across from her. She'd have to remember to ask the host to remove the extra chair next time, she thought.

"Hello, Horace."

"What you drinking? Want another?"

"Actually, I'm about to leave."

"Glad I caught you then. I was planning to call you on Monday but catching you here will save me some time."

Rachel tried not to be annoyed that he thought his time was more valuable than hers.

"One of my Red Cross board members is about to resign, and I wonder if you'd be willing to step up to the plate?" he charged right in.

"I don't know, Horace. I really try not to get involved in too many boards. I've already overextended myself, as it is."

"Will you at least think about it over the weekend? I'll have my girl call you Monday to get your answer."

Rachel knew there was no point in arguing. They said their good-byes and Horace rushed off on his next important mission, his cell phone ringing in his wake.

When Rachel asked Cindy for her check, she said Horace had paid the bill.

As she stood up to go, she was surprised at how light-headed her one Harvey Walbanger had left her and decided to hail a cab for the ride home. The evening was muggy and the thought of walking even one block in the heat made her dizzy.

As she stepped out the front door of the hotel, a taxi pulled up, and the doorman opened its back door for her.

When he said, "Good night, Ms. Springer," Rachel remembered TV personality Charlie Rose saying his favorite restaurant was the one where everyone knew his name.

*   *   *

Rachel had barely gotten her Danskins off and was drawing a bath when her doorbell rang.

"Damn," she cursed under her breath as she turned off the faucet. She entertained the idea of not answering the door, but her curiosity got the best of her, as always.

When she looked out the long glass panel beside the front door, she saw Susan standing on the stoop.

"Are you all right?" she asked, stepping into the foyer. "I saw you get out of a taxi and was worried. You always walk home on Friday afternoons."

Rachel laughed and hugged her friend.

"I was just tired. You worry too much. My god, you must have driven your kids nuts. In fact, how does Jim survive?"

"Rachel, somebody's got to worry about you," Susan said, breezing by Rachel and into the back of the house. Rachel followed her.

"I was just getting ready to take a bath."

"I won't stay long then," Susan said, sitting down on a stool at the kitchen bar. "So, how are things going?"

"*Things* are going fine."

"Good."

Pause.

"So, how about Wolf Trap? We've still got those extra tickets."

"You know the biggest difference between you and me, Susan?"

Susan just looked at her.

"I work for a living, and you don't. In fact, I've worked all my life – since the cows came home, literally – and unless you're hiding something from me, you've never had to work to pay your bills a day in your life."

"And?"

"On the weekends, I like to rest. I get tired. I like to relax. Saturday mornings I just want to be alone. I love you. I appreciate your invitations, but I think I'll 'just say no'."

Susan hopped off the stool, kissed Rachel on the cheek and headed for the front door.

"Not a problem, honey. Anything you want me to bring you from the Market?"

"Some tomatoes, if you see some that look any good."

"You got it. Enjoy your bath," she called back from the street.

When Rachel went back upstairs, the water she had already drawn was cold, so she turned the handle all the way to the left to warm it up and then sank into the full tub. She reminded herself to look into adding jets. She could really use the bursts of water against her lower back this evening.

She laid her head back and closed her eyes. Life was good – jets or no jets.

*   *   *

A half hour later, the tip of her braid wet where it had dipped into the bath water, she padded around in her bare feet on the cool kitchen tile floor. She wore nothing under her lavender silk kimono and the heady freedom from constricting bra and panties felt so good that she thought it was almost worth wearing them all week just so she could take them off.

Rachel sighed with satisfaction as she rummaged through her refrigerator to find salad fixings. A couple leaves of Romaine lettuce, some dried cranberries, a not quite yet shriveled carrot and one spear of broccoli would make a perfect dinner, she thought.

As she started to wash the lettuce, she felt a wet nose nudge her calf and looked down to see Ralph standing at her feet.

"Gee, I'm sorry, Ralph. I don't know what's wrong with me. Here, it's Friday. Why not blow it all out," and she poured out twice the amount of Alpo she normally gave him.

Ralph wagged his rear end appreciatively and went at his food with great gusto.

Rachel finished making her salad and sat down at the kitchen table to eat it and read her mail. A bill from Lord & Taylor, a newsletter from AARP and a note from Nancy Triplette, a cousin who had bought the family farm several years ago.

"Dear Rachel, Howard and I are planning our 25th wedding anniversary and hope that you will be able to come. We'll be sending out formal invitations soon, but wanted to issue a personal word of welcome to you in advance. We hope you'll come stay with us a few days here on the farm. You know, we've always got a bed made up for you."

Rachel put the letter down and looked at the opposite wall where the picture of Greenmont, her father's farm, hung in a place of prominence. She looked lovingly at the wide front porch, the long driveway lined with daffodils, the huge concrete pot of coleus, the dairy barn with rusty silo where she and her father used to find stray kittens hiding.

And she missed home.

*   *   *

Ten years ago, Rachel's 72-year-old father died of a heart attack out in the fields on a tractor alone. His body lay undiscovered until the next day when the hired man reported for work and found the tractor missing. The thought of her father dying alone and lying in the cornfield all night Rachel nightmares for a long time.

Her brother Edward considered returning to the farm to see if he could keep the place running, but Rachel talked him out of it.

Her brother was a veterinarian living in Boone, North Carolina at the time of their father's death. Rachel knew Edward could manage the farm and might even enjoy doing it, but his wife Ethel would hate it. She didn't even like visiting the place.

Rachel knew a move to the farm would be the end of the marriage and absolutely refused to put her stamp of approval on Edward's tentative plans. Fortunately, he still listened to his big sister and gave up the fantasy.

They leased the farm for a couple of years to a young couple who wanted to try their hands at getting back to nature. Nature wasn't very cooperative, and the Edmonds moved back to Richmond, Virginia, many thousands of dollars poorer but wiser.

That was when the farm was bought back into the family by the Tripletts.

Rachel was relieved to be able to visit again, although saddened by all the changes – some minor ones, like the way the house was furnished. None of the familiar family antiques greeted her the first time she went back. They had been replaced by Nancy and George's latest craze in furniture. Stipley went well with the plain farmhouse, but Rachel was sorry not to be able to sink into all the old familiar overstuffed chairs and sofas.

Other changes were more drastic, like the new interstate highway that passed dangerously close to the house now. The last time she visited about a year ago, Rachel could hear the traffic when she rocked on the front porch.

Still, she was eager to return and picked up the phone to call her cousin.

"Hello, Nancy. It's Rachel. Just called to thank you for giving me a heads up on your party. When's it going to be? I want to get it on my calendar."

"So glad you called. Looks like we're going to have to move it forward. George's mother is going to have surgery next month, and we want to do it before then. Can you come weekend after next?"

Rachel consulted her datebook and told Nancy she'd cancel an engagement penciled in that Saturday so she could make the trip.

When she hung up the phone, she felt herself getting excited already.

"Ralph, we're going home," she said as she turned out the kitchen lights and led him upstairs to the top floor to meditate.

Rachel began her meditation practice in law school and still sat on the original zafu she had then. Susan, seeing it recently, encouraged her to replace the somewhat faded and flattened purple cushion, but Rachel couldn't part with it. A lot of meditating had been done from that spot over the past three plus decades.

As she crossed her legs under her knees and straightened her spine in preparation for her practice, Ralph jumped up on the window seat to stand guard. Rain had begun to fall in a gentle lullaby on her new tin roof. She congratulated herself on spending her money so wisely. There was nothing quite so soothing as rain on a tin roof, she told herself, and no better way to transport herself back in time to the farm.

As she began to count her breaths, the drops picked up and quickly became a deafening downpour. Rachel had a hard time at first staying focused. When lightening lit up the room and Ralph leaped from the window seat and out of the room in terror, she opened her eyes.

Outside the rain was falling in sheets. The streetlight behind Mr. Moser's house looked like the beacon from a lighthouse in a storm. Rachel watched the rain pour for a while and wondered if John Turner were downstairs. She usually heard him come in from work, but couldn't remember any sounds from downstairs all night.

Of course, he could have come in while she was on the phone and she just wasn't aware of it.

This is silly, she thought. He's a grown man. I certainly don't need to be worrying about him on rainy nights.

Still, she wondered if perhaps there were some way she could find out whether he were home. She could call Susan and ask her if she saw any lights. No, that would just encourage Susan's obsession with matching them up – make her friend think she cared. No, she would just go back to meditating and let that go.

The rain slowed up some, and Rachel did let go of her thoughts of her tenant. After a few attempts, she found her breath deepening and finally the rain stopped – or she stopped hearing it.

Chapter 7

Rachel was shocked when she looked at the clock the next morning and saw that the time was 9:45, three hours later than her alarm rang on weekdays. Normally an early riser even on weekends, she was immediately disoriented by the lateness of the hour – even saddened by the thought of those hours she had missed.

Then fear struck as she wondered why Ralph hadn't waked her up to be fed and walked. She laughed when she saw him curled at the foot of her bed snoring.

"You must have needed the extra sleep, too," she said to him as she swung her legs over the side of the bed and slipped her feet into her terrycloth mules. "We must be getting old, Ralph."

Ralph wagged his tail and bounded down the stairs in denial.

The automatic coffee maker had brewed the French roast at the usual time, and it waited in the pot, cold. Rachel considered starting a fresh pot, thought better of the idea and nuked a cupful and took it outside onto the back deck.

The mid-morning humidity hit her in the face like a damp cloth, but old habits die hard. She took her usual position at the ice cream parlor table and sat in her favorite of the two chairs, facing Mr. Moser's house to the east.

The sun had risen three hours past the point in the sky she was accustomed to seeing it, and she marveled at the difference the mid-morning light made in the colors of the trees. The green of the leaves appeared more yellow, the bark a lighter shade of brown. Her pink impatiens were already beginning to wilt a little with the rising temperatures. The birdsong she always enjoyed had already been replaced by the sound of traffic.

Then she heard voices on the other side of the fence.

"Check," said John Turner's voice.

"That sure didn't take long," Mr. Moser's voice came back.

Rachel heard John laugh and then silence again as presumably the two men continued their chess game.

Rachel smiled to herself as she imagined her neighbor's delight at having found a more challenging chess partner.

"Good move," she heard John say.

"Thanks. I been playing chess all my life, I guess. How bout you?"

"Just took it up a couple years ago. I'm sure you can teach me a lot."

"I don't know about that, but we'll see. You play with Rachel yet?"

Uh-oh, Rachel thought. Here we go. Another matchmaker.

"No, I doubt she plays. She's a mighty busy lady."

"She is at that," Mr. Moser said in what Rachel interpreted as a disapproving tone. "But you should ask her. She's smart as hell. Maybe you could teach her a thing or two."

"Maybe I could," John said, then, "Checkmate."

*   *   *

After a busy week, there was nothing Rachel enjoyed more than a day with absolutely nothing on her calendar. She loved the sense of anticipation of a blank day ahead. The possibilities were endless – napping on and off for hours, launching off on some adventure across town. Just walking a few blocks to Dupont Circle presented guaranteed excitement.

By the time Rachel ate her breakfast of oatmeal and bananas, took a quick shower, made her bed and walked Ralph, the hands of the kitchen clock pointed to noon.

I sure don't want to do this very often, she thought as she sat down in the den with her *Washington Post* to see what she might want to do with her day.

A baby panda bear making its first appearance at the zoo appealed to her, but was nixed when she thought of the long lines and the stench that she would surely face in the heat of the afternoon. A Georgia O'Keefe exhibit was at the National Art Gallery but, again, the lines deterred her.

She settled on a late lunch at Mrs. Simpson's and a four o'clock chamber concert at the Phillips Gallery.

A perfect plan, Rachel thought with great satisfaction as she climbed the stairs to change into a cooler blouse and walking shoes.

She considered calling the new lady lawyer in town, but decided against it. Charity begins at home, she thought, and she was starved for some quiet.

As she looked through her closet for something short sleeved and sheer, she was suddenly struck by a desire to shop for something new – a thought that rarely presented itself. Rachel wore clothes because the law required it. Shopping was a necessity and not a form of entertainment in her book.

But she took note of the fact that her inventory of short sleeved and sheer was sorely lacking and made a stop at Lord & Taylor part of her plan.

There were plenty of boutiques along the way to Mrs. Simpson's, but Rachel knew the clerks at the larger department store and didn't want to brave a new frontier that morning.

She grabbed a pale green short-sleeved hemp blouse and matching skirt, threw on a pair of Easy Spirit walking sandals and was off on her mission, with the promise of Mrs. Simpson's heavenly chocolate mousse followed by Mozart to look forward to.

The Dupont Circle metro station was crowded, and Rachel had to stand in line to buy a fare ticket. There just is no escaping lines in this city, she thought as she inched closer to the machine spitting out tickets. When she finally got to the head of the line, the machine kept rejecting her only dollar bill. As she tried to iron out the wrinkles, a voice behind her said, "Need help?"

Rachel turned around to face her savior, a skinny black boy who towered over her by several heads, his own head covered in dreadlocks down to his waist.

"Here, why don't we trade. I've got a bunch. Maybe one of these will work," he mumbled as he shoved a fistful of ones toward Rachel.

"Thanks. I sure appreciate it," she said as the fare machine sucked the crisp new bill up like a giant toad swallowing flies.

The kid grinned at her and stepped up to get his own card, chains rattling at the pocket of his low-slung baggy jeans.

Rachel remembered the words of Stella DuBois in the play, *Streetcar Named Desire*, "I've always depended on the kindness of strangers" and thought that sometimes strangers could be pretty strange.

The D.C. metro system was the perfect place to find the bizarre, if that's what you were looking for. Every day was another lesson in weird and even after so many years in the city, Rachel never stopped being amazed at some of the things she found there. It was why she either walked or rode the subway. She hated to miss the show.

She deliberately sat next to an empty seat when she got on the train, hoping that someone entertaining would sit next to her. Very rarely was she disappointed.

Within seconds of choosing her seat, an elderly woman got on, loaded down with several shopping bags.

"Had a good morning at the stores?" Rachel asked, by way of greeting.

"Oh, no. This is stuff to be returned," the woman answered, settling herself and her overstuffed bags as comfortably as she could in the small space.

"My goodness. You must have as much trouble as I do shopping if you're having to take back all that."

"Do it every Saturday. Not a problem. Love to shop, just don't need all this stuff. Just cause you don't need things don't mean you can't buy it, you know."

The woman looked up at Rachel, beamed with satisfaction and then seemed to shrink into herself.

Rachel knew the signs when people wanted to talk and when they wanted to be left alone. She always respected their boundaries because she had her own.

When the train reached Metro Center, she said good-bye, and the two went in opposite directions.

Rachel wanted to get her little bit of shopping done before lunch so she could relax for the rest of the afternoon. Lord & Taylor was just a short walk from the subway entrance and she knew the department in the store where she believed short sleeved and sheer might be and made a beeline for it.

On the way there, she passed a mannequin dressed for a night of clubbing, complete with slinky little black dress, four-inch silver spiked heels, huge rhinestone earrings. She stopped to stare.

"Now, that's *you*, Ms. Springer," a voice behind her laughed.

Rachel turned around to see the store manager approaching.

"I'm sure we've got it in your size. Want to try it on?"

"Where in the hell would I wear it, if I got it?" Rachel shot back. "I didn't even wear something like that when I had the body to wear it."

The two women commiserated briefly about aging gracefully and then the manager asked Rachel if there were anything she could do to help her.

"No, I think I've got a pretty good idea of what I want. Just became disoriented momentarily. Thanks for asking, though."

Moments later she was in a dressing room, trying on a very simple silk blouse that suited her well. She asked the clerk for three of the same style in soft shades of pink, blue and lavender and was on her way out of the store within fifteen minutes.

The shopping bag of blouses swinging at her side, she walked toward the restaurant, picking the shady side of the street where the temperatures felt 10 degrees cooler. When she reached the corner, she crossed in front of the stopped traffic and walked the half block to Mrs. Simpson's.

"Good afternoon, Ms. Springer. So nice to see you," the host greeted her. "I'm sorry, but your usual table is occupied. May I seat you in the other corner?"

Rachel assured him that would be fine and looked to see who the lucky person was who had landed in the window seat.

A young couple held hands across the white linen tablecloth, gazing adoringly into each other's eyes.

Well, if I can't have it, I'm glad it's such a deserving pair, she thought.

The waitress brought her unsweetened tea almost before she could get seated and her bag placed on the chair opposite her. She ordered a broccoli quiche and salad, took her copy of the *Washington Post* crossword puzzle out of her purse and then realized she didn't have a pen.

When she got up to go to the front desk to borrow one, she noticed that the young couple at her table were looking at a map together. As she got closer to them, she stopped and spoke.

"Can I help you find some place?"

"Thanks," the young man said. "We're trying to find the Phillips Gallery."

"If you wait long enough, you can just follow me there. I'm going to a four o'clock concert."

They both insisted they didn't want to be a bother, and Rachel began to wonder if perhaps they really just wanted to go alone. As she was on the verge of giving up and started to point out where the gallery was on their map, the girl said, "If you're sure you don't mind . . ."

"Not at all. We've got plenty of time, so relax. If you haven't had dessert yet, I highly recommend the chocolate mousse."

About a half hour later, the couple joined their newfound tour guide at the register and thanked her again for offering to show them the way.

"My pleasure. I usually walk, but it's sort of a hike. We could share a cab and have more time to look around the gallery before the concert if you'd like."

They agreed that was a good idea and followed her to the corner to hail a taxi.

"Where are you from?" Rachel asked from the Yellow Cab's front seat.

"Charlotte, North Carolina," Bruce Cochrane said.

As the cab raced toward their destination as if on its way to a fire, Rachel learned that he and his new bride, Linda, were on their honeymoon and staying at the Hotel Lombardy on Pennsylvania Avenue.

"What an excellent choice. Have you walked to Georgetown yet?"

"We loved it," Linda said.

"You must try the little bar at the Watergate, too," Rachel advised. "The Harvey Walbangers are pretty strong though. Be careful."

The cab screeched to a halt in front of the Phillips Gallery, and Bruce insisted on paying the fare.

"Thanks," Rachel said, not usually being on the receiving end of such generosity. Actually, she thought, it felt pretty good. Maybe she could get used to it.

"You all enjoy yourselves the rest of your visit."

"Maybe we'll see you at the concert," Bruce said as he shook her hand.

"Save us a seat," Linda chimed in.

Rachel assured her she would and went downstairs to the gift shop to speak to Belinda, a friend who volunteered there on Saturday afternoons.

"My goodness, you look lovely today," Belinda cooed from behind the register. "What's up?"

"Not a thing. How about you? How was Vermont?"

"The kids are fine. Harold was a pain in the ass, and I'm glad to be home, though. Going to the concert?"

Rachel told her she was and pulled out the blouses she had bought earlier.

"What do you think?"

"They're you. What more can I say?"

"Is 'they're you' a good thing or a bad thing, in your opinion?"

"A good thing, sweetie. Why do you ask?"

"Just thinking," Rachel said and then, "Can you join me for the music?"

"No, I'm not off until five."

"Well, come on in then, if you can. Looks like it's a long program."

Rachel bought a chocolate truffle before she left and went back upstairs to wander through the rooms, naturally gravitating toward her favorite painting, "The Boat Party."

She took a seat on the bench in the middle of the room and gazed at the work of art, reflecting on the way the light today seemed to cast a spotlight on one of the characters more than the others.

Rachel felt her tense shoulders ease down into their blades, her heart open up, the lines in the middle of her brow smooth out.

It can't get much better than this, she thought as she got up and moved toward the concert hall to find her seat and two extras for her new friends.

The musicians were already tuning their instruments when she moved to the front of the room, toward the windows and their heavy velvet drapes.

She took a seat on a folding metal chair and put her shopping bag and purse in the two to her left.

As she sat waiting, she gazed around the room as it quickly filled up and was surprised to see John Turner sitting near the front. She took the opportunity to study him.

The sun was shining on his red hair, causing it to appear lit from within. She couldn't see the freckles from that far way, but she knew they were there and smiled at the thought.

As though he felt her stare, John turned and met her eyes directly.

Rachel waved and he returned the gesture. Just then, Bruce and Linda came in the room and took their seats, handing her a program. When Rachel looked back at John, he was turned the other way.

*   *   *

At the end of the concert, Rachel looked for John but didn't see him. She wondered if he had left before the final piece to avoid the rush.

"Thanks again for your help," Linda interrupted her thoughts, holding out her hand. Rachel reached over to hug her and then Bruce, saying, "My father always told me you only shake hands with people you don't like."

The young couple asked for directions back to their hotel, and Rachel set out for the walk home. The sun was beginning to set, and the temperatures had cooled to a comfortable 75 degrees. She thought about what she would eat for supper and decided to stop by Zorba's to get Greek take-out. She'd been craving baklava for a while and figured it would be a sweet way to end such a sweet day.

The restaurant courtyard was crowded with people enjoying the cool evening, watching the passersby and eating what, in Rachel's opinion, was some of the best Greek food in town.

She wound through the tables and into the little restaurant where she placed her order for souvlaki at the counter in the back. Ten minutes later, she was on her way home with spicy smells wafting out of the bag beside her. Ralph would be able to smell her a block away, she thought.

As she turned her corner and walked toward her house, she noticed people crowded around the front door across the street and realized it was Susan and Jim, John Turner and a blonde she didn't recognize. They were carrying picnic baskets and coolers out to a large black Lincoln SUV.

"Yoohoo, Rachel," Susan called. "Sure you don't want to go to Wolf Trap with us? I'm sure we could finagle an extra lawn ticket for you."

"Thanks, but I'm looking forward to an evening at home," Rachel said, realizing now John's reason for leaving the Phillips early.

"I'm sorry, Rachel – This is Ann Spellman," Susan said. "She works with John and Jim on the hospital project."

Rachel and the tall blonde shook hands, and Rachel wished them all a safe trip and a good time at Wolf Trap.

Ralph was waiting to be let out and bounded out the door. As she grabbed his leash and followed him back down the walk, she noticed that John and Ann Spellman were sitting in the backseat together, and Jim was at the wheel of Ann's car.

"Interesting," Rachel muttered as she reached for a bite of baklava. Sometimes, one shouldn't have to wait for dessert, she thought.

*   *   *

When Rachel got back from walking Ralph, the black Lincoln had left. She swallowed a large lump in her throat. With no more baklava to comfort her, she decided to settle in her den with the souvlaki and try to find a good movie to watch.

After discounting *Sleepless in Seattle*, *My Architect*, and *The Wild Parrots of Telegraph Hill* as movies not very comforting to someone struggling with a growing lump in her throat, she decided that the second season of Larry David's *Curb Your Enthusiasm* was a safe bet. Edgy humor was just what she needed.

She had just finished the last bite of pork and pita and the second show of the season when the phone rang.

When she answered it, Mr. Moser was at the other end.

"Saw your lights on and was surprised. Thought you were going to Wolf Trap with John. Anything wrong?" he shouted, evidently having trouble with his hearing aid again.

"No. I'm fine."

"But I thought John told me this morning you were going."

"No. Susan asked me to, but I decided to stay home."

"That's not what John said," her neighbor insisted.

It took Rachel several tries to convince Mr. Moser that perhaps he had misunderstood and that she was fine, going about her evening exactly as she had planned.

"Okay, if you're sure. I really like that young man. He's a fine chess player, you know."

Rachel didn't know, but she told Mr. Moser she was very glad he had found a partner and that she, too, thought John Turner was a "nice young man."

"I'll let you go," Mr. Moser said. "Must be a hell of a movie to choose it over John Turner, though."

They said good-bye, and Rachel went back to Larry David, disappointed to find that the last few shows were not as entertaining as the first.

The digital clock beside Rachel's bed glowed 12:32 a.m. when she heard the car doors close across the street. Susan's front door opened, closed and then silence. She waited to hear John's door, and, after several minutes dragged by, she considered getting up to peer out the window to see what her tenant and the leggy blond were doing.

Instead, she tried meditating to let go of the impulse.

Breathe in.

Breathe out.

She was just getting out of bed when she heard the downstairs door. She held her breath this time until the Lincoln roared away from the curb.

Rachel settled back into bed and fell asleep with a smile on her face.

Chapter 8

Sundays were Rachel's favorite day of the week. She loved getting up around seven o'clock and knowing that the whole day stretched ahead of her with absolutely nothing to do.

As she walked downstairs to make coffee, she realized she wouldn't be able to sit out back wearing just a nightgown anymore now that she shared the space.

Damn, she said to herself as she grabbed a shawl and the *Washington Post*. Maybe renting the downstairs apartment wasn't such a good idea.

She was even more rattled when she saw John had already beaten her outside.

"Good morning," he greeted her brightly as she stepped out on the deck. "Mind if I share the morning with you? I can go back inside if the answer is 'yes.' Be honest."

My god, the man was chirpy for so early in the day, Rachel thought. She was a morning person, but not a chirpy one.

"No, you're fine," she insisted, but softly, hoping her voice level would give him a clue of her need for quiet. "I'm surprised you're up so early, though, after your late night."

John jumped up to pull her chair out from the table. "I hope I didn't disturb you coming in. Peter Paul and Mary went on a little long, and then we stopped in Crystal City at some club Ann wanted us to see."

"How was it?"

"Okay. I'm not really a club kind of guy. The Phillips yesterday was more my speed. Did you enjoy the music? I was sorry I had to leave before I got a chance to speak to you."

"Very much," Rachel said as she opened the arts section of the *Post*. "Want to see part of the paper?"

"Thanks," John said as he reached for the sports section.

Rachel took a sip of coffee and breathed a sigh of relief. Birds sang. The breeze lifted the heavy heads of the hydrangea bush. The smell of bacon frying next door and very faint strains of Bach from the neighbor on the other side comforted her.

Life is good, Rachel mused. This sharing isn't too bad. Breathe in. Breathe out.

She looked up from her paper at John, and he smiled.

*   *   *

Vying for first place with morning coffee and the paper in the "heavenly things to do on Sunday" contest was an early afternoon crossword puzzle and a nap.

Rachel had just settled down in the den on the couch when she heard the front door open, and Susan's voice yoohooed down the hall.

"There you are," she sang as she bounced in the den. "I was hoping to catch you before your nap. Just got home from church and wanted to tell you all about last night."

Rachel looked longingly at the puzzle she had just begun.

"John is to die for," Susan began. "I wished so badly you were there instead of Ann Spellman. She's just not our kind of person. I'm sure John would have been much happier with you in the back seat with him. She just talked and talked and talked – all the way there, all during the concert, all the way home. My god, the woman is a non-stop chatterbox and then . . ."

"So, did you enjoy the music?"

"Mary has gained an awful lot of weight, you know, and that mumu she wears all the time didn't help matters, but her voice is still the same. Put us all in the mood to dance."

Rachel nodded.

"We went to a club."

"So I heard."

"To dance."

"That's what John said."

"He's a very good dancer, Rachel."

"Well, I'm not, so it's a good thing I wasn't there," Rachel said, picking up the crossword puzzle as a hint that, as far as she was concerned, the conversation was over.

"Maybe next time," Susan said, kissed Rachel on the top of her head and rushed out of the den, high heels click-clacking down the parquet floor to the front of the house.

"Maybe," Rachel muttered to her back.

*   *   *

Ralph wasn't as much of a napper as Rachel, but he tried to be tolerant as long as he could. When his need to either get outside or have some company got beyond his ability to contain it any longer, he pulled at Rachel's braid.

From deep within her nap, she felt the tug. She tried to ignore it, but Ralph was as stubborn as she was, and the tugs grew more insistent.

Finally, she sat up. "Okay, okay. What is it?"

In answer, Ralph ran to the front door and stood with his tail thumping the floor.

"No rest for the weary," Rachel grumbled. With those words, memories of her grandmother Springer came flooding back to her. That had been one of her favorite refrains.

"No rest for the weary," Nana said as she rolled out biscuit dough onto the floured counter top or swept the long front porch that wrapped around three sides of the rambling Kentucky farmhouse.

Grandmother Springer was a farmer's wife who never stopped the hard work that finally stopped her in her tracks with a heart attack at 60 years old, long after she became a widow and ran the farm alone.

Because Rachel's father had his own farm to manage in Virginia, her visits to her grandmother were either alone or with Edward. As her brother grew older and was needed more and more in the family's own fields, Rachel went to Kentucky by herself.

It was her grandmother's "No rest for the weary" that convinced her that she didn't want to live the rest of her life on a farm. Unlike her father, who lived and breathed with such gusto on the land, the work seemed to suck the life out of his mother. Eventually, it literally did.

Her granddaughter seemed to be her only joy in life and, for that reason, Rachel continued the summer visits as long as her grandmother lived. When she got the call that Nana had died in her sleep, Rachel's first thought was that she finally would have some rest.

"Come on, Ralph. Let's go play," she said, grabbing his leash.

The sidewalk was wet from a shower that had come up while she slept. Wet cement had a wonderful smell, she thought – so many different ingredients let loose after a good downpour – spilled food and drink, cigarette butts, animal pee. It all got mixed together and then steamed off the hot sidewalk in an aroma that was pure city.

Rachel loved it.

Ralph splashed through several puddles, sniffed his favorite spots, and took off down the street like he was late for a very important date.

A breeze cooled the afternoon off. As she approached Dupont Circle, Rachel thought it would be nice to sit on one of the benches for a few minutes. They were wet, so she went into the drug store to buy a dry paper to sit on.

Back outside with her copy of the *National Enquirer*, she walked over to her favorite bench and sat down to watch Ralph make his rounds. First, the water fountain, then several trashcans, a small clutch of homeless men playing checkers, a mother pushing a baby stroller.

Finally, he came back to sit at her feet, satisfied with a job well done.

Rachel reached down to scratch behind his ears, his reward for sharing his love around the Circle – taking on that responsibility for the family while Rachel sat on the sidelines watching, ready if needed.

Evidently, all was well that afternoon. If Ralph felt that some young mother or dirty wino needed Rachel's attention, he always came over and nudged her with his nose.

She was glad he felt satisfied with the well-being of the Circle that afternoon. She was in no mood to socialize.

No sooner had that thought crossed her mind than she sensed someone approaching her bench. She looked over her left shoulder to see a young girl plodding toward her – backpack bowing her down. She looked like she was walking the Appalachian Trail rather than out for a Sunday afternoon in the city.

Her hair was hot pink and heavily gelled into porcupine quills, her nose pierced, every inch of exposed skin tattooed. As she got closer, Rachel noticed the startling color of her eyes. Rachel knew that her own eyes had an impact on other people because of their unusual color, and as she faced this young woman, she thought, this must be the way people feel when I look at them.

"Mind if I sit beside you a minute?" the girl asked.

"Not at all," Rachel said as she scooted over to make room on the wooden bench. The battered backpack bumped her as the girl struggled to take it off so she could sit down.

"Sorry, ma'am. Didn't mean to slam you," the girl said with a very slow Southern drawl. "Don't mind me. Just need to rest awhile."

"No problem," Rachel assured her. Ralph edged closer to the girl, looking up at her with love-filled eyes.

"Nice pooch. What's his name?"

"Ralph. Appears as though he likes you."

"All dogs like me. Can't say the same for people, but I got no gripe with dogs."

"Where are you from? Your accent is pretty deep south, I'd guess."

"Yeah, it's deep. Deep as hog shit."

Rachel waited for the answer to her question but decided not to push the issue. One more question, and then she'd stop.

"First visit to DC?"

"I guess so, but I been here six months now so I guess I ain't exactly visiting no more. Guess you could call me a city girl now. At least I been here longer than anywharst else."

Rachel smiled at her seatmate and continued scratching Ralph's left ear. She figured she would let the girl make the next move.

"You live around here?"

"Yes, I do," Rachel said, remembering Edward's advice when she moved to the city: Don't talk to strangers. In fact, don't even make eye contact. You're setting yourself up for disaster, if you do.

"I moved here five years ago. Are you planning to stay?"

"Don't know," the girl said, leaning back and surveying the Circle. "The winter was pretty cold. Thought I might head on toward Florida in a couple of months."

All the questions Rachel always wondered about homeless people came pouring into her mind. "Does your family know where you are? How do you bathe? When did you last eat?" and most importantly, "Are you afraid?"

Instead, she said nothing.

"You got a cigarette I could bum?"

"Don't smoke. Sorry."

The girl looked at her for a while, seeming to take in every inch of her, from her Birkenstocks to the beads at the end of her braid.

"You got real perty eyes, ma'am. Anybody ever told you they looked like a lilac bush?"

"Yes, once, a very long time ago, somebody made that very comment," Rachel said, remembering a boy she had dated in high school. What was his name? Joe, Joey – yes, Joseph Parker. Wonder whatever happened to the kid?

"My daddy used to tell me my eyes was so perty he could smell em. Funny thing to say, don't you think?"

Rachel laughed and stood up, Ralph at her heels.

"Guess we'd better get on home. Nice to meet you Miss . . ."

"Chelsea. I like your dog, ma'am. You're lucky to have him."

"Yes, I am," Rachel said as she attached the leash to his collar. "He is a good dog and a fine judge of character."

*   *   *

Monday mornings were always a mixed bag at Springer & Associates. The phone rang all morning as people looked for a lawyer to clean up their weekend catastrophes. Rachel and Georgia tried to get to the office early to hold their beginning-of-the-week meeting before nine o'clock.

When Rachel arrived a little before eight, Georgia was pouring herself a cup of coffee.

"My, you're up and at 'em early," Rachel greeted her.

"Morning. I've got to leave a little early. Mike needs to have some kind of medical test done today, and I have to drive him to the appointment."

"Everything all right?"

"I hope so. It's just routine, but you know how they can be."

The two exchanged reports of their weekends and then went into Rachel's office to talk about the upcoming week over fresh pastries Georgia had brought from the bakery down the street.

They covered court dates and case deadlines, went over the details of several new cases and closed a couple of files. As always, the meeting ended with Rachel's least favorite item of business – overdue accounts.

That out of the way, Rachel looked at her calendar and pushed it across the desk to her assistant.

"Does this all look up to date to you?" she asked. "If so, I think I'll take next week off to go down to the farm. Nancy called to invite me to their wedding anniversary party, and I think I'll stay for a few days. Thought I'd make a vacation of it if my schedule allows."

"I'll check to make sure, but I'm fairly confident nothing will interfere," Georgia said.

With that, the phone rang, beginning another hectic day.

"Let's lock up the office and walk down to Dean & Delucca's for lunch today," Rachel suggested after Georgia hung up.

"I've got to leave early, remember. I was going to just work through lunch."

"Don't."

"You're the boss."

*   *   *

Many of the phone calls that morning required Rachel's attention, leaving her feeling like she had been spinning wheels for three hours instead of moving through her list of things to do. By the time the lunch hour arrived, she was ready to escape the office.

"Quick, let's get out of here before that damn phone rings again," she said to Georgia as she grabbed her purse and headed for the front door, Ralph trotting behind her.

"I'm right behind you," Georgia answered, switching the phones to the answering machine and turning off her dictaphone machine.

Ralph strained at his leash as Rachel locked the front door.

"How's your new tenant working out?" Georgia asked as they took off at a fast clip toward Dean & Delucca.

"I don't really see much of him, but I guess that's a good thing," Rachel laughed. "He's quiet, doesn't smoke and, so far, no late partying."

"That's what you wanted, so I guess all's well. It'll be good to have him in the house while you're away at the farm, too."

"I hadn't thought of that, but you're right."

"How much longer is he staying?"

"The lease was for six months, so I guess he'll be moving out sometime around Christmas."

"I bet he'll be glad to be home with his friends and family for the holidays."

"Yes, I'm sure you're right. He's got a grandson he talks about a lot, and I know he misses him. In fact, he told me the other day that Ben is coming for a visit this weekend."

"How do you feel about sharing a house with a rambunctious little boy? That sure will be different."

"Maybe he'll be quiet like his grandfather."

"Obviously, you've never been around children much."

"Gee, thanks, Georgia. Something else to worry about."

*   *   *

Rachel tied Ralph to their favorite patio table, and she and Georgia went inside to place their lunch order. Near the counter, Mr. Lopez stacked bottles of virgin olive oil. Rachel nodded to him, and he responded with a wide grin.

She smiled and turned her back to say to Georgia, "You know who that is, don't you?"

"Mr. Lopez. I forgot to tell you he stopped by with his wife and kids one day last week to pay Stan's bill."

"How did they seem?"

"Everybody was fine. Wish all our cases were that easy."

"Georgia, I think you've missed an important point. We didn't make any money on that case, remember?"

Looking sheepish, Georgia placed her order.

By the time they finished their salads and started walking back to work, the temperatures had climbed into the 90s, and Rachel took off her black linen jacket.

"It's going to be a hot summer," she said. "I'm looking forward to escaping to the farm. Why don't you take the week off, too? We don't have anybody right now who needs hand-holding while I'm away."

"You sure?"

"Take a break. You and Mike go somewhere cool, too."

"If you're sure . . ."

"I'm sure."

The phone was ringing when they opened the door, and as Georgia rushed to answer it before the answering machine kicked in, she said, "Think I will."

*   *   *

Late that afternoon, after Georgia had left and Rachel was manning the office alone, she heard the front door open and close. Ralph's ears pricked up, and he leaped out of the window seat and dashed out front.

"Afternoon, Ralph," she heard John Turner say.

Rachel looked at her watch, curious as to what he was doing away from work and was surprised to see that it was after five o'clock.

She got up from her desk, smoothing her skirt, and walked out to greet him.

"What a nice surprise," she said.

"What a great location you have here."

"Yeah. We got real lucky with this spot. Started out with an office in Crystal City and when this building went on the market after the death of one of my clients, I grabbed it."

"Where's Georgia?"

"She had to take her husband to a doctor's appointment. I know she'll be disappointed she missed your visit."

"Tell her I still think longingly of her chocolate chip cookies," he said. "Since your boss is gone, why don't you call it a day and let me walk you home."

Rachel said that sounded like a good idea and went back in her office to turn off her computer. When she stepped outside, John and Ralph stood with Luke Carter and his French poodle.

"Afternoon, Luke," Rachel said as she locked her front door. "I see you've met John."

"Yes, we've just been catching up on old times. John and I went to MIT together."

"Small world," John said.

"I hate to cut this short, but I need to get home," Luke said. "Susanna has invited some folks over for dinner, and she'll kill me if I'm late, but call me sometime, John, and we'll get together."

"Definitely," John said and the two men shook hands and said good-bye.

As they set off toward home, Rachel asked John when he was at MIT.

"Graduated in 1970. Luke was in the class behind me, but we were in the same dorm and got to be pretty good friends. I was sorry when we lost touch."

"He's a nice guy. He moved into the building next to me a couple of years ago, and I've enjoyed getting to know him. Seems like our dogs are on the same schedule."

A few minutes later, one of the sudden summer showers that made Rachel wish she was more disciplined about carrying an umbrella began to splatter the sidewalk and they dashed under the awning of One Step Down, a Caribbean restaurant and bar a couple of blocks up M Street.

"Let me buy you a drink, and we'll sit here and wait out the rain," John suggested.

"Great idea."

Ralph sat down next to John's feet, and he reached down and scratched his left ear.

Boy, that man learns fast, Rachel thought.

"So, is Ben still coming this weekend?" she asked after the cocktail waitress had taken their drink orders.

"Actually, he arrives tomorrow," John said. "His parents were able to get away from work earlier than they thought, so I'm taking over. In fact, that's why I was down in Georgetown this afternoon. Needed to pick up a few things for the visit."

"Doesn't seem like you had any luck," Rachel laughed, indicating his empty hands.

"I'm having it delivered tomorrow. Just an inflatable mattress and a DVD player."

"I know you're looking forward to it. When will I get to meet him?"

"Come on down tomorrow evening and have supper with us. I know he'll want to meet Ralph."

"Hear that, Ralph? We've got a date."

Ralph wagged his tail.

The rain lasted long enough for them to enjoy one drink and then stopped and the sun came out, causing the steam to rise off the sidewalk like a sauna.

"Welcome to DC in the summertime – humidity 100 percent," Rachel said.

"Doesn't bother me in the least. Sure you don't want another drink?"

"No. One was perfect."

John felt himself sigh with relief. Living with a woman who could never get enough to drink had left him gun-shy around women who drank at all. The night he had danced with Linda after the Peter Paul and Mary concert had brought back vivid memories as he smelled the alcohol on her breath. If he had any thoughts of kissing her goodnight, that offensive smell had squelched the desire.

"You're not much of a drinker," he said to Rachel.

"No. Does that bother you? If you want another, by all means go ahead. I don't mind."

"Quite the contrary. I'm ready to go."

"Tough week?"

"Just a lot to get done. I'm trying to clear my plate some before Ben comes. Susan has offered to watch him for me half days if I need help, but I'd really like to spend as much time with him as possible."

"He'll love Susan. She's raised a boy of her own, and she loves kids."

"How about you? Do you have any children?"

"Never been married. Ralph's my only family, except for a brother in Arkansas. We're pretty close, but don't see each other very often. Work keeps us both busy. Which reminds me, I'm going to be gone week after next to a family reunion in Virginia and will leave you some phone numbers in case you need to reach me."

"Sure. I'll be happy to look after things. What about Ralph?"

"He's going with me. He loves the farm."

"I'll miss seeing him," John said. "Be sure to bring him down tomorrow night. Will six o'clock work?"

"We'll look forward to it," Rachel said, noticing a longing in the pit of her stomach as John reached down again and stroked Ralph's black coat.

*   *   *

When Rachel walked into the den, she was surprised to see how late it was. The news was over so she decided to fix herself a salad and eat it outside instead of in front of the television set.

The rain had left her impatiens looking as luscious as a picture in House and Garden. Raindrops still hung on the petals, and the green leaves looked good enough to eat.

Rachel dried off an Adirondack chair as well as she could and then laid a clean towel down to sit on.

As she ate her tuna salad and fresh tomatoes Susan had shared from her garden, Rachel wondered if perhaps John would come outside to enjoy the coolness of the evening. But after she finished the last bite and lingered even longer over her iced tea, she finally realized it wasn't going to happen and was surprised that she was a little disappointed.

Later, as she locked the doors and turned out the lights to go upstairs, she noticed him sitting alone in the chair she had dried off.

She considered going back out but went to the third floor to meditate instead.

Chapter 9

The next morning, Rachel heard Ben before she saw him.

Squeals of delight drifted up from the courtyard to the third floor. When she opened her eyes and saw Ralph standing at attention at the window, ears alert, tail thumping the window seat with great passion, she thought she knew the cause of such enthusiasm.

But by the time she finished her practice and made her way downstairs, all was quiet. When no noise filtered up from the downstairs apartment, she decided John must have taken Ben sightseeing. Just as well she give them some time alone anyway, she thought, trying not to be disappointed that she was going to have to wait until later to meet John's grandson.

Rachel went on with her plan to spend some time in the office, trying to clear her desk a little before her trip to Virginia. She put on some faded jeans, a loose cotton shirt and her favorite pair of old Birkenstocks, called for Ralph and headed for the door.

On the way to Georgetown, she stopped at the hotel, One Washington Circle, to grab a quick breakfast and read the front page of the paper – her treat for working on a Saturday.

"Good morning, Ms. Springer," the hostess greeted her. "Off to work, are we now?" her Scottish brogue growing heavier as the conversation progressed.

"Yup, you caught me. My habits always get me in trouble. If I want to keep any secrets about what I do, I'm going to have to let go of some rituals."

"Well, don't let go of this one. We'd miss you," the pretty little redhead said as she led Rachel over to her corner booth.

"Thanks, Margaret."

"French toast and bacon?"

"Actually, I think I'll just have fruit and yogurt this morning. I'm trying to lose my usual five pounds."

"Coming right up," Margaret said and disappeared into the kitchen.

Rachel waved to several other regulars scattered throughout the cozy café and thought how comfortably familiar her life in Washington was. She had successfully created a small town atmosphere within the large city, and it suited her well.

Her cellphone rang and she reached in her pocketbook to find it. Georgia's name popped up on the screen.

"What's up?" Rachel said, surprised by her assistant's weekend call.

"I tried to reach you at home, but too late. I forgot you were planning to spend some time in the office today."

"I'm on my way there now. Why?"

"Rachel, Mike's going in the hospital tomorrow for surgery on Monday. They found some tumors in his colon. It may be serious."

Rachel stood up and walked outside to carry on the conversation in privacy.

"What can I do for you, Georgia? Do you need me to come over there now?"

"No, there's nothing you can do now. I just wanted you to know I won't be in the office on Monday. I don't know how long I'll be out, Rachel."

At that, Georgia began to weep, and Rachel was overcome with the helpless feeling she had experienced only a few times in her life. The last time was when her father died.

"Georgia, I'm coming over there. You're home, right?"

"Well, yes, but it's not really necessary. We're just resting. I guess I need to pack a few things. They want us to be at the hospital around seven tomorrow morning."

"I'm on my way. Do you need for me to pick anything up for you on my way out?"

Georgia assured her that they didn't need anything, and they said good-bye.

Rachel quickly paid for her breakfast and walked outside to hail a cab. She gave the driver Georgia's address in Bethesda and told him she'd want to stop at a grocery store along the way.

When she spotted a "yuppie market," as Georgia called the upscale specialty stores, she asked him to wait for her while she went inside.

As she picked up a bouquet of fresh daisies and several cold salads, she marveled at how quickly life could change and prayed that she could help her friend deal with her recent turn of events.

She thought about Georgia's desk, covered with pictures of Mike, Mike and the children, Mike surrounded by bowling trophies, Mike and Georgia on their recent cruise. What would Georgia do if she lost him, Rachel wondered.

"There are worse things in life than being single," an old maid aunt once said and Rachel figured this was one of them. Losing someone you've spent most of your life loving is surely harder than never loving, she thought.

She was shocked when Georgia greeted her at the front door, smiling as if nothing had changed. Mike stood behind her, beaming like he didn't have a care in the world.

"Rachel, I wish you hadn't done this," Georgia said. "I feel bad enough leaving you alone next week, and now I'm taking your Saturday, too."

"Nonsense," Rachel said, moving toward the cozy kitchen that opened into the great room where they stood. "I'd much rather be with you than at my desk any day. So, Mike, how are you feeling?"

"Ready to get this over with," he said, typically short on words.

"Rachel, I've called the temporary service, and they're sending over that nice young woman we used last Christmas when I was gone. You remember Rebecca, don't you?"

"Yes, and thanks. I could have done that, though. You're too good to me."

"I think she'll be a big help, and I hope to be back before you get too attached to her and decide you don't need me anymore."

"Trust me. That will never happen. What time is the surgery on Monday?"

"They've scheduled it for 8 a.m., and, if all goes well, he should be out of recovery and back in his room later that afternoon if you want to stop by to see him."

"I'll be there at eight."

'But what about . . .'"

"No problem. I'll let the temp service know where to find the key. Rebecca knows what to do. She'll be fine. It's you I'm worried about."

*   *   *

The cab ride back into the city was less stressful after seeing Georgia and Mike handling the prospect of surgery so well. Their life had always been like a fairytale romance, Rachel thought. Perfect in every way. No crises with children. No marital problems. Mike's medical problem was the first big test they had faced, and Rachel had been afraid they might not have the tools to handle it.

What she saw when she got to their house erased that fear. She observed a couple whose love for each other was shoring them up to face the stormy seas ahead – together.

With that reassurance to comfort her, Rachel went on to the office to get some paperwork cleared off her desk before she went home to get ready for dinner with the boys downstairs.

She wondered if she should take Ben a welcoming gift, and, if so, what? Her experience with children — let alone little boys — was pretty limited. She decided Ralph would be her gift and tried to concentrate on her clients.

Thoughts about how long her right hand would be gone, and how she could possibly survive without her, reminded Rachel to call the temp agency to let them know that Rebecca would arrive to an empty office Monday. She left a message and hoped someone would get it and call her back some time during the weekend.

In any event, Rachel knew where *she* would be Monday morning at eight o'clock. She knew Rebecca was a resourceful girl and that she could leave instructions for her.

Breathe in. Breathe out.

                    *   *   *

When Rachel strode up the front walk to her house, she smelled an aroma that brought back memories of her grandmother. Without a doubt, chicken was frying, she thought as she was flooded with visions of her grandmother killing and plucking the poor, unfortunate bird and flopping it in the frying pan before it had barely stopped squawking. She smiled to herself as she imagined John downstairs in an apron, covered with flour perhaps, preparing her supper.

Rachel ran upstairs to take a quick shower before heading down to meet Ben. She admitted that she felt shaky about the evening. What in the world did you talk to a five-year-old about? Nothing in her experience had ever prepared her for the challenge.

"Ralph, it's up to you, buddy. You're in charge. I'll follow your lead."

Ralph shook all over with excitement – whether from the smell of fried chicken or because he sensed her own high energy, she wasn't sure. When she opened the front door, he dashed out and made a beeline for the downstairs apartment.

The door opened before he even got to it, and Rachel was met by a miniature copy of John standing there with his arms stretched out to welcome the dog. A darker shade of John's red hair and those same moss-green eyes. Ralph seemed to intuitively know not to frighten the boy by jumping up on him and stood calmly to let himself be hugged.

"Ralph likes to have his ears scratched," John said, stooping down to show his grandson the proper ear scratching technique.

"Hi, Ralph. I'm Ben," the little boy introduced himself, seriously.

Ralph licked him on the nose, and Ben ducked his head and squealed.

"And this is Ralph's friend, Rachel," John said, drawing her into the circle of dog and boy.

"Hey, Ben. Ralph seems to really like you. You must be a nice boy."

"I am," the child announced, looking up at her with wide eyes. "I'm being very quiet so I don't bother you upstairs. You like quiet."

Rachel laughed. "Well, you don't have to be *too* quiet. Are you having fun with your Granddad?"

Ben launched into a long list of all the things they had seen and done that day, including the Air & Space Museum, the Washington Monument and a barge ride on the C&O Canal.

"Tomorrow we're going to the zoo. Wanna come? We could take Ralph."

"I don't know," Rachel said, looking at John doubtfully.

"Sure. Come along if you'd like. We'd love to have you. But right now, I think we've got some supper to eat. Ben's favorite – fried chicken, green beans and potato salad. A real southern boy at heart."

The three gathered around the small kitchen table, and Rachel was impressed to see Ben bow his head and reach for her hand to say grace before the meal. Holding his little hand in her left hand and John's big one in her right felt safe, she thought, and she was reluctant to let them go after the "amen."

Ben had evidently been taught that children should be seen and not heard at the dinner table. He sat quietly, gnawing at his drumstick and doing a good job of cleaning his plate of vegetables.

"What a good eater you are," Rachel said when it was time for dessert.

"Granddad cooks good," Ben said, beaming at John and then announcing proudly, "I'm going to sleep in a sleeping bag tonight. We might even sleep outside."

"Now, that sounds like fun," Rachel said.

"Do you want to sleep with us?"

Rachel and John looked at each other like they had both been plugged into an electrical socket. Recovering quickly, they laughed.

"Ben, I think Rachel likes to sleep alone."

"Yes, but thanks for the invitation, Ben. It feels good that you asked. Maybe another time," Rachel said, trying not to look at his grandfather.

*   *   *

John and Rachel decided to head to the zoo early, to avoid the heat of the day and the zoo smells that it intensified.

At nine o'clock she heard the downstairs door open and close and little feet hopping up her front steps.

She opened the front door just as Ben was about to ring the buzzer.

"Good morning, Ben. How was the sleeping bag?" Rachel greeted him, but the little boy was too busy hugging Ralph to answer.

"We decided to sleep inside," John offered. "Ben saw a rather large bug with millions of legs and long feelers right outside our door, and we figured we might sleep better indoors. We may try a campout next year, when he's six."

"Good plan. I don't like bugs either, Ben."

"You don't? Wow, that's cool. Is Ralph going to the zoo with us? Can I hold his leash?"

"He sure is, but I'd better hold the leash. Sometimes he gets really excited when he sees a squirrel and tries to run where he shouldn't."

Ben looked disappointed but quickly recovered when his grandfather asked him if he'd like to help him carry the picnic basket.

"Hope you don't mind leftover fried chicken," John said.

"It's the best kind. I'm embarrassed I haven't brought anything to contribute to lunch."

"You've brought you. Now, let's go see if we can find the elephants."

John hailed a cab and loaded people, dogs and picnic baskets into the back seat. Traffic was heavy as people drove to Sunday school, but they finally stopped in front of the entrance to the zoo. Rachel was impressed by Ben's patience as he stood holding his grandfather's hand. John looked like a man who had just been told he'd won the lottery as he beamed down at the boy.

"You've got a real jewel there," Rachel said to him.

"His parents are doing a fine job raising him."

"When are they picking him up?"

"Friday is the plan. They'll stay overnight and then leave to go back to New York the next day."

"I'll be leaving Thursday to go to Virginia. They can stay upstairs while I'm gone."

John thanked Rachel again for the invitation, and they discussed where she would leave the key. She told him she was sorry she wouldn't get the opportunity to meet the rest of the family, and he assured her they would be equally disappointed.

Just then, Ben gave a shriek and went running off to stand in front of a picture of giant snakes outside the reptile house.

"Can we go in here first, Granddad?"

"You're not afraid of snakes?" Rachel asked.

"Oh, no. Just bugs."

"Just like me," she said. "We're funny, aren't we? Bugs are so little, and we're so big, and yet we get scared."

"But bugs are sneaky," Ben explained. "Snakes aren't sneaky."

Rachel agreed that bugs were indeed sneakier than snakes and got a huge smile as a reward for her understanding.

Ben finally tired out after touring the Reptile House and watching the bears, tigers and monkeys, and they decided to find a shady spot for their picnic before moving on to the elephants.

A grassy knoll near a small fishpond made a perfect spot to spread the blanket John had squeezed in the basket. Rachel spread it on the ground while he walked a short distance to buy drinks.

As she took out the food and placed it on the blanket, she noticed Ben looking at her intently.

"Why is your hair like that?" he finally asked.

"Like what?"

"Long, like a little girl's hair."

"I don't know, Ben. I guess I just haven't thought about cutting it."

"What's that on the end of it?" he asked, pointing to the beads at the end of her braid.

"They're just some pretty beads I found one time on a trip. They remind me of how much fun I had there with some friends."

Ben looked thoughtful for a minute, and then said he'd like to have something to remind him of his trip to Washington.

"Well, we'll find you something, then," Rachel said. "To remind you of Ralph."

"And you," Ben insisted, and Rachel felt a catch in her chest.

John sat down with three lemonades just as she was about to reach out for a hug.

"I'm sorry I didn't think to ask what you wanted to drink," John apologized.

"Lemonade is perfect," she said.

"She likes lemonade. Just like me," Ben smiled

"And me," his grandfather agreed. "Aren't we lucky."

Chapter 10

Rachel got our of bed at five a.m. Monday so she could shower, eat breakfast and practice her yoga and meditation before taking a cab to the hospital. She knew that if she cut out any of her morning routine, her day suffered.

The temp agency had left a phone message Sunday afternoon while she was at the zoo. They had notified Rebecca of where the key was hidden, and she was going to call Rachel that morning for instructions.

Rachel said a prayer for Georgia and Mike as she locked the door and stood outside to wait for the cab.

Traffic was typically snarled with Monday morning commuters, and she was glad she had allowed herself plenty of time. The Yellow Cab pulled up to the front door of the hospital at 7:45.

A volunteer at the information desk directed Rachel to the appropriate waiting room where she found Georgia's children huddling around their mother. It wasn't clear who was comforting whom.

Georgia stood and walked over to Rachel as she came in the room.

"They just took him in," she said, fighting back tears.

"At least they're on time," Rachel said. "I'm sorry I didn't get a chance to tell him 'good luck.' How are you holding up?"

"Fine," Georgia said automatically, then added, "Not really. I'm scared to death. What if they can't get it all? What if he's dying" What if . . ."

"No more 'what if's," Rachel said, wrapping her arms around her friend. "You take it easy. I'm right here. Let me help you for a change. Right now I want you to take a walk with me down to get a cup of Starbucks coffee."

"No. I can't leave," Georgia almost shouted, looking shocked at the suggestion. "Suppose they need me?"

"Georgia, relax. It's going to be a long morning. Trust me."

"Go on, Mom. Take a walk. We'll be here, and we'll come get you if the doctor comes out," son, Mike, Jr.,

Still reluctant to leave her post in the waiting room, Georgia allowed herself to be led away to the little café on the main floor.

"Did the temp agency get in touch with Rebecca?" she wanted to know.

"They did. But, you're not supposed to be thinking about work now. Here, what do you want to eat with your coffee? A pastry, perhaps?"

Georgia laughed and said she didn't think she'd ever eat sweets again. She said that everybody she knew had stopped by the house the day before with a plate of chocolate chip cookies, and she had overindulged in her chocolate addiction.

"I feel hung-over," she moaned "Coffee will be just fine."

"I just realized, I don't know how you drink your coffee," Rachel admitted. "You're always fixing mine, but I don't think I've ever – in 20 years – brought you a cup of coffee."

Georgia laughed. "It's about time you did. And I think you can handle it. I take it black.

*   *   *

Three hours later, the surgeon pushed through the swinging doors, and Georgia leaped to her feet. The family gathered around her like a protective shield.

"Mike did well," the doctor said. "We were able to remove all the tumors and they looked benign. We're having the lab do tests, and we should know something for sure within a few days. He's resting in recovery now and should be in his room within a few hours. Why don't you all go take a break and come back at around two o'clock. You should be able to see him then."

"And, how are you doing," he asked Georgia as he turned to walk back through the doors.

"Fine," Georgia said and then laughed when she saw Rachel shake her head. "Well, at least better than I was several hours ago. That was pretty scary."

"Good girl," Rachel said. "Now maybe you'll let me get you some lunch."

"Just because you were able to fix my coffee, don't get cocky and think you can handle lunch," Georgia teased.

"Humor me, just this once. I promise I won't make a habit of it."

"Promise?"

"Promise."

*   *   *

When Rachel arrived at the office, she saw Rebecca watering the plants in the front of the building.

"Welcome back," she said. The attractive blond turned at the sound of her voice and gave her a smile that seemed to light up the whole block.

"Ms. Springer! How good to see you again. How are things at the hospital?"

Rachel gave the shortened version of the report and led the way inside. Georgia's desk was almost covered with cellophane-covered plates of chocolate chip cookies.

"Clients have been bringing them in all morning," Rebecca explained. "Georgia's got quite a fan club."

"She sure does. I'll take them by the hospital this evening when I go back. Any business go on while I was out, or was it just cookie deliveries?"

Rebecca handed her a stack of phone messages, and Rachel went into her office to return calls. One was from a potential client who had gotten her name from Stan. She decided to get that behind her first since it might require more time than some of the other more routine calls requesting confirmations on court dates.

She dialed the number and the phone rang four or five times before an elderly woman answered it. Rachel identified herself and asked to speak to Mrs. Ruth Proctor.

"This is Mrs. Proctor. Who is this?"

"Rachel Springer. Stan and I work together. I believe he told you to call me about a legal matter."

"Oh, yes. Thank you for returning my call, Ms. Springer. I need help changing my Will, and he suggested I call you."

"I'd be happy to meet with you, Mrs. Proctor. When would you like to stop by?"

"Stan said you'd come here. I'm not able to get around much these days, and I don't live far from your office."

Rachel silently cursed Stan for volunteering a house call but agreed to pay a visit before she left for Virginia. She got the address and hung up with a promise to be on time. Mrs. Proctor said she hated to be kept waiting more than almost anything.

Rachel rolled her eyes and wondered why she let herself get involved in some of the things she did.

Even after all these years, I've never learned to say 'no,' she realized as she dialed the next number.

*   *   *

Mike's room looked more like a place to have a party than to recover from surgery. Balloons, cards, gifts and baskets of flowers greeted Rachel when she arrived with her chocolate chip cookie delivery. Georgia came to the door to help her with the bags, and Rachel hugged her as soon as she could free her hands.

"You look like a different woman than you did this morning," she said to her friend.

"I feel like a different woman. The doctor said they got every bit of tumor, and he'll go home tomorrow as long as he feels good."

"My goodness, Mike. Don't scare us like that again."

"I'll try not to," he laughed. "Guess you were worried about losing Georgia."

"You're damned right I was. But I'm pretty fond of you too, so don't pull any funny stuff again."

Georgia launched into lots of questions about the office, and the two women had a good laugh about Stan's referral service, wondering how Mrs. Proctor had gotten hooked up with a private eye.

"Wish I could go see her with you," Georgia said when Rachel told her the Capitol Hill address. "That's a beautiful street, and she probably lives in one of the mansions. Can't wait to hear all about it."

"I'm going tomorrow after work, so you won't have to wait long. I'll call you and tell you all about it Wednesday morning."

*   *   *

An envelope with "RACHEL" printed on it was taped to the front door when she got home. It was covered with what looked like fingerprints of jelly and sealed with a ragged piece of dirty Scotch tape.

Inside, a piece of lined paper had been folded carefully several times into a lopsided square. Spread out under the porch light, brightly colored pictures of several figures danced across the page above the labels "GRANDAD," "BEN," "RALPH" and "ELEPHANT." The largest, somewhat lumpy, figure featured a long rope of hair with a huge red ball at the end of it. The name "RACHEL" was framed in a heart.

A note in John's handwriting at the bottom read, "Come downstairs if you get home before 9."

Rachel looked at her watch and was disappointed to see that it was almost 9:30, and there was no light downstairs. She unlocked her front door and went into the foyer, feeling smacked in the face by its emptiness.

Ralph bounded down the stairs and lunged against her legs in greeting.

"Come on, boy. Let's get some fresh air. It's stuffy in here."

Ralph crashed through the kitchen and out into the backyard, Rachel right behind him with the picture. She lit several citronella candles and fell heavily into an Adirondack chair to watch Ralph make his rounds. He finally settled at his favorite bush.

Within minutes, she heard footsteps behind her and turned to see John coming toward her with a tray. He set it down on the table near her.

"Thought you might like a little toddy," he said.

"Smells like jasmine tea."

"What else?"

"Thanks, John. I do need a toddy."

"How were things at the hospital?"

Rachel gave him a full report of Mike's surgery, the doctor's prognosis and Georgia's bravery through it all, and then told him a little bit about the rest of her day at the office.

"And what about your day?" she finally asked.

"Ben went to Susan's this afternoon while I checked in at the project site. That's where Ben did your picture. Did you find it?"

"How rude of me. That should have been the first thing out of my mouth. What a gift! John, he's the most precious child. How much you must love him. You must hate the thought of his leaving."

John Turner looked up at the stars and didn't say anything for a while. Rachel sat with him in silence, knowing that something was passing between them that didn't need words.

Finally, he looked at her.

"I can't explain it, Rachel. I love Ben in a way I've never felt for a child before – never felt for anyone before, maybe. It's like we understand each other on a level that transcends age and experience. It's the closest thing I've ever felt to God."

Rachel nodded.

Ralph nosed up to the table to check out the cups of tea and get his ears scratched.

"I loved Ben's picture of Ralph. The tail is so proud – like a banner on four feet."

"I loved the picture of you."

"But did he have to make me look so lumpy? My god, I didn't realize I appear so large to him. Maybe I need to lose more than five pounds."

"Nonsense. Making you the biggest character in the picture was his way of paying you a compliment. Did you notice the braid?"

"Yes. I'm afraid he thinks I'm too old for one."

"Just the opposite. He loves it. In fact, he thinks you're perfect."

"Must be because we're both afraid of bugs."

"I think it's more than that."

As if on cue, a tiny voice pierced the dark.

"Granddad, I can't sleep."

"Well, why don't you come out here with us and have a little toddy," John said.

Ben dashed across the brick courtyard, looking carefully around him for bugs along the way. When he spotted Ralph sitting beside Rachel's chair, he made a beeline for the dog.

"Thanks for the beautiful picture, Ben," Rachel said. "I'm going to take it to work with me tomorrow so all my clients can see it."

Ben beamed up at her. "Did you show Ralph?"

"He loved his tail, especially. You're quite a good artist."

"Yes, I am," Ben said and looked at her lap longingly. Slowly, he stood up and inched a little closer until he was standing as close as he could get without actually touching her.

Rachel wasn't sure what to do and looked at John for guidance.

"Ben, would you like to sit on Rachel's lap for a minute before you go back to bed?" John asked.

Without a word, Ben climbed up into the old wooden chair with Rachel and grabbed on to her braid. When his little face turned up to hers, the starlight reflected in his eyes, and she felt something in her chest move.

Rachel looked over Ben's head at his grandfather, and they smiled at each other.

Chapter 11

When Rachel left for work the next morning, she saw Susan standing at the end of her walk, wearing her ratty lavender chenille bathrobe and scanning the front page of the *Post*.

"Mornin, neighbor. What's the good news?" Rachel called across the street to her.

"My god, honey, where have you been? I haven't seen hide nor hair of you in ages," Susan squealed as she came hobbling across the street in her bare feet.

Rachel told her the short version of the news about Georgia and Mike and agreed to meet her for lunch later to catch up.

"Don't be late. I've got a really tight schedule, trying to get everything done before I leave for Virginia."

Susan promised to get to Rachel's office by 11:30 so they could walk down to the riverfront together for an early lunch.

At 11:45, she breezed in beneath a large hot pink floppy straw hat. A sunflower yellow sleeveless dress and bubblegum pink beads around her neck completed the whirlwind ensemble.

After the initial shock of such a flamboyant entrance, Rebecca was about to ask her to take a seat when Rachel came out of her office.

"You're late, Susan," she said on her way to the front door. "Now, we're going to get stuck in a lunch line."

"Late? I thought I was early. Didn't we say noon?"

"We were going to be *eating* by noon. You were going to be *here* at 11:30. Susan, you've never been early a day in your life, but come on, let's get going. Maybe we'll get lucky and everyone will decide to eat at their desks today."

The two set off, down the hill toward K Street to find a café with no line and a view of the water, dotted with sailboats and sparkling under the sunny September sky.

Luckily, a new, barely discovered outdoor café had several empty tables, and Susan and Rachel were seated immediately by a good-looking young man in white shorts and navy blue polo shirt.

"See, no problem," Susan beamed. "You're always getting all worked up over nothing. Here we are, with the best tables in DC and you were fretting we'd be stuck in a line."

Rachel studied the handwritten menu and didn't respond.

"What'll it be ladies?" the waiter named Rhett asked. When they hesitated, he launched into an impressive list of specials, and they both decided on the asparagus quiche and a glass of iced tea.

Rhett had barely turned his back before Susan attacked.

"So, how are you and John doing? What's Ben like? When are his parents arriving?" she fired off, hardly taking a breath between questions.

Rachel, trying to be patient, explained that Ben's parents were scheduled to arrive Friday but that she would be gone to Virginia by the time they got to DC.

"But then you won't get to meet them, will you? That's too bad. It's very important that a man's children like you, Rachel. But now, Ben – he's obviously crazy about you. I saw that darling picture he drew. Isn't he precious? Don't you just want to eat him up?"

"Yes, he's a very sweet boy, Susan. You're very kind to offer to babysit while John works."

"It's just no problem at all, Rachel. It's the least I can do."

Susan looked at her expectantly for a few minutes longer and then – never one to exercise much restraint – she got right down to business.

"How are you and John getting along? Any romance yet? You're just so perfect for each other, Rachel."

"I don't know what you mean 'perfect for each other,' Susan. Nobody's perfect for me – except maybe Ralph. We *get along* just fine. Nobody's been perfect for me in 62 years. Why would John Turner be?"

Susan suddenly turned serious and leaned closer to Rachel and took her hand.

"Rachel, do you really want to spend your old age alone, lying in some smelly nursing home with nobody to visit you, tied up to tubes and messing in your diapers with nobody but some crabby knock-kneed underpaid nurse's assistant around to care for you?"

"My god, Susan, stop it. This is ridiculous. You're not looking for romance for me. You're looking for a caretaker. How morbid."

"Of course, there can be a little romance along the way, but ultimately, Rachel, you need to start being more realistic about your future. Jim and I worry about you."

"Well, you can stop worrying. I've done just fine so far, and I don't see any reason why I won't continue to."

Rhett arrived with their lunch plates right as Susan was preparing her second line of attack.

"Let's eat, if you don't mind," Rachel said, interrupting her before she got started. "I've got a client coming in at one o'clock and *I* don't plan to be late."

*   *   *

Rachel finished reviewing the answers to interrogatories with her high-maintenance, highly peroxided blond divorce client and walked her out to the lobby. She was surprised to see John and Ben sitting there.

She escorted Mrs. Beaver to the door and turned to greet them.

"What a nice surprise," she said to Ben. "What are you guys up to this afternoon?"

"We walked down to get an ice cream cone, and Ben wanted to see where you and Ralph work. I hope you don't mind that we stopped by without an appointment."

"Want to go get some ice cream?" Ben asked.

"I wish I could, Ben, but I have to work."

"Can Ralph go with us?"

"Come on in here and ask him," Rachel laughed, leading the way into her office where Ralph lay sleeping on the window seat. He lifted his head groggily at the sound of voices and then leaped to attention when he saw his new little friend.

Rachel went to her desk and pretended to check the calendar.

"Looks like he's free for the rest of the afternoon, lucky dog."

"We'll bring you some back, okay? Do you like chocolate? It's my favorite," Ben said.

"Mine, too."

"See, Granddad, I told you she'd say chocolate was her favorite. Cool, huh?"

"Very cool," John agreed.

Rachel hooked Ralph's leash to his collar and off the three went, agreeing that they would take Ralph home with them and that Rachel could pick him and her ice cream up after work.

As she watched the figures fade into the crowded streets of Georgetown, the vision of herself tethered by tubes in a nursing home superimposed itself in the background, and she shivered with something close to dread.

Just then, the intercom buzzed, interrupting her thoughts. She sat down to take a call from Mrs. Beaver, who wanted to ask again when she could expect to hear from her husband's attorney.

"Relax, Mrs. Beaver. Relax," Rachel said. "All is well. Trust me. I really do know what I'm doing."

But, after she hung up the phone, Rachel wondered if that was true.

*   *   *

During the taxi ride to Capitol Hill later that day, Rachel thought about her upcoming trip to the farm and realized that there was a twinge of regret this time about leaving home. It was an odd reaction, compared to her past experience. Greenmont had represented "home" for so many years. Even though someone else was living in the sprawling old farmhouse, it still felt like hers.

Suddenly, Rachel realized that she didn't want to leave Ben. That she was already missing him – and his grandfather. That their living downstairs in her house made it feel more like home than the farm where she had grown up.

"Amazing," Rachel muttered.

"Ma'am?" the cabdriver asked, thinking she had spoken to him.

"Nothing. Just talking to myself."

The cab slowed down and stopped in front of iron gates in a six-foot brick wall. Rachel paid the driver, got out and pushed the buzzer. Mrs. Proctor's voice crackled over the intercom.

"Mrs. Springer, you're right on time. Bully for you. Do come in."

Rachel heard the lock click open and pushed the gates aside.

Ahead of her lay a long, flagstone walk, bordered on each side with ancient boxwoods. She walked through the towering tunnel of bushes and up to the front door of a brick Georgian mansion.

Before she reached the top step, the front door was opened by a handsome young black man with high cheekbones and startling blue eyes, and dressed in a crisp white linen butler's jacket.

"Please come in, madam," he said, reaching out for her briefcase.

"I'll keep it with me, thank you."

"Yes, madam. Right this way, please. Mrs. Proctor is waiting for you in the library."

Rachel followed him through the dim, wide foyer and down a long hall filled with massive oil portraits of distinguished old men. When she reached the library, she recognized in her client the same hawk-like nose predominant in each painting.

"Thank you for coming so quickly, Mrs. Springer. Forgive me for not getting up to greet you. This damned broken hip is hell."

Rachel restrained herself from laughing at her elderly client's ribald language and instead offered her condolences.

"Please have a seat here," Mrs. Proctor said, pointing to a chair opposite her own. Above the fireplace between them was the only portrait of a woman Rachel had seen on her tour so far.

"That's my mother," her hostess said.

"What a regal-looking woman."

"Hummph. She was a regal bitch."

Rachel didn't know what to say to that, so she rummaged through her briefcase, stalling for time. Pulling out a legal pad, she asked Mrs. Proctor how she knew Stan.

"I hired him to follow my niece, Ramona."

Rachel waited for her client to provide the rest of the story. Satisfied that Rachel was listening, the old woman went on.

"I was planning to leave everything to Ramona, you see. I have no children of my own. No other living relatives at all, in fact. Everything was going to the girl. Then I began to suspect that the silly thing had ignored my advice and was seeing some scoundrel who works at the Pentagon. The *Pentagon*. Can you imagine that?"

When Rachel showed no signs of being horrified by the idea of working at the Pentagon, Mrs. Proctor proceeded.

"You *do* know what that means, don't you, Mrs. Springer?"

"He's a Republican?"

"Quite so," the old lady said, looking like she had just smelled something rotten. In fact, she appeared to be trying to rise from her seat to escape the very thought of her only living relative in the clutches of the enemy.

The young black man appeared out of nowhere to assist her with her cane.

"Thank you, Robert. Help me over to my desk, if you please."

At the dainty French provincial lady's writing desk, Mrs. Proctor found the framed picture she was looking for and brought it over to Rachel.

"This is Ramona."

Rachel looked at the picture of a tiny blonde, astride a huge shining black horse. The girl was decked out in fox-hunting clothes and carried her crop like a royal staff.

"Charming," Rachel said.

"Yes. She has had a charmed life. Beauty, all the finest schools, traveled all around the world. I've seen to it all since her parents died in a boating accident when she was 16. Now, she's throwing it all away. For a *Republican.*"

Rachel knew without a doubt that offering any consolation — something like, "Well, once I had a very good friend who voted for Nixon" — would be a waste of her billable hours, so instead, she asked how she could help.

"I want to change my Will. I'm disowning the girl. I want to leave everything to the animal shelter."

As if on cue, a huge yellow tabby cat made its grand entrance and leaped into the old woman's lap, turned in a circle several times and settled down with his head buried under her left armpit.

Mrs. Proctor stroked behind his ears and introduced him as "Henry."

"Henry has more sense than most people, you know. Henry came from the animal shelter several years ago, and I know they'll appreciate my gift."

"I'm sure they will, Mrs. Proctor," Rachel said and then asked for a copy of her old Will and a few other bits of information she needed to update it. They made an appointment to meet again in a couple of weeks so the Will could be signed and notarized.

On the way out the door, Rachel remembered for the umpteenth time that she needed to write her own Will, something she continued to put off. Her conversation with Susan and now this scene with Mrs. Proctor had begun to shake her conviction that perhaps she could somehow escape the inevitable.

As the cab pulled away from the curb, she turned back to find Mrs. Proctor staring out the library window.

The sunset reflected off hundreds of other empty windows, framing the picture of the old woman and the cat.

Chapter 12

Rachel was glad to see that the lights were on in the basement apartment when she got home. A note on her door read, "Don't forget your ice cream. We'll keep Ralph."

Beneath the words was a picture of a black dog licking what appeared to be an ice cream cone. Just in case Rachel couldn't identify them, the words "RALF" and "ICE CREEM" were scrawled at the bottom of the ragged sheet of the page of yellow construction paper.

Rachel quickly scanned her mail, checked her answering machine and decided nothing was more important than what waited for her downstairs.

She did stop long enough to change from her navy blue pumps into her Birkenstocks and then ran out the back door and around the side of the house to knock on John's door.

Ben answered it in mid-knock. His face looked like he had just been told there was no Santa Clause.

"What's the matter, Ben?" Rachel asked as she kneeled down to his level to look him in the eye.

"They didn't have plain chocolate. We had to get it with nuts. I hate nuts, don't you?"

Rachel weighed her answer carefully. So far, she'd been batting a thousand in the game of things she had in common with Ben, and she certainly didn't want to blow her winning streak over a few nuts.

"Actually, Ben, I think nuts in chocolate ice cream make eating it more fun. I don't always like to eat them either, but I sure do enjoy picking them out. Sort of like hunting for Easter eggs."

Ben thought about that seriously for a few minutes, and then his little face broke into a huge grin.

"Can I try it with yours? I've already had mine."

"Now wait a minute, Ben. Rachel may not have had her supper yet. She may want to wait," John interrupted.

"Oh, I never wait for chocolate ice cream – with or without nuts," Rachel said, definitely hitting a home run with Ben with that comment.

"Cool," the little boy pronounced. "Let's eat it outside."

Ralph led the way out to the back courtyard, John following with her dish of ice cream and two spoons.

"How was your day?" he asked.

Rachel told him about her meeting with Mrs. Beaver and her trip to Capitol Hill, and they laughed together over the contrast between the two clients.

"You sure have a fascinating life here in DC," John said. "I don't guess you'll ever want to leave it. It seems perfect. Wonderful house, great neighbors, Georgia to help with the challenging and lucrative practice you love. All in a city that's one of the most exciting places to live in the country. You've made a wonderful life for yourself, Rachel Springer. In fact, I've never met a woman who seems as happy as you. Have you always had it all together like this?"

"Pretty much."

"I don't mean you haven't worked hard to get it. I'm sure you have, but I don't see any scars to hint at suffering along the way."

"No, I haven't suffered, but maybe I've sacrificed some."

When John looked quizzical at her answer, she said, "There's never been a Ben in my life."

"You never married."

"Never even came close. Well, there was one time, but something told me it wouldn't work."

"Do you get lonely?"

"Do you?"

"Yes."

"So do I, but maybe everybody does, and that's just life. I've got Ralph."

"And me," Ben piped up, startling the adults who hadn't realized he was listening.

"And you," Rachel said, handing him a spoonful of plain chocolate ice cream.

*   *   *

The next morning, Rachel was up early and in a cab on her way to the rental car office before her downstairs neighbors woke. She left a note saying goodbye, telling them where the key to her front door was hidden and a phone number in case they needed to reach her in Virginia.

The streets were still relatively empty as the cab made its way across town to the Hertz office. The sky was early morning clear, and Rachel inhaled a deep exhaust-free breath and thought about how grateful she was to be Rachel Springer.

The car rental agent greeted her by name as she walked in the front door with her small overnight bag.

"Where to this time, Ms. Springer?"

"Down to the farm. Want to go with me?"

"Wish I could. Maybe next time."

Rachel signed the rental contract and walked out to the freshly washed silver Grand Am. While she continued to be thankful she didn't own a car and didn't have to keep up with oil changes, inspections and tags, she did enjoy driving occasionally. Especially south, during the fall when the leaves were beginning to change in the Virginia countryside.

The drive from the city to Abingdon took about six hours, and Rachel had brought along a book on tape that she figured should take about the same time as the drive. She waited until she got off the beltway and onto Rte. 29 before she turned on *The Shipping News* and began to listen.

She stopped once along the way for a bathroom break and arrived late afternoon, just as she had planned.

As she turned off the main highway onto the windy gravel road that led a mile toward Greenmont, Rachel's mind was flooded with memories of all the times she had ridden that same road. Sunday mornings with her father and Edward on their way to church. In the crowded school bus. With her father in the pick-up truck to the seed store. With boys into town to a movie.

As she passed an almost invisible lane that snaked through the dense woods, she smiled to herself as she remembered parking beneath the trees to neck.

When she finally approached the long driveway from the road up the hill to the house, she caught her breath at the change since her last visit. Almost every one of the giant maple trees that had lined it were gone, leaving the landscape looking like Ralph the time she had to have his fur shaved. He had hidden under the bed for days in embarrassment.

"What in God's name happened to the trees?" were the first words out of her mouth when her cousin greeted her at the front door.

"Oh, Rachel. I'm so sorry. Didn't we tell you? Some horrible disease got into them, and we had to have every one cut down."

"I've never seen anything so cruel," Rachel said, collapsing down onto the top porch step.

"Several neighbors around here had the same problem. It was heartbreaking, but unfortunately, there wasn't a thing we could do to save them."

Nancy took Rachel's bag and led her into the kitchen where fresh coffee and a plate of cookies waited.

The two cousins sat and talked, catching up on less devastating news – births, marriages, the new farm manager – and then Rachel said she'd like to take a shower and rest a while before dinner.

"Of course, dear. You know where your room is," Nancy said. "And welcome home."

Rachel climbed the creaky stairs, remembering the nights she came home late from a date, trying to avoid the loose boards so she wouldn't wake her father. She smiled at the banister made smooth by all the little bottoms that slid down it.

Her room overlooked the cow pond across the field. Several Holsteins stood in it – just like she pictured them so often when she thought about the farm.

Nancy hadn't changed the room much since she and her husband bought the farm. The same slightly frayed and faded white dotted Swiss curtains hung at the windows, the same worn rag rug covered the floor, the painting of the old man praying over a loaf of bread and bowl of soup. Even Rachel's childhood four-poster bed was still centered between two small closets.

She fell into the feather bed and immediately drifted off into a nap that was more from relaxation than tiredness. As she sank into sleep, she heard the soft lowing of cows being herded to the barn to be milked, and her father's face floated before her.

He smiled.

*   *   *

Rachel almost fell out of the bed when she glanced at the clock on the bedside table and saw that two hours had flown by since she lay down. She jumped up just as a knock came at the door.

"Rachel, are you about ready for supper? Simon is taking a shower, and we'll be ready to eat in a few minutes," Nancy said.

"Be right down."

Rachel had forgotten how early farmers like to eat and decided to forego her own shower. Instead, she washed her face and changed into a pair of jeans and sweatshirt. She searched in her suitcase, found the box of Godiva chocolates she had brought as a gift for her hostess and left the room.

The aroma of peach cobbler floated up the stairs to meet her as she opened the door.

"Hope you're hungry," Nancy greeted her when she walked into the kitchen.

"I am. What can I do to help?"

"Fill the glasses with ice, pour the sweet tea, and we'll be all set."

Simon's huge bulk came through the dining room door just as Rachel filled the last glass. He lumbered over to where she stood and embraced her in a bear hug that smelled of Old Spice.

"You look as fresh as a new born calf, girl. DC must still be agreeing with you. Don't know how you stand it," he said.

Rachel smiled and offered her condolences for the lost trees. Always the optimist, Simon moved quickly from that tragedy to fill her in on the new farm manager.

"In fact, George is joining us for dinner," he said. "I think you'll like him. He's a bachelor. About your age. And we try to have him over for dinner as often as we can. I think he's lonely."

Oh, no. Here we go again, Rachel thought. Another match-maker.

As if on cue, George Mobley walked in the dining room, and she was introduced to a ruddy-faced man with a silver ponytail almost as long as her own braid.

He focused on the bead at the end of her hair immediately, and they smiled at each other as though they shared a secret joke.

"Evenin', Ms. Springer. Glad to make your acquaintance," he said as he came around the table to shake her hand and pull out her chair.

"Why, thank you. And please, call me Rachel."

*   *   *

After a dinner of pork chops, turnip greens, mashed potatoes and cornbread, the four took their cobbler and coffee outside to the lawn chairs gathered under a huge oak tree in the side yard. A full moon had already begun to appear low on the horizon.

"Bet you don't get a sight like that in DC," Simon said as they sat enjoying the cool night.

"Au contraire. I sat under a full moon not too long ago out back in my courtyard. You all need to come stay with me sometime so I can show you that the city really isn't all that evil."

Simon looked doubtful, but Nancy's eyes lit up.

"Can't leave the cows," Simon said.

Rachel remembered her father saying that more than once and could feel traces of her old resentment at being trapped on the farm. She wondered if Nancy felt the same need to escape.

"Perhaps Nancy can come for a weekend some time," Rachel said and then saw the look that passed between the two. She realized it would be a cold day in hell before her invitation was accepted.

George broke the uncomfortable silence by asking Rachel what had taken her to Washington. Her cousin poured more coffee while she talked about leaving the farm for law school, her short career in a large DC firm and her realization that she wanted to work for herself.

"How about you? How did you get to Greenmont?"

"You want the long or the short story?"

"Suit yourself. I've got all night."

"Well, since these folks have already heard most everything, I'll stick to the bare bones and hope for another chance to fill you in on some of the details later."

George pulled out a pipe and a pouch of tobacco. "Mind if I smoke?"

"Not at all. Reminds me of my father. That isn't Prince Albert, by any chance?"

"How'd you guess?"

Slowly and with great care, he filled the pipe, tamping the tobacco down with a well-worn tool Rachel figured had heard many stories.

George had grown up in Montana on a horse ranch and joined the Army when he was 17. His parents gladly signed permission for him to enlist, hoping that the discipline of military life would rein their rowdy son in some. For years, he had been in and out of some scrape or other. Nothing serious, but troubling, nonetheless.

When he was sent to Vietnam, his mother had some doubts about her decision to let her oldest of four children go, but his father was confident that "a few hard knocks" would toughen him up.

Six months later, he stepped on a land mine and was sent home with only one leg.

"I didn't notice a limp," Rachel said to the silence into which he had lapsed.

"I've had many years to straighten it out. I think you'd notice something if you saw me with my pants off."

At her age, Rachel was always surprised when she blushed, but she could feel her face flame up and hoped he couldn't see it in the dark.

"Did you go home when you were released from the Army?"

"No, I didn't go home. I took my disability pay and did some traveling."

George said he had always loved photography. He bought himself a camera and a notebook and spent about a year crossing the country, snapping pictures and interviewing interesting characters he met along the way.

When he finally got tired of wandering, he settled down in rural Louisiana, married a widow with two kids and learned to farm.

"But she got tired of going to bed with a gimp, and one day she disappeared."

"With the kids?"

"No, she left all three of us."

"Did you try to find her?"

"Some things are best let go, and she was one of them."

When the last of the two children left home for college, George decided to relocate again and landed in Virginia.

Rachel sat in the dark, listening to the tree frogs and wondering what to say to a man who had lost so much.

"I'd love to see some of your pictures. I caught a shutterbug, too, but I've never done anything like what it sounds like you've done."

"Save your compliments until you've seen my shots. How about tomorrow afternoon?"

Rachel looked over at Nancy. Her cousin assured her that they had nothing on the schedule that would keep her from walking across the field to George's house.

The date made, George got up, thanked his host for dinner, shook hands with Rachel and said he'd look forward to seeing her around five the next day.

As he walked into the dark, Rachel saw the ragged limp.

*   *   *

Disoriented, Rachel wondered where she was and what had waked her up. She looked at the clock on her bedside table and saw 4:30. A rooster crowed.

As her head dropped back onto the feather pillow, she remembered her grandmother's words, "No rest for the weary."

Minutes later, the clatter of pans drifted up from the kitchen, followed closely by the smell of coffee and the slam of the backdoor. Simon leaving to milk the cows, Rachel thought.

She tried to go back to sleep but quickly gave up. Slipping on her plum-colored velour jogging suit, she decided to take a walk to the barn to watch the milking.

As she passed the bedroom next door, she could hear Nancy moving around inside. "I'm going for a little walk. Be back in a minute," Rachel said.

"Breakfast'll be ready shortly. Don't be too long."

When Rachel walked through the open barn door, George looked up from where he sat beside one of the cows.

"Didn't expect to see you up so early, city girl," he teased.

"Your rooster had other ideas. Mind of I try my hand at the milking? My father taught me years ago, and I'm curious as to whether I've still got the touch."

George got up from his stool so she could sit down. Rachel was surprised but delighted to find that the milking at Greenmont was still done the old-fashioned way. With only a few cows, kept for the family's own personal needs, milking by hand was a manageable chore.

Within minutes, milk was ringing into the tin bucket, and Rachel inhaled its warm sweet smell.

"You're a natural," George said. "We'll have to get you a little Jersey cow to take back to the city with you."

Rachel pictured Ben's ear-to-ear grin at finding a cow in the courtyard. He needs to be here with me, she thought. And his grandfather. She couldn't quite visualize John as a farmer – the kaki pants with the perfect creases, the starched white shirts didn't fit in the picture.

She looked over at George and noticed the hole in the left knee of his jeans and had a similar problem visualizing him in DC – about as much trouble as a cow in her courtyard.

"What are you smiling at, city girl?"

"Nothing. Here, I'd better get back to the house and see if Nancy needs help with breakfast. Will you be joining us?"

"Reckon I will. Mighty hard putting in a full day's work without something on my stomach."

As she walked back to the house, Rachel wondered what her life would have been like if she had kept the farm and had waked every day with the demanding crow of a rooster rather than alarming national news. Certainly, she felt healthier this morning than she had in a long time.

But she did miss her downstairs neighbors.

Chapter 13

Rachel sat playing the old upright piano in the parlor when she got the phone call that changed her life.

When she heard her neighbor's voice on the other end of the line, alarms went off in Rachel's head.

"There's been an accident," Susan said.

Within seconds, Rachel went through her list of friends and family, conjuring up scenes. She held her breath and waited for the room to stop spinning.

"It's Ben's parents. John just called to tell me they died in a car accident early this morning. He's on his way to identify the bodies now."

Rachel sat down on the ladder-back chair next to the telephone table in the hall. She pictured John Turner, driving alone to some hospital morgue. She couldn't bring herself to visualize his grandson, Ben. Across the street at Susan's. An orphan. The little freckled face sobered by such an unfair life.

"Does Ben know?"

"As much as a five-year-old *can* know."

"Where did it happen?"

"Near Centreville. Semi hit them head-on. John said the driver fell asleep at the wheel."

"How is John?"

"In shock."

Susan's uncharacteristic restraint was an indication that she, too, had been broad-sided. Caught up so suddenly in the middle of a family tragedy. Catapulted from occasional babysitter to grief-counselor.

"I'll come right home. Be there by dark."

"Right. I knew you'd want to be here. Sorry to be the bearer of such horrible news."

"Thanks for calling. And, Susan . . ."

"What?"

"Thanks for being my friend."

*   *   *

As Rachel sped from southwestern Virginia toward her home in Washington, D.C., she was glad she had decided to leave Ralph with John. Ben had been so heartbroken when she told him the dog was leaving for a week that she couldn't bring herself to tear them apart. Ralph loved the farm, but some sixth sense had told her to leave him – that his place was with Ben.

When she walked into Susan's living room and saw the boy and the dog curled up asleep on the rug together, she knew that something powerful had guided her.

But where was that power earlier today on Rte 55, she asked herself.

Susan pulled Rachel into the kitchen.

"Let him sleep," she whispered. "He's had a rough day."

"Heard from John?"

"No. I'm sure he's busy making arrangements."

Rachel looked across the street to her house and the basement apartment.

"I think I'll go over and see if there's anything I can do. Call me on my cell phone if Ben wakes up."

She left by the back door so she wouldn't disturb the sleeping boy and walked across to her side of the street, wondering what to say to a man who had just lost most of his family.

When she knocked softly on his door, he opened it almost immediately.

Without a word, he pulled her to him. She could feel his body trembling, but no sound escaped. She led him over to the sofa and cradled him in her arms like a baby. Finally, the sorrow broke free in a deep wailing. It was a grief like Rachel had never experienced, and she wondered if there would ever be an end to it.

She remembered once coming upon the scene of a baby bird that had been killed by a cat. A whole flock of birds sat in the branches of a tree, screaming at the cat below. Finally, all but one bird left, and Rachel listened to that lone mother bird screaming until she, too, stopped and flew away.

John's sobbing ended as abruptly, and he took a handkerchief out of his back pocket and wiped his face.

"I saw you come out of Susan's house," he said. "How's Ben?"

"Asleep with Ralph."

John smiled. "I wanted to get myself together before I go bring him . . . bring him home." He looked at Rachel. "Johnny and Patty named me as his guardian when he was born."

Rachel watched as fear mixed with grief in John's eyes. Rearing a boy was leagues away from weekend visits, no matter how you looked at the picture.

"Will you go back over with me?" John asked.

"Of course. Are you ready?"

"Ready as I'll ever be."

John got up from the sofa like a man who had aged 50 years.

"Thanks for coming back," he said. "I'm sorry your trip was interrupted."

Rachel murmured something – she didn't know what – and shut the door behind her.

When they climbed the steps up to the street, they saw Ben and Ralph sitting on Susan's front steps. Instead of jumping up to greet her, Ben stayed rooted to his seat, clutching Ralph's collar. Ralph, sensing the boy's need for an anchor, sat beside him, wagging his tail as a welcome to his mistress.

"Hey, Rachel," Ben said.

"Hey, Ben. Thanks for taking care of Ralph for me. He looks very well-fed and happy. You did a good job."

"I love Ralph."

"He loves you, too," Rachel said as she sat down next to him.

Ben turned deep brown eyes up to her, and she waited.

"A truck ran into my Mommy and Daddy and they're in heaven now. They're not ever coming home."

"I know, Ben. I'm so sorry. My Mommy and Daddy are there, too, and I miss them a lot."

Ben looked at her more intently.

"When you were little like me?"

"I was little when my Mommy died and big when my Daddy died."

"Little is worse, right?"

"Little is worse."

Choking back his own grief, John struggled to explain to Ben that he would live with him now. In Washington for a while and then back in New York.

"No. We can't leave Ralph," Ben wailed, and the floodgates finally broke.

Chapter 14

Later that night as she perched on her meditation zafu in Washington, bathed in city moonlight streaming in through the lone window of her attic room, monkey mind ran wild with thoughts of how she could help John; where Ben could go to kindergarten next month; where she could find friends for him; the fact that they needed more room and might move to a larger apartment.

Again and again she refocused on counting her breath, never counting any higher than three before losing focus again. Thoughts of the farm surfaced several times, and she remembered she had missed her date to see George's pictures. Ah, the road not traveled, she thought as the image of his mischievous twinkle further disturbed what were supposed to be the calm waters of meditation.

The soft ping of her zen alarm signaled that her allotted 30 minutes were over. Ralph jumped off the window seat and came over to lick her face.

"Good, boy. I missed you, too."

Rachel put her cushion and the cashmere shawl she wrapped like a cocoon around her shoulders in their corner basket and went downstairs to fix her toddy of jasmine tea.

She peered out the kitchen window to see if John might be in the courtyard and was disappointed to find the Adirondack chairs empty. Probably wants to stay close to Ben, she thought.

The funeral was to be day after tomorrow in Johnny and Patty's hometown. John had invited her to stay in his spare bedroom, but she told him she'd probably just fly up for the day. He and Ben would stay for a few days more, gathering the things he would need for the next several months.

Since she had already planned to be gone all week anyway in Virginia, her work wouldn't be affected by the trip. All she had to do was schedule the flight. She'd do that tomorrow. Tonight she'd try to accept the fact that she couldn't do much of anything to help John.

*　　　*　　　*

Susan offered to drive John and Ben to the airport to catch their flight to New York the next morning, but John decided to take a cab.

Rachel heard the driver toot his horn as she poured her first cup of coffee.

She grabbed Ralph's leash, snapped it to his collar and the two went out to say goodbye.

Ben looked sleepy but a lot more rested than his grandfather as they came out the basement door. He wore his Scooby Doo backpack and carried a Gameboy.

He brightened when he saw Ralph.

"Is Ralph coming with you to New York?" he asked hopefully.

"'Fraid not. He'll stay here and keep the home fires burning."

"What time does your flight arrive?" John wanted to know. "I'll meet you at the airport."

"Absolutely not. You'll have your hands full. I'll see you at the church. Are you sure there's nothing I can do for you?"

"Be there," John said and turned to put his suitcase in the trunk of the cab. When he turned back to her, she was hugging Ben good-bye.

"Don't forget Ralph," she said to Ben, who was about to climb into the backseat of the Yellow Cab.

"Wow. Thanks for reminding me. I almost forgot. And don't you forget Granddad."

"Never," Rachel said and opened her arms.

*　　　*　　　*

Rachel decided to go into the office to check her mail since she was in town.

Georgia was a welcome sight, manning her desk again. In control. Rachel called her from the road the day before to tell her about the accident.

"How are they?" Georgia asked as soon as Rachel walked through the door.

"Numb. On their way to New York. Ben wanted to know if I was bringing Ralph to the funeral."

"Poor kid."

"It's John I'm worried about. Imagine trying to raise a child at his age."

"It's going to be tough, but it sure will give him some way to channel his energies instead of having them sapped by grief."

"Is that the way it works?"

"We'll see, won't we."

"How's Mike?"

"Doing great. Anxious to get back to work. I practically have to tie him down," Georgia laughed.

Rachel smiled sympathetically as she walked into her office. She'd only been gone a few days, but the stack of mail was still overwhelming. She'd never been able to convince Georgia to throw away junk mail, which accounted for half of the envelopes on her desk. Georgia was terrified she'd discard something important, despite Rachel's reassurances.

Rachel sighed as she sat down at the desk and began tossing unopened credit card company solicitations into the trash.

The phone rang, and she waited for the intercom. Sure enough, the buzzer sounded, and Georgia announced that Horace Gilbert was on line one.

"Morning, Horace. How are you?"

"Not good. Need you to meet me at the club tomorrow at three p.m. Got a little deal you've got to look over."

"Can't do it, Horace. I'm leaving early tomorrow for a funeral in New York."

"Can't it wait? This is a damned crisis."

Rachel waited for a few minutes to see if Horace would catch his mistake, and when he didn't, she tried to be patient with the self-centered S.O.B.

"Horace, it's a funeral. Two people have died."

"Oh, yeah. Right. Well, I guess I could bring it to you this afternoon maybe. Let me look at my calendar."

Rachel took a deep breath, thinking of all the times she had catered to her client. She had spoiled him. Led him to believe her world revolved around him and his needs and whims.

"I'll be there at two o'clock," he announced.

Rachel considered telling him that she was actually on vacation this week, but decided to be grateful for some small concession on his part. He *had* offered to come to her office, after all, rather than demand she ride across town to his club.

"See you then," she agreed and noted it on her calendar.

That's when she noticed that she had written, "Susan's birthday" on the day's date.

Talking about self-centered, she thought. Rachel was horrified that she had forgotten her best friend's big day. Not even a card. What could have possibly been so important that she had let the day slip up on her like this?

John's face immediately popped into her mind.

As she dialed Susan's number, she pooh-poohed the idea that she could be acting like a fickle 16-year-old, forgetting her friends as soon as a good-looking man came on the scene.

"Hello," Susan said on the second ring.

"Happy birthday to you. Happy birthday to you. Happy birthday, dear Susan. Happy birthday to you," Rachel sang somewhat off-key.

"Oh, my god, spare me," Susan moaned.

"What's wrong with you? You always love your birthday."

"I've never been 60 before. I think I'll skip birthdays from now on."

"Good luck. It doesn't work. I've tried. So, what you got planned in the way of celebrating? Can I take you to lunch?"

"Don't you have enough things on your plate, getting ready for tomorrow?"

"Not too many that I don't have time for you. Where you want to go?"

"The Mayflower."

"The Mayflower? Okay. You got it. Meet you there in an hour." Rachel started to say goodbye with her regular, "and don't be late," but instead said another, "Happy birthday" and hung up.

*   *   *

As usual, Susan was late, and since Rachel had to be back in her office to meet Horace at two o'clock, lunch was short.

The dining room was crowded for a mid-week day, and they were crammed at a small table near the serving station.

"Sorry I didn't call first to reserve a better table," Rachel apologized. "Forgive me?"

"Absolutely. So, how was the farm? I guess you're horribly disappointed to miss the party. I know how much you looked forward to it."

"Actually, I'm only going to New York for the day. I'll probably drive back to Virginia in time to be there when the rest of the family arrives on Saturday."

"You're not staying to help John? What if he needs you? What if Ben asks you to stay? You really do need to consider staying, Rachel. You might not get back to Virginia. You might not even get back here, in fact."

"My, god, Susan. Take it easy. John hasn't said a word about needing me. He's got lots of friends up there, I'm sure."

Susan looked at her across her glass of white wine.

"Here's a toast to you," Rachel said, changing the subject. "Another wonderful year of poetry and pink pedal pushers. You're a dear friend, Susan, and I love you. But you really must learn to stop fixing me. I don't need fixing."

"I'm not so sure," Susan said and took a sip of wine.

*   *   *

Rachel read through Horace's latest get-richer-quick contract, brought a couple of points to his attention and took it out to Georgia to redraft.

While they waited for the revision, Horace paced around the office, picking up magazines and flipping through them.

"You're mighty quiet today, Horace. You're not worried about this deal are you? The changes I've made are minor. Shouldn't be a deal-breaker. It all looks pretty good to me."

"Nah. I know it's gonna work. It's not that."

"What is it, then? You're acting like you hear a ticking time bomb."

"You hit the nail on the head, Rachel. Dr. Smith wants me to go in for some tests. Says my ticker ain't quite right."

"I'm sorry to hear that, Horace, but I hope you'll do what he says."

Horace didn't answer and continued pacing.

"You *are* going in for the tests, right?"

"Not sure. What do I do if he wants something more serious done than tests?"

"You do it."

"I don't know, Rachel. I just can't see myself laid up in some hospital with tubes sticking out of me. Who'd run my business? I don't trust a soul. Well, you maybe."

"Maybe?" Rachel laughed. "Horace, you're impossible. Tubes sticking out of you for a couple of days would be a hell of a lot better than *you* stuck six feet under, don't you think?"

"Good god almighty, Rachel. Don't say that."

Georgia saved the day by interrupting the going-down-hill conversation with the freshly-typed document, which Horace grabbed on the way out the door in his hasty retreat.

"What was that all about?" Georgia asked.

"Horace has heart problems."

"I wondered when somebody would figure that out. Want to make a bet on whether he'll do something about it?"

"I think we'd probably bet the same way on this one and unfortunately, I'm afraid Horace would be the loser."

Chapter 15

Rachel took a cab to Ronald Reagan International Airport, arriving more than an hour before her 6:55 flight to La Guardia. She hoped the steady rain falling on Washington had already hit New York and moved on. Funerals were bad enough on a sunny day. Rain was almost too much to bear, she thought.

As she sat, drinking her bad airport coffee and reading the front page of the *Post*, her thoughts shifted to Ben and what he was able to understand about his recent life changes. Children are so resilient, she had always heard. Children live more in the moment.

Still, she remembered the deep despair she felt when her mother died. Of course, she had been 10 instead of five, and Rachel hoped the age difference was in Ben's favor. Perhaps five more years of worldly wisdom had created the sense of doom she experienced. She remembered the heavy pall that hung over her house for a couple of years after that day at the grave, and she promised herself that she would do anything to save Ben from it.

She remembered the powerlessness she felt in the face of her father's grief.

It was after her mother's death that she asked her father to teach her to milk. She decided that being beside him in the barn during those early morning hours would help her father start his day on a happy note. She learned to milk, but his depression seemed to deepen rather than lift.

As her father sank further and further into his black hole, little Rachel asked herself what she was doing wrong. Why she wasn't good enough.

Sitting in the airport, Rachel experienced one of those "Aha" moments people pay psychiatrists millions of dollars to achieve.

Rachel saw the wall she built to protect herself from feeling that failure ever again. Don't get close. Don't feel.

And she knew that she had to prevent Ben from building that wall.

*　　*　　*

John finally gave up insisting he meet her at the airport and gave her his son's address instead. Rachel arrived a couple of hours before the funeral.

The cab stopped in front of a brick colonial house with a huge weeping willow in the front yard.

Ben sat under it.

As Rachel slammed the taxi door shut, he came running toward her.

"You're here! You're here! I've been waiting for *hours*."

Rachel picked the child up, holding him in her arms for the first time. He buried his face in her neck and grabbed her braid.

"Where's the red thing?" he asked suddenly.

"What red thing?"

"The red Mexico thing. It's gone."

"Oh, no, Ben, you're right," Rachel said reaching for her bare braid. "I have no idea where it is. I guess I've lost it."

"Don't worry, Rachel. I'll find something else for you. Come on. We'll look in my room."

Rachel picked up her purse and followed him into the house.

Voices came from the back.

"Let's go find your grandfather first," she said.

Ben took her hand and led her to the kitchen where a half dozen people were gathered around a round oak table.

John sat with his back to the door, a pretty brunette pouring coffee into the cup sitting on the table in front of him. Her hand rested protectively on his shoulder.

"Granddad! She's here!"

John jumped up, spilling some of the coffee as he rose.

"Rachel! I didn't hear the cab," John said as he pushed his way across the room to her. "I'm so sorry I didn't come out to greet you."

"That's okay. Ben was waiting outside for me," Rachel said and reached out to him, not sure whether to shake hands or hug. She felt eyes watching and decided to follow John's lead.

He gave her a sideways hug and pulled her into the group to make introductions. His brother, Ted, and his wife, Marcie, and their teenage twins, Angus and Peter. His uncles, Mark and Andrew.

"And this is my friend, Alicia Townsend," he said, indicating the woman pouring more coffee.

Alicia nodded.

"Rachel lost her red Mexico bead," Ben said, breaking the awkward silence.

John look puzzled.

"The bead I wear on the end of my braid," Rachel explained. "It's really no big deal."

"I'm going to find her something in my room," Ben said. "Come on, Rachel. Let's go upstairs."

"Ben, Rachel probably would like to sit down and have a cup of coffee," Alicia said, finally speaking.

"NO," Ben shouted. "She wants to find it NOW with ME."

"Sure, Ben, let's go look," Rachel said. "You're so sweet to want to help me."

Delighted that he had won at least one battle in what must feel like World War III, Ben grabbed her hand and pulled her out of the room.

"That's Mommy and Daddy's room," he said as they passed a closed door. "Want to see it?"

"No, I want to see *your* room."

Ben seemed relieved and ran down to the end of the hall to a sunny space filled with toys, books and pictures of his family. Rachel's eyes lit on a picture of Ben at the beach with what must have been his parents. The woman was a tall, athletic-looking blond who could have been a Miss Clairol. The man looked like a younger version of John.

Ben saw her looking at the picture.

"That's Mommy and Daddy."

"They look like nice people, Ben. Just like you and your grandfather."

Ben pulled away from her and started rummaging through his toy box. Finding nothing, he began searching through his drawers.

Triumphantly, he presented her with a red leather cord with shells at each end.

"How about this?"

"That's perfect, Ben. Thank you so much. Do you want to tie it in my hair for me?"

Ben made a feeble attempt and when she could sense he was getting frustrated, Rachel took over for him.

"Perfect. I feel so pretty."

"You *are* pretty," Ben said.

Rachel convinced him they should return to the kitchen to see what was going on. When they entered the kitchen, all conversation stopped. Rachel sensed something was terribly wrong.

Alicia came toward her.

"Ben, are you sure you want to give this away?"

Ben didn't look at her and didn't speak.

John walked over to where they were standing and touched his grandson's head.

"Ben? Alicia just asked you a question."

Still nothing.

John looked at Rachel who felt clueless as to what was going on.

"That cord belonged to Ben's mother. They made it together at the beach last year."

"Oh, Ben," Rachel said, kneeling down to the child's level. "You should keep this." She started to take off the gift.

"NO," Ben shrieked. "I want YOU to have it for your hair. You NEED it." And with that, he ran from the kitchen, sobbing.

"I'm so sorry, John. I didn't know."

"Of course you didn't. We shouldn't have even said anything. And you do look very pretty wearing it," John said and gave her a hug – a real hug.

Alicia frowned.

*   *   *

Rachel rode to the graveside service with Mark and Andrew. They followed the funeral home limo carrying John and Ben. The little boy waved out the back window throughout the short trip to the cemetery.

When they arrived, about 50 people had already gathered around the funeral home tent. Rachel questioned John's decision to bring Ben when she saw the open graves, side-by-side.

As she stepped out of the car, Ben ran over to her.

"Are you going to sit with me?" he asked.

"No, Ben, but I'll stand in the front, close to your seat, so you can see me, okay?"

Ben didn't say anything but nodded his head. The crowd seemed to create a shyness she hadn't seen in him before.

John came over to where they stood, smiled at her and took his grandson's hand to lead him over to their front row seats under the tent. The wind was flapping its edges, making a loud drum-like sound above which the minister was forced to shout his greeting to the friends and family gathered. Even though Rachel stood almost beside him, she could barely hear his words.

All too soon, whatever he said came to an end, and he leaned over each member of the family, whispering words of comfort. Finally, John and Ben rose and walked to the two caskets, waiting to be lowered into the gaping holes in the ground. They each placed roses on the tops and then walked slowly back to the waiting limo.

As Rachel left, she saw that beside each of the two roses lay two toy Matchbox cars.

Reaching for a Kleenex, she felt the first drop of rain hit her cheek.

*   *   *

The house was already beginning to fill when Rachel and John's uncles walked in. Again, Alicia appeared to be acting as hostess, this time carrying a tray of cucumber sandwiches through the crowd.

"So nice of you to come all the way from Washington for the funeral," she said as Rachel took a bite of a tiny triangle. "Johnny tells me you're a great landlord."

Rachel was glad she had a mouthful of cucumber so that she had time to process her response. She had plenty of experience to recognize jealous girlfriends when she spotted one.

Alicia waited for her comeback.

Rachel smiled and said, "I've been very glad to have John – and Ben – downstairs."

"I guess you've started looking for a new tenant."

Fear ran through Rachel's veins like cold water. John walked up just as she was about to ask Alicia what she meant.

"Thanks again for coming, Rachel," he said. "It meant so much to Ben to have you here – and to me."

"You're welcome, John. I'm glad I could be here. When will you be coming back ho. . . – to Washington?"

"Probably Monday. Not sure yet, but it looks that way."

Rachel resisted looking at Alicia and instead said she needed to call a cab and get to the airport, herself.

"Sure you don't want somebody to take you? I'm sure one of my uncles would be glad to help."

Rachel declined the offer, trying not to be disappointed that he hadn't made it himself. But how *could* he have left a houseful of guests for the hour or more round trip to La Guardia.

Rachel chastised herself for being so childish.

Out of the corner of her eye, she saw Alicia finally smile.

*   *   *

Ralph was waiting in Susan's living room window when the cab pulled up. She paid the driver and walked across the street to rescue him before she went home.

When Susan opened the front door, a wiggling mass of fur and tongue bounded into her arms. She buried her face in his neck, inhaling the smell of pure love.

"He's missed you," Susan said.

"I missed him, too. A lot."

"So, how was it? When are they coming home?"

"Everything went fine. Very lovely service. Lots of support from friends and family. And they're coming back Monday, maybe. But it's not really 'home,' Susan. Their home is in New York, remember?"

"You know what I mean. How long will they be here, do you know? Are they going to stay in your apartment?"

"My god, Susan, I don't know. John's just lost his son. We haven't talked about his rental agreement."

"You don't need to get snippy with *me*, Rachel. I'm just curious."

"Sorry. I guess I'm tired. Think I'll go lie down for a while. Thanks for taking care of Ralph for me."

"Want to come have supper with us later? We're having leftovers, but there's plenty here for you too, if you want to come."

"That sounds good. What time?"

Susan told her to come back whenever she got up from her nap. They'd wait and didn't mind eating late. Jim had a meeting anyway and probably wouldn't get home until after seven.

Rachel kissed her friend on the cheek and walked across the street to the big empty house waiting for her.

*   *   *

After a long soak in the big garden tub and a half-hour nap on the sofa in the den with Ralph, Rachel felt more like herself. The lost, frightened little girl she had felt like in New York had been someone she hadn't seen in a long time. She breathed a sigh of relief as she looked around at the familiar world she shared with Ralph. *Her* world.

No green-eyed girlfriends here.

She slipped on her Birkenstocks, hooked Ralph's leash to his collar and locked the front door.

Jim still hadn't gotten home, and she was glad to be able to enjoy Susan alone for a little while.

"Still doing the poetry thing on Saturdays?" she asked, determined to steer the conversation away from John.

"Yes, I am. In fact, I've joined a little writers group that meets on Wednesday nights at the Java Joint. I just love the people. You need to find yourself something like that. You really do need to do something besides work all the time."

Rachel laughed at her friend. She never gave up.

Jim walked in the kitchen and saved her from further makeover attempts.

"Hey, Rachel. Good to see you. How was it?"

Rachel filled him in on her quick trip and said she thought John might be back on Monday.

"Good. We were afraid we might lose him. In fact, my boss had even started poking around for a replacement as soon as the news of the accident hit the office. We can't afford to lose time on this building. Having Ben here was enough of an interruption. Prolonged absences just wouldn't cut it. But John's so good at what he does that we hated to have to find someone else."

"Yeah, I know what you mean," Rachel said. When she saw Susan's eyes twinkle, she rushed to explain herself. "When Georgia was out because of Mike's surgery, I was devastated. Having her back made me feel like I'd been saved from a sinking ship."

Leftovers at Susan's house were always a smorgasbord of international delights: Indian lamb kebabs, fried rice, a few slices of pizza, cold fried chicken. Rachel ate like she was starving.

"Didn't they feed you up there in New York?" Susan asked as Rachel went back for seconds.

"I don't know why I'm so hungry. I just feel like I can't get enough. Hope this doesn't last long. I'll be as big as a house by next week."

"What you need is to join a gym. I know just the place. It's right . . ."

"Enough! Enough!" Rachel shrieked. "I'm fine. Really. I don't need a gym. I don't need a poetry group. I just need another slice of pizza and to get back to my old routine."

Susan looked hurt.

"Sorry to shriek like that, sweetie, but sometimes you really are too much. I'm fine. Really."

"I just want you to be happy, honey. You know, sometimes people eat too much when they're not satisfied with their lives."

"I'm happy, Susan. Really. Now, what's for dessert?"

Chapter 16

Rachel slept late the next morning. Finally, at 9:15, she rolled out of bed. The trip to New York had been short, but it must have taken a lot out of me, she thought.

Ralph rushed to the back door to be let out. As she opened it for him and stepped out onto her back deck, she heard the Moser's next door, discussing their plans for the day. A few doors down, a child squealed at some early morning surprise. She could hear traffic picking up on Dupont Circle, just a block away.

Life was good.

She left Ralph outside to enjoy his morning rounds and went back inside to make coffee. Susan had shared an apple walnut muffin she had bought at the Episcopal Church bizarre down the street. Rachel put it in the microwave to warm up while she waited for the coffee to brew. The smell of warm apple reminded her of her grandmother's kitchen.

I need to learn how to bake apple pies, she thought. Ben would love it. He'd be downstairs, playing, and smell the tempting aromas wafting down and come running up to see what I made. I'd serve him a glass of milk and a still-warm slice of pie.

She smiled to herself at the fantasy. Then reality set in, and she began to worry that the basement apartment was too small and that John would have to find a larger place.

Why not ask him if he'd like to move upstairs? There was certainly plenty of room. Three bedrooms, a huge den.

Ben would be thrilled, she felt sure, but what would John think?

Maybe she'd run the idea by Susan. No, Susan would definitely misunderstand.

Ralph stood at the door, pawing to come in.

"Ralph, what do you think of this idea?" she asked him, knowing full well what he would say, if he could.

*   *   *

As Rachel brushed her teeth, she glanced in the mirror above the sink and noticed the cord Ben had given her. She had woven it into her hair so she wouldn't lose it. The two shells dangled just below the end of her long braid.

Rachel smiled when she remembered how delighted the boy had been to be able to help her. He'd be back day after tomorrow – she hoped. Panic suddenly hit at the thought that maybe John would change his mind about coming back Monday – or coming back at all.

Maybe the wiles of the lovely Alicia would divert him – convince him he needed to stay in New York.

Maybe she should call to see how they were doing. The day after was hard. All the distractions of planning the funeral over, the company gone, the plates of food reduced to crumbs.

Maybe she should leave him alone.

Suddenly, she felt like a 16-year-old girl whose mother has told her girls shouldn't call boys.

This is ridiculous, she said to herself and picked up the phone. John's home phone number lay where she had left it on the counter with her other important numbers.

After several rings, the answering machine clicked on, and John's voice said, "Thanks for calling. We're out right now, but please leave a message, and we'll call you right back."

"We?" Who is "we?" she worried as she hung up.

*   *   *

As soon as Rachel walked into the office Monday morning and saw Georgia at her desk, she knew she was looking at the right person to advise her in her dilemma.

They went through the usual Monday morning routine – "How was your weekend? Blah, blah, blah" and "How was *your* weekend? Blah, blah, blah." Then they got down to business, running through the calendar for the week, talking about past-due accounts and anything else that needed two heads instead of one.

Finally, business aside, Rachel broached the subject that had been weighing on her mind since she had gotten back from New York.

Rachel was never one to beat around the bush.

"Georgia, what do you think of my asking John if he'd like to move upstairs so he and Ben would have more room? That basement apartment is much too small for them to live in together for any prolonged period of time, don't you think?"

Georgia looked like she had just been asked what she thought of Rachel flying to the moon. Stalling, she took a sip of coffee.

"I knew you'd think I was crazy," Rachel said, not waiting for an answer. "I'm sure John would, too. He'll probably want to move out into the suburbs, closer to the project and nearer good schools."

"Wait a minute there, Boss. You didn't give me a chance to say anything. I think it's a great idea. I was just a little surprised, that's all. You've never had a roommate – at least, not as long as I've known you."

"Never."

"Maybe it's about time. When do they get back?"

"Tonight. Think I should say something right away? You know, so John won't be worrying about what to do? Or should I wait a while and let him settle back into work? Or maybe . . ."

"Stop, Rachel. You're making too big a deal of this. Just go ahead and give the man the option. If he says, ' no,' drop it."

"What will he think?"

"That you've got more room than you know what to do with, maybe? It's not forever, Rachel. Just another three months."

"Right. Another three *and a half* months, to be exact."

"Three and a half months, and they'll be gone, and you'll have all that room to yourself again."

"Right."

Rachel got up from her desk and walked over to the window seat where Ralph lay.

"I guess the vote's unanimous, old boy."

Ralph wagged his tail and licked her fingers.

*   *   *

Rachel had a four o'clock appointment to deliver Mrs. Proctor's Will. Georgia went with her to notarize it. The butler would be the witness.

They locked the office and drove Georgia's Honda Civic over to Capitol Hill. When they pulled up in front of Mrs. Proctor's iron gates, Georgia let out a whistle.

"My god, Stan's dealing in the big time these days, isn't he? And she's leaving all this to the animal shelter?"

"That's the way the Will reads, doesn't it? You typed it."

"Some people have more money than they have sense."

Rachel laughed and rang the buzzer.

"Come on in. You're late," Mrs. Proctor's voice crackled over the intercom. Robert opened the door and showed them to the library where their client sat before a blazing fire. In the warm October afternoon, the temperature in the room felt like it was well over one hundred degrees.

Rachel took off her jacket before she sat in the bentwood rocker near her client.

"Is the room too warm for you? I do love a fire, and I thought I felt a little chill in the air."

"It's lovely, Mrs. Proctor. Georgia, are you all right?"

"I'm fine," Georgia said as she mopped her brow, opened the briefcase and took out the document to be signed.

"Mrs. Proctor, have you had any second thoughts about changing your Will since we last met?"

"My what?"

"Your Will. We're here today so you can execute your new Will, leaving your estate to the animal shelter."

"The animal shelter?"

"Yes, ma'am. You decided to cut your niece, Ramona, out of your Will and leave everything to the animal shelter."

"Oh, yes," Mrs. Proctor said and then launched into an explanation of her niece's misadventures for Georgia's benefit. "Now, what do you think of that?" she asked Georgia.

"I'm sure you know what you're doing, Mrs. Proctor. After all, it *is* your money."

"You're damned right it's my money, and there's no way I want even a penny of it to fall into the clutches of some money-grubbing no-good Republican. Where do I sign?"

Rachel went through her pre-signing script, asking her client if she was of sound mind or had been coerced into changing her Will. Finally, the signing and witnessing were done, and Rachel and Georgia gathered up their things and prepared to leave.

"Guess that's that," Mrs. Proctor said.

"Yes, ma'am. Call if we can ever help you again."

"Can't imagine what for, but you never know. Life's always full of surprises," Mrs. Proctor said.

"You're right about that," Georgia said and winked at Rachel.

*　　*　　*

Georgia dropped Rachel off in front of her house at about 5:30.

"Want to come in for a drink?" Rachel offered.

"No, Mike's making supper, and I don't want to keep him waiting."

"How nice."

"Maybe you'll get some of that special treatment soon," Georgia said as she pulled away from the curb.

Rachel couldn't tell if anyone was downstairs yet or not. She went in to let Ralph out. Still no noise from downstairs. Then she saw the light blinking on her answering machine.

Oh, no, they're not coming, she thought.

The message was, in fact, from John, calling to let her know their flight had been delayed and they were coming in a couple hours later than planned.

"Just didn't want you to worry," he said.

How considerate, Rachel thought.

Then another tiny voice, "I love you, Rachel."

Rachel smiled. "I love you too, Ben," she whispered to herself.

She looked in the refrigerator for something to eat for supper and thought of Georgia going home to a lovely dinner.

As she sat eating a bowl of cold cereal, Rachel couldn't help but feel a little sorry for herself.

She took the bowl into the den and turned on the news to distract herself. A hurricane along the coast, war in Iraq, local crime rates up. Not a good way to lift one's spirits, she realized.

She finished her granola and decided to take a walk up to Dupont Circle while it was still daylight.

Ralph thought that was a good idea and off they went.

Mrs. Moser stood in front of her house next door, watering her pansies.

"Good evening, Rachel. How are you?"

"Great. Your pansies look especially pretty this year."

"Thanks. Every year, I say I'm not going to bother, but Mr. Moser always pouts, and I give in and plant a few. Says they make a house look like a home. You should get yourself some."

"Maybe I will," Rachel agreed and caught up with Ralph who had made it all the way to the corner already. She clasped the leash to his collar, and they crossed the street together, Rachel thinking about the difference in a "house" and a "home."

The Circle seemed to suffer from more homeless people than usual. She looked around for Chelsea, the young girl she had met almost a month ago. She thought about how much her life had changed since then and wondered if anything major had happened in Chelsea's life.

Funny how some people could go for days, months, years without any significant changes in their lives and others faced them constantly.

Rachel admitted her own life had been fairly stagnant for a long time. Recent turns of events were certainly making up for it, she thought.

She found an empty bench and sat watching Ralph circle the rag-tag encampment, looking for an interesting handout perhaps. Lots of ear scratching tonight, but not much else.

Finally, he shuffled over and plopped down at her feet, disappointed.

"Bad night for begging?" Rachel asked.

"Yes, ma'am," a voice answered form over her left shoulder. Startled, Rachel turned to face a woman pushing a stroller. A little girl, who looked to be about three years old, sat slumped over, asleep like a rag doll.

"I was talking to my dog. He likes to come up here and get all kinds of good things to eat. Things I don't give him at home."

"Me, too."

Rachel didn't know what to say to that, except that she hadn't brought her purse with her.

"You live near here?" the woman asked.

"Pretty near. Maybe I'll see you next time we come. I'll make sure I bring my wallet."

"Sure. That's what everybody says. But they don't."

The young mother walked away.

"I will. I promise," Rachel called after her. She hated the way the homeless always made her feel so guilty. Even after more than 10 years of living among them every day, she still hadn't gotten used to the sight of the people begging – especially the young women with children.

She thought of Ben and how she would have felt if that had been him in the stroller.

She wrote her address on a piece of paper and ran over to give it to the woman.

"Here, stop by later, and I'll help you," she said as she handed her the slip of paper.

The woman looked like she had seen a vision of the Virgin Mary appear on the side of the bus stop wall.

"Thank you, ma'am. Thank you. I promise I won't bother you. I promise I won't come knocking on your door again. Just once."

"I'll be going home in a few minutes. In fact, if you want, you can come with us."

"Thank you, ma'am."

"What's your name?"

"Belle Mason and my little girl's name is Mary."

"Pleased to meet you, Belle. I'm Rachel Springer, and this is Ralph."

Ralph sniffed the child's little hands, waking her up. A smile spread across her whole face – a smile like she had just found a long-lost friend.

"Where do you live?" Rachel asked.

"We've been staying at the shelter, but we're trying to find someplace else. It's not a good place for children, if you know what I mean."

"I can imagine. Well, actually, I can't imagine. I've never had children."

"Bet you've never been homeless either."

"No, I haven't."

"It's the pits."

"Let's go on back to the house, and I'll give you enough money for a couple of nights in a motel. Get a few good nights of rest and a good bath."

"Thank you, ma'am. That's mighty kind of you."

They left the Circle and walked side-by-side back to Rachel's house. Rachel was thankful Mrs. Moser had finished watering her pansies. She felt sure her neighbor would not approve of what she was about to do. Which made her wonder what the Moser's would think of her proposal to John.

When Rachel turned down her walk, Belle stopped dead in her tracks.

"You live *here*?" she asked.

Rachel turned back to her and nodded. The girl refused to move another inch. Rachel retraced her steps to where she stood, rooted to the sidewalk.

"What's wrong?"

The girl just stood and stared. Finally, "You're not going to believe this," she said.

"Try me. I hear a lot of unbelievable stories in my line of work."

"This was my grandmother's house."

Rachel was speechless. Of course. "Mason" had been the name of the estate from which she had bought the house.

"Elizabeth Mason was your grandmother?"

"Sure enough. Hard to fathom, isn't it," the girl said, looking down at her child. "We've come on some hard times recently."

"You wait right here with Ralph and let me go get my purse," Rachel said and started up the walk. Suddenly, she felt ashamed of herself, keeping them waiting on the street like dogs. "Or would you like to come in?"

"May I? It would be kind of cool to see the place again."

Rachel opened the door wide. Belle took Mary out of the stroller and carried her into the foyer. The light from the kitchen illuminated the long hall leading to the back of the house.

"The place looks just the same," Belle said. "You like living here?"

"Very much. I feel lucky to have it."

"Granny would like that. She loved this house like it was a person. More, in fact."

Rachel thought of Mrs. Proctor and the changed Will and wondered if this child's homelessness might have a similar explanation. She gave her a couple hundred dollars from her emergency cash fund.

"Thank you, ma'am. I really appreciate this. Mary and I, that is. Come on, Mary, let's get out of Ms. Springer's way. I'm sure you've probably got dinner to fix for your family."

"No, I don't have a family. It's just me and Ralph."

Belle gave her a look of pity and patted Ralph on the head.

"Good thing you've got a dog."

"Yes, a very good thing."

*   *   *

A couple of hours later, Rachel heard the basement door open and movement in the apartment below her. She waited a few minutes and then dialed John's number. He answered on the first ring.

"John, it's Rachel. Have you all eaten? I've got plenty of chili left over if you're hungry."

"Thanks, Rachel. I was hoping it was you. Ben was pretty hungry by the time we landed, so we ate at the airport."

"How was the flight?" Rachel said, disappointed that he had eaten, taking away her excuse to see him.

"Uneventful. Ben's exhausted. Why don't you let me get him in bed, and I'll meet you out back in an hour."

Rachel's heart soared like a young girl's. When she hung up the phone, she looked at herself in the mirror and saw a flush in her cheeks. Was she nervous? Excited? Sick? Georgia had advised her not to make a big deal out of her offer. Not to take it personally if John decided to turn it down. But the thought of losing her housemates – of having an empty apartment downstairs – left her feeling like she had a hole deep in her stomach.

To pass the hour, she moved into the den and curled up on the overstuffed chintz sofa to flip through the new issue of *Shambala*. She started several articles that interested her but couldn't get past the first paragraph.

The phone rang, rescuing her from her futile attempts to concentrate.

The call was from a telemarketer. Not even a live one. Rachel listened for a couple of minutes to the recorded message, announcing that she had been selected for a free trip to Hilton Head Island and then hung up. She looked at her watch. Only 30 minutes had passed. Rachel contemplated what she could do for the next half hour. She decided to check her email.

The usual string of unsolicited spam, which she deleted without opening. A message from her cousin, Nancy, saying they missed her and hoped she'd come back soon. A memo from the neighborhood association president announcing the upcoming monthly meeting. Rachel noticed a message sent by someone she didn't immediately recognize. She was on the verge of hitting the "delete" button when she realized it was from George, the farm manager.

Curious as to how he'd gotten her email address, she opened the message. Her curiosity was satisfied immediately.

> *I bribed your cousin into giving me your email address. Hope you don't mind. Told her I'd quit if she didn't. I can be quite persuasive. Don't hold it against her. Sorry to hear of the emergency that took you home before I got the chance to share my photographs, but hope you'll come again soon. I enjoyed your company. Never seen a city girl milk a cow before. George.*

Rachel smiled to herself. She was just starting to compose a reply when she heard the downstairs door open. She closed and saved George's message and dashed to her own back door, Ralph right behind her.

John got up from his chair as she came toward him. Ralph rushed ahead of her and brushed against his legs in greeting. He stooped down to rub Ralph behind his ears. When he stood up, he lost his balance and Rachel reached out and grabbed his arm to steady him.

He brought his other arm around her and pulled her close. They stood wrapped in each other's arms, listening to a siren in the distance. Rachel felt like she had come home.

She tilted her head up for a kiss. John's lips were gentle at first, exploring the edges of her mouth and then his hunger overcame him and he seemed to want to consume her.

How long had it been since she had been kissed like this, she wondered, and then gave herself up to the moment, realizing that none of that mattered now. She lost herself in the smell of his neck. Some pepper smell she couldn't identify, but told herself to ask about later.

The grizzle of his chin chafed her face. But it was his broad shoulders and back that she yearned for. That she didn't want to let go of. Even though she realized that John was the one whose life was so precarious at the moment and that it was *he* who *needed* her support, she felt safety and protection in his embrace. It was a feeling she hadn't allowed herself to want for a long time. Maybe a *very* long time.

"You feel so good to me," John said, finally breaking the silence.

"Ummmm," was all Rachel could bring herself to say. It was as though she was afraid words might break the spell.

Reluctantly, they parted and sat down in the two chairs.

"You need a glider out here," John said.

"Or a hammock," Rachel said and then was embarrassed by how forward that sounded.

"Perfect idea. Let's get one tomorrow."

"Let's," Rachel said, warmed all over by the sound of "us."

For a while, they sat in silence, looking at each other with new eyes. John's hands were one of his best features, Rachel decided. Long elegant fingers with neatly clipped nails on a broad firm base. She found herself longing to feel them on her body. Stopping that fantasy before it went too far, she asked, "So, now what?"

"You mean about the hammock? Well, I thought you'd know where to buy one."

"No, what are your long-range plans? Now that Ben will be staying with you?"

"I was hoping you'd have a suggestion," he said, looking her in the eyes, his expression full of hope.

"Actually, I did have an idea, John, and it's sounding better and better to me," Rachel said and smiled. "Why don't you and Ben move upstairs with Ralph and me. There's plenty of room. I've got three bedrooms and lots of space all over the house to spread out in. What do you think?"

"I don't have to think. I know. And Ben will love it. All we'll need to do is look into finding a school for him, and we'll be settled."

"At least until your project is completed."

John sat in silence for a while, seeming to try to look into the future. A frown creased his brow.

"At least," he said. "But right now, why don't we move into my living room. At least until we get that hammock, we can get closer to each other on my sofa and be able to hear Ben if he needs me."

He helped Rachel up from her chair, and they walked inside, hand-in-hand.

"What about Alicia?" Rachel asked as soon as they sat down on his couch and he had pulled her to him.

"Alicia?"

"Aren't you two dating?"

John didn't laugh and shrug her question off as she had been afraid he might. Instead, he held her hands in his and took his time with his answer.

"We did date. In fact, we were seeing each other quite a bit before I left to come down here. She's a lot of fun, and she was always very good to me."

"I could see that."

"What do you mean?"

"During the funeral. She was the perfect hostess."

"Yes, she was, and she was always an interesting dinner companion. She'll make someone a perfect trophy wife."

"So, like I said, 'What about Alicia?'" Rachel asked, moving further away from John.

"I'm not looking for a trophy wife, Rachel. I've had a trophy wife, and she got pretty tarnished over the years. I want solid gold, and I think I've found it. I think I'm falling in love with you, Rachel. And I know Ben is already there. Fallen head over heels, in fact."

"But, I'm a lot older than Alicia. Probably older than you. I'm more grandmother material than mother material for Ben."

"I don't care what you call the material. I think it works really well."

John reached for her hand and pulled her back toward him and into his arms. His kiss moved from her lips to her eyes and down her neck to the hollow in her collarbone. Rachel trembled beneath the touch of his hands in her hair. He tugged on her braid.

"I want to see your hair loose. When will you take your braid apart for me?"

"Soon," she said in a croak and then laughed as she cleared her throat.

"I hope so, Rachel. Gosh, I guess I'm going to have to start thinking about babysitters again."

"I think you've got a very willing and able volunteer right across the street."

"Susan! Of course. Looks like things are falling into place then, doesn't it. When do you want us to move upstairs?"

"How about tomorrow," came a little voice from inside the bedroom.

"Ben Turner, I thought you were sound asleep," John said, jumping up from the sofa.

Looking wide-awake, Ben ran over to the sofa and fell into Rachel's lap.

"I think tomorrow sounds perfect," she said. "I'll go right upstairs and tell Ralph."

"Tell him he can sleep in the bed with me and Granddad."

Rachel looked at John.

"Doesn't sound like I needed three bedrooms after all."

"We'll see about that," John said under his breath.

Chapter 17

Rachel didn't wake up singing the next morning. She woke up feeling like the song, itself. Improvisational jazz, perhaps, but the beat was strong.

Meditating proved difficult. Thoughts raced around in her head. Staying in the moment was almost impossible. Every time she thought she had anchored her mind, it escaped into the future. Sometimes as far into the future as worrying about how old she would be when Ben graduated from high school. Or even if she would be alive. Every time she felt fear and doubt creep in, she acknowledged them and observed them pass as she counted her breath.

When the ping of her alarm signaled the end of the half hour, she rose from her zafu and moved downstairs to let Ralph back inside.

Thank god, the skies are sunny, she thought.

John told her he would take the day off to move his and Ben's things upstairs. They discussed asking Susan to occupy Ben during the transition but then decided he needed to be part of the experience. So much of what had happened in his life recently had been out of his control that they agreed it was important that he not feel left out of the move, too.

Being part of a family decision made her feel like a child, rolling down the hill behind her grandmother's house. Deliciously dizzy.

As she sat at the kitchen table, sipping her second cup of coffee, Rachel suddenly realized she should make plans for supper – not a regular part of her routine. Her meals were always impromptu stops at the market and a glance at the deli section where she picked out something that looked good to eat.

She called Georgia late last night to tell her she wouldn't be going to the office and warned Susan about the activity that would be going on across the street. Both women congratulated Rachel on the news and, of course, offered to help.

Rachel thanked them and tried to downplay the event.

Now, she wished she had taken Susan up on her offer to bring supper over later.

Maybe it wasn't too late. She'd start being domestic tomorrow. Just as she picked up the phone to call her friend, she spotted her pink bathrobe across the street and dashed to the door to catch her.

Susan saw her coming and stopped.

"My, don't you look spry this morning. Going to a fire?"

"Not exactly, but I do have a few things on my plate today, and I wondered if you . . ."

"Would fix supper? You know I will. Ben loves my fried chicken. How about I serve it around six?"

"You're wonderful," Rachel said, hugged her friend and dashed back across the street, Ralph on her heels, confused by all the early morning dashing.

John said he'd probably have everything in boxes and ready to move upstairs by late morning. They'd take a break for lunch and then spend the afternoon unpacking boxes. Rachel voted for skipping the boxes, but he insisted that a move was a move, regardless of how short the distance, and a move required boxes.

Rachel remembered several moves she had made – quite successfully, in fact – using garbage bags and pillowcases, but she decided not to argue. It was, after all, *his* move, regardless of the fact it was into *her* house. As long as she let him deal with disposing of the empty boxes. Fear set in at the thought of moving clutter.

Breathe in. Breathe out.

*   *   *

Rachel's plan was to make the spare room at the front of the house Ben's room. It was furnished with twin beds and featured a large walk-in closet he could use as a toy hideaway. She made a note to buy new bedspreads and curtains to replace the frilly flower-covered ones she had used for years.

John would sleep in the room across the hall from him. A large bathroom next door would be convenient for him. Rachel spent some time removing items from the vanity drawers and small linen closet so he and Ben would have plenty of room for their own toiletries.

She felt satisfied that John would be comfortable in his new room. She upgraded to a queen-size pillow-top mattress just a year ago and the new plain forest green comforter gave the room a masculine touch. A leather recliner in the alcove overlooking the courtyard would be a nice place for him to rest when he wanted privacy.

The third floor would remain her own retreat.

John called shortly before noon to say they were just sitting down to lunch and should be ready to start hauling boxes within a half hour, if she was ready to be invaded.

She decided to take Ralph for a walk to kill the remaining time. She was in the mood for street food and headed for their favorite hot dog vendor at the Circle.

Deejee had parked her cart in her usual spot near Revco Drug Store and a long line formed. Rachel stood at the end of it with Ralph, both of them enjoying the smell of chili, cheese and onions.

She hardly recognized Belle and Mary. Only the pink stroller looked familiar – not the people attached to it.

"Hi, Ms. Springer," Belle said, smile washing over Rachel like a warm summer shower.

"My goodness, Belle. You look fabulous. And, Mary, I believe you've grown an inch since I saw you last."

"You were right. The hotel really did make a difference. We especially loved the big bathtub, didn't we, Mary? In fact, she didn't want to get out of it. We really got our money's worth. Well, I guess it was *your* money's worth. Thanks, again."

"Let me buy you a hot dog, "Rachel said, ordering three – two all the way and one plain. Mary held hers in her chubby little hands and had a great time gumming it.

"Seeing my grandmother's house again helped, too," Belle said. "Made me remember who I am. I've got some things in the works I'm hoping will get my life back on track. Don't want to jinx anything by talking too much about them, but I've got my fingers crossed."

"I'll cross mine, too."

The three sat on the bench near Deejee, eating their hotdogs and throwing pieces of bun to the pigeons. Mary squealed every time a bird got near her and begged for more bread.

"She's a precious child. You're doing a good job with the mothering part of your life, obviously."

Belle looked at her daughter and smiled. "The loving is easy. It's all the other stuff that's hard."

And then a thought hit Rachel that made her sure she had lost her mind. She hesitated only a few seconds before she asked, "What are you doing this afternoon?"

"My usual – nothing," Belle laughed.

"Would you like to come home with me and play with a little friend of mine while his grandfather and I get some moving done? I'll pay you."

"Sure. Sounds like fun, doesn't it, Mary?"

Mary threw another piece of bread and squealed. Ralph contained himself as long as he could and finally made a lunge at one of the birds, causing the whole flock to scatter. Mary wailed.

"Looks like a good time for us to leave," Rachel said and led the little group up the street.

A small stack of boxes waited outside the front door when they arrived. On top sat Ben's stuffed Pooh Bear, apparently eager to see his new home.

Mary reached out to it and cried, "Pooh."

"Yes, that's Pooh, but he's not yours," Belle said to her. "Where's your blanket?"

She was trying to distract the child with her ratty blanket when John and Ben came up the walk.

"Hey, there, guys," John said.

"John, this is my friend, Belle, and her daughter, Mary. Belle said they will play with Ben so he won't get bored."

Mary was still shrieking, "Pooh" at the top of her lungs. Ben hesitated briefly and then reached for the bear and handed it to the little girl in the stroller.

"Here, you can hold it for a little while, but not forever. Don't forget. It's my Pooh Bear."

Mary's smile lit up the whole street.

"Thanks, Ben. That was so nice of you to share," Rachel said.

"I think she needed it more than me – at least for now."

"Thanks," Belle said. "I'll make sure she's careful with it."

"Let's get started," John said. "We should be able to get all this shifted upstairs in no time at all."

Rachel ushered Belle and the children into the den and turned on the Disney channel. Ben wanted to see his room first, so Rachel led him into the sunny room at the top of the stairs.

"Wow, this is great," he said when he saw the huge closet.

"It'll be even greater with all your toys in it," John said.

"Which bed are you going to sleep in, Granddad?"

Rachel looked at John and waited.

"I might sleep in this one tonight," he said, plopping down on the bed closest to the door, "but I have my own room across the hall. Want to see it?"

Reluctantly, Ben walked with his grandfather the few steps to the other guest room and then circled it like an animal getting the lay of the land.

"That's a big bed. I could probably sleep in it with you, if you want."

"We'll see. Let's get our stuff unpacked right now, and we can talk about sleeping later."

"When it gets dark."

"Yes," John said, "when it gets dark."

*   *   *

Ben ran back downstairs to watch a PBS special about polar bears with Belle and Mary while Rachel helped John with the boxes. He hauled; she unpacked.

She marveled at how much pleasure she felt folding the tiny shirts and jeans and putting them in the dresser drawers in Ben's room. Some nurturing gene had been activated deep within her, she thought and smiled as she felt it stir.

She placed the picture of Ben's parents on the table beside his bed so he could reach it. But when she came to his box of toys and books, she decided to let him arrange them in the closet, himself. She brought a small bookshelf in and placed it in a corner of the large walk-in closet and made a mental note to see if she could find a small child's worktable to fit in the hideaway. A stackable unit brought up from the basement would be perfect for the toys.

Pleased with the nest she created, Rachel walked across the hall to see how John was doing and was surprised to find him sitting on the bed, staring out at the courtyard.

As she got closer, she saw the tears on his cheeks.

She sat down beside him and reached out to touch his hand.

"Sometimes the pain just washes over me like a tsunami," he said. "Forgive me. I know I should be filled with gratitude for what you're doing for Ben and me – for the beautiful home you're willing to share – for the chance to be with you – and I am grateful – and excited – but sometimes this loss is bigger than all that."

"I remember the feeling. You're okay, John. I'm right here. When the tide goes back out. When the waters recede. I'll be right here."

"Thanks," John said, stood up and pulled her close. His kiss was salty with tears, and she tasted his grief.

"So, what shall I do with these empty boxes?" he asked, shaking himself back to the task at hand.

Rachel restrained herself from reminding him that she had wanted to use garbage bags in order to avoid the hassle of what to do with the boxes. Instead, she suggested they take them apart and put them on the curb for the recycle pick-up.

She looked around the room at the few books and pictures he brought and thought how lived-in the room seemed already. A colorful pillow tossed on the plain bedspread seemed to bring it to life – to create an invitation that hadn't been there before.

John saw her looking at the pillow and explained he had bought it on one of his early trips to Santa Fe.

"Next time I go home, I'll bring some of my blankets, too."

"In the meantime, I've got a few I'll share with you," Rachel said.

"One day maybe we'll make that trip west together. I'll bet we've been to a lot of the same places and enjoyed many of the same things. Experiencing them together is something I look forward to."

"Me, too," Rachel said. "But right now, let's get Ben's approval on his room. I left the toys and books for him to unpack."

"You're a wise woman, Rachel Springer."

Rachel smiled and squeezed his hand.

* * *

When Rachel walked into the den, the sight waiting there enveloped her like her favorite down-filled coat on the first chilly day of fall.

Belle sat on the sofa holding Ben in her lap. Mary snuggled close beside her, still clutching Pooh Bear. It was as though Mary had traded her mother for the stuffed animal – just "for a little while."

Belle looked like a Madonna, her love pouring out over the two children – one motherless, the other homeless.

She looked up from the television and smiled at Rachel. All the fear seemed to have been erased from her eyes.

Suddenly she asked, "Is it time for us to leave?" and the clouds rolled over the sun.

"No, not at all. I just came down to see if Ben wanted to check out his new room."

"Yeah," Ben cried and jumped off Belle's lap. "Come on, Belle, let's go."

"I saved the fun part for you – the toys. You can arrange them on the shelves, yourself. The books, too."

"In my toy room?"

"In your toy room."

Ben gave a shout and ran from the den, Ralph nipping at his heels and bounding up the stairs behind him.

"Guess we'd really better be going," Belle said. "It'll be getting dark soon, and I like to get back to the shelter before they start serving supper so we can get ahead of the crowd."

"Why don't you stay here with us for supper. Knowing Susan, there'll be enough fried chicken to feed an army. Then we'll call a cab so you won't have to walk back in the dark."

"You sure?"

"Sure."

"Belle, are you coming?" Ben yelled from upstairs.

"I'm coming. Here, Mary, take Mama's hand. We're needed upstairs." As mother and daughter slowly climbed the stairs, a plan began to formulate in Rachel's mind.

As soon as the two were out of earshot, she turned to John, still sitting in the recliner, reading the sports section of the *Post*. Rachel thought of all the years that section had been tossed, unread, into the recycle bin.

"John, if I tell you something, will you promise me you won't think I'm crazy?"

John looked up at her and put the paper down in his lap, giving her his full attention.

"I promise."

She sat down on the arm of the recliner and leaned back against his shoulder, resting her head against him. He pulled her into his lap.

"So, what is it?"

"I'm thinking about offering Belle the apartment downstairs. She could be a live-in nanny. What do you think?"

"I don't think it's any crazier than your inviting Ben and me to live up here."

Rachel sat up and faced him. "Really? I thought you'd say I was nuts."

"Really. I think it might be a good idea to check out her background first, especially if she's going to be taking care of Ben, but I get the feeling she's just a young woman who's down on her luck. Ben likes her, and he's a pretty good judge of character."

"Right. I'll have Stan do a little research for me right away. In fact, I'll give him a call now."

Rachel jumped up and moved into the kitchen to dial the private investigator's number.

Stan answered on the first ring, took the little bit of information she could provide and told her he'd get back to her within 24 hours.

Rachel hung up the phone and ran upstairs to see what her ever-expanding family was doing.

Chapter 18

Stan called Rachel at the office the next day at around three o'clock. He'd found no surprises but was still checking.

Rachel was relieved and went out to tell Georgia her latest news. Georgia wasn't as enthusiastic as she had been about John's move upstairs. Always playing the role of the protective mother, she expressed concerns that Stan's background check couldn't cover.

"What if somebody she met at the shelter decides to visit and they're the kind of person who wouldn't have passed Stan's background check. Suppose they find out where you live and rob you blind. Suppose . . ."

"Whoa. Slow down. I trust this girl, Georgia. I don't believe she'd put me in any kind of danger. I think she's ready to make a fresh start, and I doubt that means dragging the homeless from the shelter with her."

Georgia still looked doubtful but moved on to more practical matters.

"Want me to draw up a lease? Maybe month-to-month?"

"Thanks. That's probably a good idea. It's a trade. Room and board for babysitting, plus some kind of pay. I'll talk to John tonight about how much to pay her and let you know tomorrow."

"Have you talked to her about this?"

"Not yet, but I think she'll be as thrilled with the idea as we are. Did I tell you the house used to belong to her grandmother?"

"Wow. That's pretty powerful stuff, Rachel. Wonder if she likes chocolate chip cookies. I could . . ."

Georgia's cookie plan was interrupted by the ringing of the phone.

Rachel walked back into her office to organize the files she needed to take to court. Tucked in one of them hid the picture Ben had drawn of Ralph and the ice cream. She made a note to buy a frame. And a hammock.

*   *   *

Rachel felt distracted all day. Concentrating on work had never been a problem in the past. In fact, over the course of her career, she had realized that she had become a workaholic. But that had definitely changed – at least for the moment – as she focused on her housemates and wondered what they were doing.

Ben was spending the day with Susan, who planned to take him to the Air & Space Museum in the morning and then shopping for a few school clothes in the afternoon.

John was checking out schools.

Rachel felt jealous of both of them as she sat waiting for her case to be called.

Maybe it was time to retire, she thought. She could be a stay-at-home grandmother. Or perhaps she could just cut back on her caseload so she could be at home when Ben got out of school in the afternoons. Or maybe . . .

Just as Rachel was at risk of really projecting into some even more absurd possibilities, she heard the Clerk call, "Monroe vs. Payne," saving her from completely "flying off the handle," as her grandmother used to describe such flights of fancy.

As she walked out of court, Michelle Arrington, a new lawyer in town, called to her.

"Where've you been, Counselor? Haven't seen much of you lately."

"Sorry I haven't been in touch more. How are you doing? I hope you're feeling at home by now."

"I am. I love D.C. Want to grab some lunch next door?"

Rachel's immediate reaction was to turn down the offer so she could check on things at home. She almost had "no thanks" spit out when she reined herself in. She really had to be careful not to lose herself – her own life – in all these new people who were becoming part of it, she told herself.

"Sure, that sounds great," she said, proud that she had been able to do what was not coming easily.

The two women were able to get to Chico's deli counter before the lunch crowd converged. Rachel ordered a black bean burrito, knowing she'd regret it later but deciding to live dangerously.

She and Michelle grabbed the window table in the front and spread their lunch out before Michelle said, "So, what's new? You look radiant. At the risk of offending you, I'd say you look ten years younger. No, make that 20."

Rachel laughed.

"Well, I have had my safe little world turned upside down recently."

"Wow. Your life always seemed so perfect to me. What's happened?"

"I guess it did look pretty perfect. And it's not that this new life is any better, but it's significantly different."

And then Rachel told the story of being talked into renting her downstairs apartment to John; about their evolving friendship; of falling in love with Ben and feeling a mothering part of herself being activated; and finally, about the accident and her decision to ask John and Ben to move upstairs.

"So, is this just a roommate arrangement, or are you romantically interested in Granddad?"

Rachel blushed.

"Okay, you don't even need to answer that. I can tell by the color of your face."

Michelle reached across and squeezed Rachel's hand.

"This is great. You deserve it, Rachel. Whatever 'it' turns out to be. As long as it's good."

Rachel felt fear in the pit of her stomach and took a bite of burrito to smother it.

*   *   *

Stan called later in the afternoon, just as Rachel was packing her briefcase to go home. Georgia had already left, so she answered the phone herself.

"I've finished checking out Belle Mason," he said. "You want the good news first, or the bad news first?"

"Just give it to me straight, Stan."

"Okay. I'll give it to you chronologically. How about that?"

"That makes sense."

Stan was a no-nonsense man and went right to work, spitting out all the information he had been able to gather on Ben's potential nanny.

She had been born 25 years ago in the little town of Warrenton, Virginia, about 45 minutes southwest of Washington. She graduated from Fauquier High School, went a year to George Mason Community

College, where she was working toward an associate degree in nursing before she dropped out.

Her parents were blue color workers. Her father drove a beer truck. He mother worked at the local Safeway. She was the youngest of six children. Got in a little trouble involving underage drinking at George Mason. Flunked out of a couple of classes her last semester.

"Here's the doozy," Stan said. "She got a DWI two years ago and served a little time for it."

"Anything since then?"

"Nothing else on her record. Never had a real job, doesn't look like. No credit problems – just no credit. Looks like her parents are still alive, but I'd say if she's living on the streets, she must not have much of a relationship with them."

"Would you let her live in your house and take care of your child, Stan?"

"Rachel, I did what you asked. I got the sheet on the girl. Don't ask me the hard stuff."

"But, you're such a good judge of character, Stan. I trust your judgment."

"This one's beyond my field of expertise. This one requires some heart, and I'm afraid I learned to shut down in that category years ago when I started this work."

"Well, ultimately, it's John's decision anyway – at least about Ben. Thanks, Stan."

"When do I get to meet your fellow?"

"He's not *my* anything. But I do want you to meet him – soon."

"Want me to run a sheet on him?"

Rachel hesitated just a minute and then laughed. "I'm assuming the hospital did that before they hired him as a consultant, but thanks."

They hung up after making a promise to get together soon. Rachel liked Stan and wanted to include him in her new life. He'd been a friend for a long time and had earned the privilege of being included in the warm circle that had so miraculously appeared around her as if dropped from the heavens into her lap.

Rachel thought that it was fortunate that she had been sitting down in a position that would create a lap when her new blessings arrived. If she had been doing her usual running, those blessings would have fallen by the wayside.

*   *   *

When Rachel arrived home, Ben was in Susan's front yard, playing ball with Ralph. Susan sat on the porch, watching.

"Rachel," Ben shouted. "Look what I taught Ralph."

Rachel stopped and gave her undivided attention as Ben rolled the ball to Ralph, who grabbed it in his mouth and carried it to Susan, who rolled it back to Ben.

"That's it," Rachel said. "I'm quitting my job tomorrow and staying home. You guys are having all the fun."

"But you've got to admit, coming home is a lot more fun when you've got this to come home to," Susan said.

"Definitely."

Rachel sat down on the front porch steps with Susan and watched Ben and Ralph run around in circles in the yard in front of her.

"Imagine having that much energy at the end of the day," Rachel said.

"He's gone full force pretty much all day. I tried to get him to take a nap after lunch, but he'd have nothing to do with it."

Rachel looked at her friend, concerned that taking care of a five-year-old might be too much for her.

"So, how are you?"

"Ready for a hot bath and bed," Susan laughed. "But first, let me give you the cake Ben and I made. John said to tell you he'd pick up a pizza on the way home."

Rachel called Ben and Ralph into the house while she went to retrieve Susan's famous German chocolate cake.

"Thanks for doing this, Susan. I'm going to talk to John tonight about asking Belle to move into the basement. If he agrees, she'll be responsible for Ben during the days. And, of course, school starts next week."

"Are you sure about Belle?"

"I had Stan check her out. Everything looks okay to me, but it's John's call."

Rachel and Ben hugged Susan goodbye and followed Ralph across the street. Ben bounced with news about all the adventures he and Susan had at the museum. He was thrilled with his new clothes and had lots of questions about school since he'd never been to any kind of organized playgroups. His parents kept him close to home since his mother didn't work.

Worried about how he would adapt to so many sudden changes, Rachel checked several books out of the library on child psychology and devoured them every spare minute she had. She hoped John was equally concerned and preparing himself, as well.

But so far, so good.

"When's Granddad coming home?" a little voice broke into her thoughts.

"He said he'd be here by 6:30."

"When's that?"

"Well, it's 6:05 now."

"When's that?"

"Tell you what. Let's go upstairs and put your new clothes away and maybe read a book, and I'll bet when we finish, it will be 6:30."

"And Granddad will be home then?"

"I hope."

"I missed him today."

"Me, too."

*   *   *

Rachel breathed a sigh of relief when she heard the front door open at 6:28. She wasn't prepared to teach any lessons on patience and disappointment yet. She hadn't gotten that far in the child-rearing books she was reading.

Ben jumped off her lap and raced downstairs to greet his grandfather, Rachel right behind him. John held Ben in his arms when she walked into the kitchen.

"Rachel missed you, too," Ben said. "She wants a hug."

"Delighted," John said as he set Ben down to make room for her. Rachel felt her whole body relax against his.

"Okay, now, let's eat," Ben interrupted. "Me and Susan made a Germum cake for dessert."

"German," John corrected him. "German chocolate cake."

"You know about Germum cakes?" Ben asked, wide-eyed.

"I love German chocolate cakes. Especially Susan's," John said.

"Cool. Well, this is specially good cause I helped."

"And this pizza is especially good because I bought it, so let's eat it while it's still hot."

The three sat down at the table with the cardboard pizza box in the middle. When Rachel lifted the lid, Ben let out a wail.

"Oh, no," he cried. "Pepperoni. I hate pepperoni."

"We'll just pick the pepperoni off your piece," Rachel offered.

"That won't work. The pepperoni juice is still on there. Mommy never makes me eat pizza like this."

Rachel looked at John hopelessly as Ben fled from the table and ran upstairs to his room. They could hear his heartbroken sobs echoing through the house.

"What do your books say to do now?" John asked.

"Haven't gotten that far yet. You had a child. What did you do?"

"We never ate pizza."

Ralph, impatient with his people's ineffectiveness, ran from the room and up the stairs.

Within minutes, the crying stopped. Rachel and John waited and were rewarded by footsteps padding toward them.

Ben bounced into the room, climbed into his chair and started picking pepperoni off his slice.

"Ralph said he likes pepperoni, and he'll eat mine."

Rachel and John looked at each other and smiled with relief.

"I think I'll add my own chapter to those books and title it "Dog Wisdom," Rachel laughed.

"It may be the one chapter that really makes sense," John said as he placed a small plate of pepperoni slices on the floor for Ralph and whispered, "Thanks, buddy."

*   *   *

John supervised Ben's bath and got him in bed by 8:00. The child was tired after his day of sightseeing and shopping.

Rachel walked upstairs to say goodnight.

"Is the bed comfortable?" she asked.

"Not as good as mine, but it's okay. Can Ralph sleep with me?"

"Sure, if he wants to. How about it, Ralph?"

Ralph circled the bedside rug a few times and lay down.

"Looks like he does," Rachel said and leaned over to kiss Ben on the forehead. "Sweet dreams."

"No, you're supposed to say, 'Night night, don't let the bedbugs bite.'"

"Sorry. Night night, don't let the bedbugs bite."

"And now you say, 'I love you, Ben.'"

"I love you, Ben."

"I love you, too, Rachel. Now, you say, 'See you at the breakfast table.'"

"See you at the breakfast table."

"Good."

"Okay, pal, now it's time for you to close your eyes and go to sleep," John said, tucking him in and turning off the light. "I'll leave the door cracked, and I'll be downstairs in the den."

"With Rachel?"

"With Rachel."

"Good."

John and Rachel held their breaths as they eased down the steps, wondering how far they'd get before Ben thought of a reason to call them back. They made it all the way to the den with no little voice stopping them.

They sat frozen on the sofa, waiting, and still nothing.

"Looks like he's going to be okay," John finally said.

"How about you? Are you okay?"

"I don't know. Who's going to sleep with me?"

Rachel snuggled up to him and turned her face up for a kiss, which he was happy to provide.

Finally, he pulled away from her and said, "So?"

"So what?"

"Who's going to keep me from being lonely tonight?"

"Who's been keeping you company every other night?"

"Nobody, but things have changed. I want you with me tonight."

"Let's take it slow, John. We've got Ben to consider, too. I want to be sure about us – that we're going to be able to sustain what we feel now – before we share a bed. I don't want to disappear from his life like his parents have."

"You're right, but let's figure it out as quickly as possible. I don't like to feel lonely any more than Ben does."

"Me neither," Rachel said and hugged him.

With her head resting on his shoulder, Rachel asked John what progress he had made on the school front, and he reported that he had met with the principal of the Montessori school and was told there was an opening. Ben was registered to start next week.

Rachel told him about her call from Stan.

"I think we should give it a try, John. How about you?"

John hesitated only a moment, but long enough to alert Rachel to his doubt. She pulled away from him and moved to the edge of the sofa so she could look him in the eyes.

"What's wrong? I thought you agreed that she'd be good with Ben and that you wanted to help her, too."

"Let me sleep on it, Rachel. Being a parent again is heavy-duty stuff. I need to be sure."

"Of course," Rachel said. "I didn't mean to rush you. I'm sure Susan will be happy to help out until he starts school next week, and we can always find an after-school program if we need to."

"And you can always offer Belle the apartment without it being connected with Ben, you know."

"Of course. No pressure," Rachel said as she stood and stretched. "I'm going upstairs to meditate now. Can I get you anything before I go up?"

"Not a thing. Will it bother you if I turn on the television and see what's on?"

"Not at all."

John stood up and pulled her to him for a goodnight kiss. "Thanks again, Rachel – for everything. This all feels very good."

"Yes, it does, John. See you in the morning."

"Don't let the bedbugs bite."

*   *   *

As Rachel walked by Ben's room, she peeked in. Ralph had moved from the rug to a position at Ben's feet on the end of the bed. He raised his head and looked at her, as if to see if he had her permission. She smiled at him, and he laid his head back down and closed his eyes.

Rachel suffered several distractions as she sat on her zafu, attempting to meditate. Images of Belle and Mary sitting on a park bench at Dupont Circle the first time she met them. John downstairs watching television alone. And the most unsettling thought – John in bed just across the hall from her room.

She sat for the full half hour that was her usual practice, but it was a long way from being a quiet sit. When the soft ting of her alarm signaled that 30 minutes had passed, she stretched with relief. She realized she missed Ralph in the window seat, standing guard.

Passing by Ben's door on her way down to the kitchen, she saw that the dog had moved again and was lying beside Ben, under the boy's arm.

John turned off the television and left the den dark. Rachel sat at the kitchen table, waiting for water to boil for tea. She picked up the *Post* and leafed through the entertainment section, looking for an event that her new family might be interested in sharing with her during the coming weekend. An ad for the circus looked like fun, and then her eye caught an announcement for a baroque concert at The Phillips. She wondered whether she should mention it to John, or if she should wait for him to make the moves.

With a tightening in her stomach, Rachel remembered why she had stayed single so many years. It sure was simpler.

Chapter 19

When Rachel's alarm rang at six o'clock, she was surprised to realize she had slept through the night without waking. She wondered if Ben had gotten up without her hearing him.

She found her answer when she passed by his room and saw that the bed was empty.

Later, when John and Ben joined her in the kitchen, she looked up and smiled. "Guess you weren't lonely last night, after all," she said to John.

He grinned like a little boy caught in a trap of his own making.

"Rachel, can I let Ralph outside?" a sleepy-eyed Ben asked.

"Good idea. Hope he didn't keep you awake last night."

"Nope. But he did want to sleep in Granddad's bed. Was that okay?"

"Sure."

"But not every night, Ben. You have your own room just like Rachel and I do."

Ben's lower lip trembled, and Rachel got up and knelt in front of him.

"Do I get a good morning hug before you let Ralph out?"

Ben threw his arms around her neck in a tight squeeze.

"Susan said we're going to visit a little girl today. She likes poems, and we're going to write some."

"Wow, wish I could go with you," John said. "Rachel, why don't you meet us at the Chinese restaurant near my office for supper. Susan is going to drop Ben off around five."

"I'm pretty sure I've got my last client at four, so that shouldn't be a problem."

"We'll wait for you."

"Sounds great," Rachel said and left the room to take her shower. When she came back downstairs to let Ralph in and feed him, her housemates had already cleaned up the kitchen, brought the paper in and left for the day.

"Come on, Ralph. Let's hit the road. Looks like everyone else is way ahead of us, as usual."

*   *   *

Rachel walked through Dupont Circle, on the off chance that Belle and Mary might be there, enjoying one of the few remaining warm fall mornings. She was disappointed to find no sign of them.

During the night, she had arrived at the conclusion that she would invite Belle to move into the apartment and not wait for John's decision about hiring her as Ben's nanny. Perhaps seeing Belle on a regular basis would help him feel more comfortable with the idea, she hoped.

Rachel stopped to ask one of the Dupont Circle regulars if they had seen the mother and child in the past day, but nobody had. She asked Deejee, the hotdog vendor, to tell Belle she was looking for her, and set off for her office at a faster clip than usual.

She noticed recently that she felt younger and stronger and wondered if it were possible that all the things she heard and read about the benefits of being around young children were true.

Seemed like the proof was in the pudding, she thought.

Mrs. Proctor and her butler were waiting in the front office, nibbling on chocolate chip cookies when she arrived.

Georgia looked at her boss apologetically.

"Morning, Rachel. Mrs. Proctor dropped by to see you. I told her you had to be in court this morning, but she said it was extremely important she speak to you right away."

"Of course, it's important," Mrs. Proctor huffed, rising to her feet with some effort. "Do you think I would have come all the way down here if it weren't important?"

"Good morning, Mrs. Proctor. How nice to see you. Come on in my office. Would you like some coffee?"

"Don't drink the stuff, Mrs. Springer. Not good for you."

Rachel decided to drop that subject before it went any further, poured herself a cup from the pot Georgia always left on her desk and pulled a chair next to the one Mrs. Proctor had plopped down in.

"What can I do for you this morning?" she asked, although she had a good idea what the nature of the emergency visit might be. She had lots of experience with very elderly clients and knew that one thing – and one thing only – occupied most of their time – preparing for their deaths.

"You've got to change my Will. Ramona has finally come to her senses and left that dreadful man," Mrs. Proctor announced. She looked as satisfied as if she had just told Rachel that her niece had been named president.

"That's not a problem, Mrs. Proctor, but certainly a phone call would have sufficed. You really didn't need to make the trip to my office. The change will be simple, and we can schedule an appointment to bring it to your house sometime later in the week so you can sign it."

"No. It needs to be signed this morning."

Rachel sat back in her chair and took a sip of coffee, taking a minute to restrain herself from what she wanted to say – that her office was not a drive-by fast Will service.

Instead, she focused on her breath, looked at her watch and tried to let go of the control she felt Mrs. Proctor trying to wrest from her.

"Well, let me see if Georgia has time to type it. I'll be right back."

Mrs. Proctor sniffed impatiently, but, to her credit, didn't say anything. Instead, she opened her purse and took out a pen.

In the next room, Georgia was already at work on the document. She rolled her eyes at Rachel and said she'd have it finished in five minutes.

Rachel took that time to retreat into the bathroom to relax the muscles in her shoulders. She could already feel them tensing from the demands of her client. She tried to shrug off the stress she felt and after a few shrugs, she felt her body let go. She walked back out to Georgia's desk just as her assistant was stapling the blue cover on the document.

"Here, see if she would like another cookie," Georgia said, handing Rachel the plate and following her into the inner office with the new Will and her notary seal.

After Mrs. Proctor and Robert left, Georgia sat down in the chair in front of Rachel's desk.

"Do you know what that was all about?" she asked her boss.

"The niece left her boyfriend, she said."

"No. I mean do you know why Mrs. Proctor was in such a rush to get her Will changed?"

"No. Do you?"

"While we were waiting for you to arrive, she told me that tomorrow is her 95th birthday, and that years ago, a fortune teller told her she would die when she was 95."

"Oh, my god. You've got to be kidding me."

"I think she was serious."

"Please don't order the flowers yet," Rachel said and then added, "but try to get her bill in the mail today."

*   *   *

The court calendar was even more crowded then usual and Rachel waited all morning to hear it called. When her motion was finally brought before the judge, she rose to approach the bench. When she picked up her yellow legal pad, a slip of paper fell onto the table. She glanced down and saw the note Ben had left on the kitchen table. "I LOVE YOU," and John's p.s., "me, too."

She stood in front of Judge Barker.

"Ms. Springer, you look mighty cheerful this morning," the crusty old man barked at her. "Care to tell us what's your secret?"

"Must be the fall weather, your Honor."

"Ms. Springer, I've seen you in front of this bench many falls, and that pink in your cheeks is something new."

"Yes, your Honor."

"Humph," the old man snorted. "Well, whatever it is, it's very becoming, so keep it up."

"Yes, sir. I believe I will."

*   *   *

The restaurant was beginning to fill up when Rachel arrived. She spotted John and Ben at a booth near the buffet and wound her way through the tables toward them.

"Sorry to keep you waiting. Traffic was snarled around Wisconsin Avenue. Have you been here long?"

John stood up and helped her remove her raincoat. "Just long enough to miss you," he said and nuzzled her ear.

"Sit next to me. Sit next to me," Ben squealed, and Rachel slid in to the booth beside him.

"How was your day?" John asked.

Rachel gave a brief account of her meeting with Mrs. Proctor and Judge Barker's compliment. John smiled. "You do look especially lovely tonight," he said.

"You look GREAT," Ben corrected him.

"Must be the gift you gave me for my hair," Rachel said, reaching up to touch it.

Ben beamed at the thought that he had contributed something and then went back to his crayons.

"What are you drawing?" Rachel asked, leaning closer to the little body beside her.

"Susan and me and the little girl we played with today. She let me ride her Big Wheel all around a giant driveway. You should have seen how fast I pedaled – faster than anybody – faster than Superman – faster than . . ."

"Okay, Ben, that's enough. We get the idea. Finish up your picture so you can eat supper," John interrupted.

Ben stuck his lower lip out but did as he was told.

"What about your day, John? How's the project coming?"

"Right on schedule. In fact, we're a little ahead of where we thought we'd be. Everyone's very pleased with the progress."

Rachel felt a knot of fear in her chest as she considered John's contract ending. The image of his leaving Washington to return to New York was not something she was ready to look at yet.

"Something wrong?" John asked. "You don't look very well."

"No, I'm fine."

The waitress approached the table to take their orders, rescuing Rachel from John's further questions.

After John had ordered spring rolls for the three of them, he reached across the table and took her hand.

"Got any plans for Saturday night?"

Rachel felt herself blush with pleasure like a 16-year-old. She jokingly pretended to consult her pocket calendar and then assured him that her dance card had one slot left.

"Good, because I'm taking you to the concert at the Phillips. Ben and his new friend are spending the night with Susan, and we've got the whole evening to ourselves."

Rachel smiled and felt her stomach do a flip she hadn't known was still possible.

*   *   *

"So what are you wearing on your date Saturday night? Do we need to go shopping? I saw the most divine outfit in the window at Macy's yesterday. It's silk and the most . . ."

"Whoa. Slow down, Susan. First of all, this isn't a date. Don't make me nervous."

"You're nervous, I can tell. That's a good sign, trust me."

"It's not a good sign, so stop being silly."

"What are you going to wear?"

"I'm not going to think about what I'm wearing Saturday night on Wednesday, first of all. Second of all, I've got plenty to choose from in my closet when I do decide to think about it."

Susan was quiet on the other end of the line, and Rachel realized she should be more appreciative of her friend's efforts to improve her life.

"But I do want to thank you for letting Ben spend the night so John can go out. That's very generous of you."

"I wish you could have seen Ben and little Monica yesterday. I wouldn't have traded that hour watching them for anything. *Anything*, Rachel."

Rachel sensed that Susan was making a point but decided to change the subject before things got any deeper.

"What are you and Jim doing this weekend? I wish you could go the concert with us."

"We've had our dating days. We'll be very content playing grandparents. Doesn't look like we're going to have any grandchildren of our own anytime soon."

"How are Walter and Brenda doing? I haven't heard you mention them lately."

"They're both busy with work. I don't even think they're coming for Christmas this year. Can you imagine? Can you even *imagine* not wanting to be with your mother during the holidays? Rachel, I swear sometimes I just feel like I'm dying. Dying a thousand trillion deaths when I think of . . ."

Rachel broke in as she sensed Susan getting wound up beyond her capacity to unwind. "Maybe they'll change their minds. Christmas is still a long time off."

"*A long time*! Honey, do you know what I'll need to do to get ready if they come? The list goes on and on. I have to . . ."

"Relax, Susan. Take a deep breath. Everything's going to be fine – regardless of whether they come or not. You've got Jim, and you've got lots of friends who'll keep you very busy during the holidays. And this year, we've got Ben."

"Suppose he and John want to go home – to New York – what then?"

Rachel hadn't even thought about the possibility, but she decided to practice some of her own philosophy.

"Susan, we're just not going to discuss that today. I'm late for an appointment. See you later. And thanks again for keeping Ben."

"Look in Macy's while you're out, if you can."

*   *   *

Rachel didn't stop by Macy's, but she did check out the fitness club she'd been passing on her way to work every day for 10 years.

The woman sitting at the front desk looked to be in her early 50s and just a little overweight. Rachel immediately felt at home – not something she experienced the few times she had timidly approached other gyms where hard young bodies thoroughly intimidated her.

The club manager gave Rachel a tour of the cardio machines and the fitness equipment. Not one to make a snap decision, Rachel told her she'd think about joining and call to schedule a demonstration of the various pieces of equipment if she decided to give it a try.

When she arrived at work, Georgia looked like she had just learned a secret.

"Did I see you going in Health for Her this morning?" she asked without even a good-morning preamble.

"My god, my life is an open book. But, yes, you did."

"What, may I ask, prompted that after all these years?"

"Nothing in particular. Want to join with me? It looks like a nice facility, and I sure could use a workout buddy. We could go at lunch together."

"I'll think about it. But I don't have a new man in my life motivating me, you know. Mike's seen this old body for many years, and I don't think he could handle it changing."

Rachel decided to ignore the "new man" comment, picked up the phone messages Georgia had retrieved form the answering machine and went into her office to return calls.

The first one was from Deejee, the Dupont Circle hotdog vendor.

"Sorry to call you at work, but I lost your home phone number," she said.

"Not a problem. What's up?"

"I thought you'd want to know the news about Mary."

Rachel's heart stopped as she waited for Deejee to go on.

"Bert told me yesterday that the reason we haven't seen Belle and her lately is that the kid is in the hospital, and they're not sure what's wrong."

"Where? Which hospital?"

"DC General. Went in Saturday, I think. That's all I know."

"Thank you so much for calling. I'll try to get there today and let you know what I find out."

Rachel hung up the phone and sat at her desk for several minutes, digesting the news. Images of the little girl sitting on the sofa with Ben and her mother flashed through her mind. Of her clutching Ben's Pooh to her little chest.

She got up and went out to Georgia's desk.

"Clear my calendar for the morning," Rachel said and told her about the phone call. "I'm going over there to see what's happening and if there's anything I can do."

"Call when you know something," Georgia said, picking up the phone to make the necessary schedule changes for her boss.

On her way to the hospital, Rachel called John on her cell phone and was disappointed to hear that he was in a meeting. His secretary asked Rachel if she wanted her to interrupt him.

"No, but give him the message that I'm on my way to DC General. Tell him Belle is there with Mary."

When Rachel hung up, she realized she wanted John with her when she saw Belle. Facing the mother's fear alone gave her cold chills.

Rachel was accustomed to helping people solve their problems every day, but this one seemed more than she was equipped to handle.

That sense of needing John's support intensified when she walked into the hospital room and saw Belle's white face leaning over the still form in the bed. Mary had an oxygen mask on her face and a tube snaking from her little arm. She was asleep.

"They're keeping her drugged," was the first thing Belle said. "I don't like that."

Rachel went to stand beside her and rubbed her back gently. Finally, Belle stood up and allowed herself to be embraced.

"You should have called me to let me know you were here," Rachel said.

"I didn't think we'd be staying. What day is it, anyway?"

"Monday. What do the doctors say is wrong?"

"Pneumonia. They can't seem to do anything, though. Rachel, I'm scared. What if she doesn't make it? She's all I've got."

Rachel didn't know what to say to that and was relieved to see John walk in the room with a bouquet of balloons, which he tied to the foot of the bed.

Belle smiled weakly and held out her arms. He leaned over and stroked Mary's tiny forehead and, at his touch, she opened her eyes for just a brief moment and smiled.

"Hey, there, beautiful. I brought you something to make you well. Some magic balloons. You just look at them real good now, so you can get out of here and come see us, okay?"

Mary moved her head slightly and sank back into unconsciousness.

"And you? How are you holding up?" he asked Belle.

"Not too well. This is definitely the hardest thing I've been through, and I've been through a lot."

"Well, we need you to make it through this, too. We've got a deal we want to talk to you about. As soon as Mary gets out, we want you to move into the basement apartment and take care of Ben for us," John said.

Speechless, Belle dropped down on the edge of the bed.

"Are you kidding?"

Rachel, too, looked shocked by John's sudden offer.

Belle glanced at her. "You want me to do this? How would I pay you?"

"That's part of the deal," Rachel said. "You take care of Ben and, in exchange, you live rent-free. It's called a live-in nanny."

"You hear that, Mary? You and Mommy have a job. You've got to get out of here, Baby, so we can go home."

Just then, a young doctor who looked like he was about 16, marched into the room. He seemed surprised to see Rachel and John. Belle made the introductions and John took charge, once again.

"What's the story, doctor? What seems to be wrong?"

The doctor referred to the chart briefly and went to check Mary's vital signs. "Still not sure, but looks like maybe pneumonia."

"You've done all the tests, I'm sure?"

"There are a few more tests we could run, I guess."

"Let's do them then," Rachel said.

"Well . . ."

"I'm paying, if it's the lack of insurance you're worried about."

The doctor scribbled some notes on Mary's chart and left the room.

"Can't have our live-in nanny stuck here in the hospital," John said. "Listen, I've got to get back to the office, but here's my phone number. Call me if those tests don't get done – today."

Belle hugged him goodbye. "Thank you, Mr. Turner. Thank you so much."

John kissed Rachel on his way out the door.

"Wow, what's going on with you two?" Belle asked.

Rachel smiled. "Not sure yet, but it feels great. I need to get going, too, but I'll try to stop by again later this evening. Can I bring you anything when I come back?"

Belle denied needing anything, but Rachel noticed that her clothes looked like she'd probably worn them since Mary was admitted on

Saturday. She made a note to go through her closet and find some things that might fit the young woman – something she wanted to do since she met her but didn't know how.

"Oh, and Georgia sends her love and said she'll be by with some cookies tomorrow."

"You all are so good to me. Why? Why are you so nice to us?"

"Don't you think she deserves it?" Rachel asked, nodding toward the bed.

"Yes."

"I rest my case."

Chapter 20

The rest of Rachel's day was a whirlwind of phone calls, questions from Georgia as she gathered information on a personal injury case, and a couple of free consultation appointments that lasted longer than Rachel would have liked.

At around one o'clock, Georgia knocked on the door and poked her head in Rachel's office.

"Aren't you going out for lunch?"

"I got in so late, I figured I'd skip lunch today. Thought I'd order something delivered."

"Who's letting Ralph out?"

"It's such a beautiful day, I decided to leave him in the courtyard. I'm going home after work to pick up some clothes for Belle. He'll be fine 'til then." Rachel rummaged through her top desk drawer and found a menu from the Chinese take-out place down the street.

"Want something?"

"No thanks, I think I'll step outside and get some fresh air though. Be back in about half an hour."

"Do me a favor and lock the front door. I don't want any interruptions while you're out. In fact, put the phone on night ring, too."

"Sure. Can I bring you anything?"

"No, thanks. Chinese will fill the bill for me today. Enjoy your walk."

Rachel realized she wasn't getting a very good start on her exercise regime. Her plan had been to go to the gym before work, but this morning she visited the hospital instead. Going to work out after the office closed wouldn't suit either, because she wanted to see Mary.

Rachel sighed and said, "Oh well, tomorrow's another day."

* * *

She didn't get away from the office until almost 5:30. Georgia was covering her computer monitor when she walked into the lobby.

"Tell Mary I'm going home to make cookies and I'll see her bright and early tomorrow morning," she said.

"If you're going before work, I'll come on in to the office and open up. Hopefully, she'll be coming home soon."

"Right, "Georgia said, but looked doubtful. "Do you think she's getting the best care available, or are they neglecting her because she's homeless?"

"John's making sure that doesn't happen."

"He's a good man, Rachel."

Rachel was quiet and pretended to search in her purse for something so that Georgia, who knew her so well, couldn't see her eyes and read something there she wasn't ready to reveal.

"You deserve him, you know."

"What I deserve is a chocolate chip cookie. Be sure to save me one. Gotta go now. See you tomorrow."

"Give them my love. And bring Ralph to work tomorrow. I miss him."

* * *

Rachel let Ralph inside and fed him before she climbed the stairs to go through her closet. Several pairs of jeans she hadn't fit into in 10 years went into a shopping bag, along with a couple of sweatshirts she had been given as gifts and never worn. It always puzzled her when friends brought her brightly colored clothes that were such flagrant advertisements for theme parks she had no desire to visit, much less advertise. She hoped Belle didn't have the same aversion to pink or cartoon characters. Maybe they'll cheer up Mary, she thought.

As an afterthought, she threw in a bottle of Chanel No. 5 hand lotion and a copy of the latest issue of *National Geographic*. If Belle didn't feel like reading, at least she could look at the pictures.

Rachel realized she didn't even know what Belle's taste in books was – or television – or any of the other likes and dislikes that made up a normal lifestyle. Perhaps Belle didn't even remember what she liked either, Rachel thought.

* * *

Deejee was just getting ready to leave when Rachel walked in the door to Mary's room. Belle's mouth was bulging with hotdog and a chili aroma hung heavy in the air.

"Smells like a ballpark in here rather than a hospital," Rachel greeted them.

"Thank god," Belle mumbled between bites. "Maybe the smell of french fries will perk Mary up. Nothing else seems to work."

"Georgia's coming tomorrow before work with the cookies. She sends her love. And here are some things I hope you can wear."

Belle peered into the bag. "Wow," she said as she squirted some lotion on her hands. "Sure you want to get rid of this? It must have been very expensive."

"I'm sure. I'm allergic to it, and it's just going to waste. Use it before it dries up in the bottle."

"I got to get back to the Circle," Deejee said. "We miss you, baby. Do what those dudes tell you and get on out of here."

Rachel watched as the two young women held each other, thinking of the way Deejee seemed to have taken on the role of mother of the homeless in the Circle. She wondered where the woman lived and what kind of family she had of her own.

Deejee leaned over and kissed Mary on the cheek before she left, leaving a little bit of ketchup behind. Belle wiped the red sauce off with a corner of the sheet. Rachel stopped herself from offering a Kleenex.

"Sorry about that," Belle apologized when she saw Rachel's frown. "I guess I forgot. I promise I'll do better at your house. I didn't grow up in a shelter, you know. Like Mary."

"I'm not worried at all. You're just under a lot of pressure right now. You'll be fine when you get out of here. What's the doctor saying today?"

"They're going to run some more tests tomorrow, and they've got her on some different medicine. We just wait now, I guess."

"I know that's hard."

"Really."

"Here's a card Ben made," Rachel said, handing Belle a sheet of lined paper with two small stick figures sandwiched on either side of a larger one. The words "ME," "MARY" and "BELLE" were laboriously printed beneath them, and they were framed by a lopsided heart. What looked like another child but with a tail had been squeezed as an afterthought into the heart above the people. The word "RALPH" sat beside it.

Belle laughed – the first time Rachel had ever heard the sound come from her.

"He really needs you, you know," Rachel said.

"He's a great kid."

"We're all looking forward to you moving in. Soon, we hope."

Belle said nothing for a few minutes. Rachel saw that she was crying and went over to stand beside her.

"Everything's going to be fine. Children are stronger than we think they are, I hear. Mary will probably be 100 percent better tomorrow and driving everybody crazy to let her out of bed."

"You think so?"

"I'd bet money on it," Rachel said, grateful for the confidence she learned to effect after years of representing clients against whom the cards were stacked.

She wished she felt the same confidence, herself.

*   *   *

When Rachel got out of the cab, she was surprised to see the house dark. She opened her front door and shouted, "Hello. Anybody home?"

Quiet answered her.

She took off her jacket, threw it on the chair beside the hall table and picked up the mail off the floor beneath the mail slot.

Didn't look like John and Ben had gotten home yet, she thought as she walked to the back of the house. Confused, she sniffed something that smelled like brownies.

When she flicked on the overhead kitchen light, she was almost knocked over by horns blowing and voices yelling, "Surprise!" Ralph ran over and jumped on her legs as John and Ben continued to yell, "Surprise! Surprise!"

The table was set with her best china and crystal and a bouquet of yellow roses.

"My god, you almost killed me with shock," Rachel said, dropping down into the closest chair. "What's this all about?"

"Ben wanted to celebrate our new home, and I thought it was a good idea. What do you think?"

"Great idea. Is that brownies I smell?"

"Yup, and I made 'em, didn't I, Granddad?"

"You sure did, pal. So, is anyone hungry?"

"I am! I am!" Ben squealed and hopped up into the chair beside Rachel, immediately knocking over his glass of water. Rachel jumped up to get a towel to mop up the mess, but John pushed her back down.

"Sit still. This is a thank-you dinner, and you're not to do anything but be thanked."

After the damage control, the three held hands, bowed their heads and Ben said the simple grace Rachel remembered as a child. "God is great. God is good. Thank you, God, for this food."

"Amen," she and John joined in.

"Who are the two extra plates for?" Rachel asked.

John looked at Ben, who seemed embarrassed by the question. When Ben didn't answer, John said, matter-of-factly, that they were for Ben's parents.

"What a nice idea," Rachel said.

"Really? You think it's okay?"

"Absolutely."

"They're here, you know. You can't see them cause they're angels now, but they're here. I can see them," Ben said and looked to see if she believed him.

"That's wonderful, Ben."

"Can you see your Mommy and Daddy angels?"

Rachel glanced over at John, who waited to hear what her answer to that would be. When she hesitated a little too long, he jumped in to save her.

"I think angel parents probably only appear to children, Ben, to let you know they're still taking care of you. Rachel is a grown-up now, and she doesn't need taking care of anymore."

Maybe I do, Rachel thought. To John, she just smiled and mouthed the words, "Thank you" as she took her first spoonful of the most mouthwatering alphabet soup Campbell's had ever made.

*   *   *

Georgia arrived at the office late, with a report from her visit to the hospital. Mary had a good night's sleep, and the nurse was drawing blood for some more tests when she walked in the room. Belle looked refreshed after a shower and wore a bright yellow sweatshirt with Mickey Mouse embroidered across the chest. The doctor was enjoying a chocolate chip cookie when she left.

"Sounds like things may be looking up, don't you think?" Rachel asked hopefully.

"Looks like it."

"Great. I think I'll wait until after work to go again. I need to do a little shopping at lunch."

"Oh?" Georgia said, surprised. After years of working for a woman who hated the very thought of shopping, it was a shock to see a twinkle in Rachel's eyes when she said that's what she planned to do during lunch.

When Rachel offered no further explanation, Georgia asked, "Shopping for what?"

"Oh, not much. John and I are going to a concert tomorrow night, and I thought I'd use that as an excuse to buy something new. I may need a new suit sometime for a bar social. You never know."

"Right. A bar social. I hope John likes spending Saturday night with a woman who looks like she's on her way to court."

Rachel let that comment sink in a minute and then said, "Maybe you'd better go with me."

"Sounds like that would be a good idea."

*   *   *

As Rachel got ready for the concert Saturday night, she was glad she had taken Georgia with her to Macy's. The tea length black crepe sheath was not something she would have bought for herself. As she turned to view the dress from different angles, she tried to see the woman in the mirror as John might.

The folds of crepe fell delicately across her curves, accentuating what needed to be and hiding what didn't. The silver silk scarf tied at her throat picked up the sparkles in the rhinestone earrings Georgia had insisted she buy to go with the outfit. Her feet felt strange in a pair of sling-back black evening slippers.

When she came into the den where John was waiting for her in front of the fire, he dropped the sports section and stood up, speechless.

"You've got legs," were his first words. "Gorgeous legs, I might add."

Rachel laughed and pretended to be shocked as she looked down. "My god, I sure do. How about that."

"Seriously, Rachel, you look fabulous. We'll have to do this often. Let's go across the street so Ben can see you."

"Well, if we're going to do that, you'll have to wait a minute," Rachel said and ran back upstairs.

When she came down again, John saw that she had taken off the silver hair clip and replaced it with the cord Ben had given her.

John smiled at her. "I love you, Rachel Springer."

Rachel stood on tiptoe to kiss him on the neck and then carefully wiped away the lipstick she had left near his ear.

Chapter 21

Rachel struggled to focus on the music as she felt the warmth of John's shoulder pressed against hers.

The plan was for Ben to spend the night across the street. Rachel's heart beat so fast at the very thought of being alone in the house with John that she was afraid he might hear it.

"Are you all right?" he asked at intermission. "You seem jittery. Aren't you enjoying the music?"

"It's fantastic. I love Beethoven, and this is one of my favorite pieces. Thanks again for suggesting we come."

John didn't push his questioning any further, and Rachel appreciated the fact that he showed concern but knew not to overdo it.

"Maybe I'm just worried about Mary," she said. "I talked to Belle this afternoon and not much is being done except watch her because it's the weekend."

"We'll go see her tomorrow. How about that?"

"Sounds good."

The lights flickered, signaling that intermission was ending.

Walking back into the concert hall, Rachel noticed the Moser's waving and nudged John to get his attention. Mr. Moser gave her the thumbs up sign and gestured to her outfit. She felt herself blush and wished she wasn't the kind who showed her emotions so easily.

John laughed when he saw the pink in her cheeks. "He really likes you, you know."

"They've been good neighbors for a long time – and good friends. When was the last time you guys played chess?"

"Not since Ben moved in, come to think of it."

"You need to get back to the board and let me take care of Ben. Mr. Moser needs you almost as much as Ben does, I'm sure."

"How about you? When are you going to play chess with me?"

The conductor walked back out, and the audience grew quiet, saving Rachel from having to let John know she had never learned the game – and didn't intend to.

*   *   *

The Moser's pushed their way over to where John and Rachel sat even before the lights came all the way up at the end of the final piece.

"Rachel, you look beautiful," Mr. Moser said. His wife beamed at her and grabbed her in a big hug.

"Come have some dessert with us before you go home, dear," she said. "I just made a chocolate cake this morning, and we'll never be able to eat it all ourselves."

"I don't know," John started to say, but Rachel interrupted him with, "Sounds like a great idea. Thanks."

"Did you all drive or take a cab?"

"Cab," John said, looking at Rachel doubtfully.

"Good, then you can ride home with us," Mr. Moser said. "I just cleaned out the backseat this afternoon and there's plenty of room for you lovebirds."

"Peter, you're embarrassing Rachel," his wife scolded.

"Can't think of anything I'd rather do than snuggle in the backseat with Ms. Springer," John teased. "Come on, let's get going."

The old blue Buick was parked a couple of blocks from the gallery. Rachel and Mrs. Moser walked behind the men, enjoying the cool fall evening.

"Mrs. Moser, we may be getting some more new family members soon," Rachel said.

"Oh?"

"Yes, John needs a nanny for Ben, and we've met a young woman who would be perfect. She's got a little girl of her own and needs a job that will allow her to stay home. She also needs a place to live, and with the basement apartment empty now, we think it's a perfect arrangement."

"Where did you meet her?"

"Oh, just out and about. Actually, her grandmother used to own my house. I guess you and Mr. Moser remember Mrs. Mason, don't you?"

Mrs. Moser stopped in her tracks and stared at Rachel. The men kept walking, deeply engrossed in their conversation about birding.

"Peter, stop," Mrs. Moser shouted. Her husband hesitated for a minute and then turned around and walked back to where his wife stood beneath the circle of a streetlight.

"Peter, Rachel is thinking about moving Ethel's granddaughter into her basement apartment."

Mr. Moser stepped backwards in an almost comic reaction and then recovered his composure.

"Well now, Mildred, that is Rachel's business," he managed to say.

Mrs. Moser looked chastised but still not convinced.

Rachel didn't know whether to push her for information or to let the matter drop.

It was only much later, as the four sat around the Moser's kitchen table drinking hot tea and eating cake, that she broached the subject again.

"What's the story with Belle Mason?" she asked.

Mrs. Moser looked across the table at her husband. He nodded his head. "You've opened the can of worms, Mildred, you might as well use them now."

"That girl broke her grandmother's heart, is what she did. Nearly killed the old woman. In fact, if you want my opinion, she did kill her."

"Belle came from a good family, went to a good school – a private girl's school out in Virginia somewhere," Mrs. Moser began.

"Foxcroft," Mr. Moser interjected.

"And her grandmother paid for it. And lots of other things, too. Her parents couldn't be bothered."

"She was a devoted grandmother. That woman did everything she could for the girl. Cute little thing," Mr. Moser said.

"Until she got to be about 16 and then all hell broke loose."

"Now, you don't have to get to cursin' like that, Mildred. You calm down now, old girl."

"Well, Ethel and I were friends, and it hurt me to see her so run down by it all."

"What happened?" Rachel asked.

"Belle got in with the wrong crowd, started smoking those marijuana cigarettes and drinking and then she just wouldn't go back to school. Finally, she ran away, and Ethel had to hire a private detective to find her."

"Where was she?"

"Right here in Washington. Can you imagine that? Right near her very own grandmother and yet living on the streets. It about sent Ethel over the edge. Her parents completely turned their backs on her. Said she couldn't come home, even if she wanted to."

"And her grandmother?"

"She had a stroke a week after Belle was found and died in a nursing home six months later."

"Poor Belle," John said.

"Poor *Belle*? How about poor *Ethel*?" Mrs. Moser said.

"Well, of course. It must have been a terrible ordeal for the grandmother, but imagine the guilt Belle felt," Rachel said.

"She *should* feel guilty," Mrs. Moser said.

Rachel and John looked at each other and silently communicated that any further discussion wouldn't be a good idea.

"But you do what you think is right," Mr. Moser said. "It's your house – right, Mildred?"

"And your grandson," Mrs. Moser said and got up to clear away the dirty dishes.

*   *   *

"So, what do you think now?" Rachel asked John once they had closed their front door and were safely out of earshot of their neighbors.

"About what?" John asked, pulling her close.

"About Belle?"

"Oh, that," John said and dropped his arms. Rachel could feel him withdrawing into himself.

"I'm sorry. I don't mean to spoil the evening for you, but I thought maybe we should talk about the plan for her to move in again. Maybe we can work through it together."

John walked into the den and turned on the gas logs. He sat down on the sofa and patted the seat beside him.

"Do you want to talk about it?" Rachel asked again, sitting down but keeping a little distance between them.

"Actually, I'd rather talk about why you seem so tense tonight. Why you're afraid of me."

"What do you mean?"

"All I wanted to do was come home after the concert and be alone with you. You seemed to jump at the chance to have that chocolate cake, seemed to me. What is it, Rachel? Is it me?"

"Of course not, John."

"You're acting completely different than you do when Ben is here. You seem like another woman tonight – like you've retreated into a hole."

"I'm sorry. I guess I am afraid."

"Of what?"

"I don't know, John. I just know my insides feel like they're shaking apart – like everything is flying in a million directions. My chest feels like it has a big leather belt strapped tightly around it to hold all the parts in place. There were times today that I felt I couldn't breathe."

"My god, woman, I had no idea a date with me would affect you so adversely," John laughed.

Rachel's downcast eyes clearly showed her disappointment in his reaction.

"I'm sorry. I don't mean to treat your feelings so lightly," he apologized. "Come here and let me hold you. Enjoy the fire, Rachel. Everything's going to be all right. With Belle. With Ben. With you and me. I love you, Rachel. Relax."

"I'm trying, John."

"Breathe. Isn't that what you say to Ben when he's scared?"

"Right. But it's hard with this damn belt squeezing my chest."

"Then take it off, darling. Take the damn thing off."

"I wish I knew how."

*   *   *

Later, as Rachel lay in bed – alone – she thought about John's suggestion that she "take off" the tightness in her chest. How easy it sounded and yet she hadn't a clue how to do it.

"What do you think, Ralph? Do I need therapy?"

Ralph leaped up on the bed and licked her face in response.

"Just like a man. You always think the answer to all problems is a kiss."

Ralph licked her again and snuggled against her as close as he could.

Rachel finally relaxed, listening to his snore.

"I wonder if John snores," she asked herself and thought she felt the tension in her chest loosen just a little.

*   *   *

Rachel woke to a gentle tapping at her door.

"Yes?"

"You awake?" John asked.

Rachel jerked upright in bed and grabbed for her robe. She tried to smooth the hair hanging wild around her face and shoulders.

"Something wrong?" she asked.

"No. I just thought you might like some coffee in bed."

Rachel felt the belt tighten as she looked down at her ratty robe. She glanced over at the mirror above her dresser, trying to see if her face looked as puffy as it usually did in the mornings. Were the dark circles under her eyes too bad?

John opened the door just a crack.

"Can I come in?"

"Thanks, John. How sweet of you," Rachel said in a tiny voice.

John pushed the door open with his foot, and Rachel saw that he carried a tray covered with a white linen napkin. On it sat a bud vase with a single yellow rose. The coffee's almond scent filled the room ahead of him. Rachel forgot her embarrassment when she spotted the flaky chocolate croissant sitting on one of her china dessert plates.

"There's the smile I was hoping for," John said as he set the tray down on the bed beside her. "And your paper, Madam. I'm going across the street to have breakfast with Ben. You enjoy your morning, and we'll see you a little later. I thought we'd take Ben to the hospital with us to see Mary this afternoon. He's dying to find out all about the hospital and what's going on there."

"Thanks, John."

He kissed the top of her head and lingered just a moment longer to caress her hair. "Nice," he said. "Like the robe, too."

Rachel laughed. "You're a desperate man, John Turner, but I love you."

John smiled, patted Ralph and left her to her coffee and croissant.

*   *   *

About an hour later, the phone rang. Rachel wasn't surprised to hear Susan's voice on the other end.

"So, how was it?"

"The concert was beautiful. Large crowd. Had dessert with the Moser's afterwards. Thanks again for keeping Ben. Did you guys have fun?"

"We had a blast, as usual. I got out some old Tinker Toys, and we spent the whole evening making a space station with them. That kid has quite an imagination, you know. And he's such a sweet boy. No problem getting him to bed at all. But speaking of bed . . ."

"Don't go there, Susan. Don't even think of going there. You're not helping."

"Sorry. I just want you to be happy."

"Sleeping with John Turner right now would not make me happy, so take it easy."

"He's a good-looking man, Rachel, and if you're not careful, somebody's going to welcome him into her bed, and it will be all over for you. Just a warning."

The belt tightened another notch, and Rachel caught her breath.

"Gee, thanks, Susan. I really needed to hear that. Gotta go now. Love ya."

"You too, sweetie. Really I do. Sorry if I upset you."

Rachel said goodbye, hung up and went to the door to let Ralph in.

"Life's tough sometimes, Ralph. Real tough."

Ralph licked her hand and headed up the stairs to the third floor meditation room, Rachel right behind him.

*   *   *

The long, hot shower felt especially good after breakfast in bed and a deep meditation to empty out all the poison from the paper.

Rachel luxuriated under the stream of hot water. When she stepped out onto the plush white bathmat, her skin was flushed and smelled like lilacs from the new bath gel she had bought on her shopping spree with Georgia.

She dried off slowly with a heavy white bath sheet and lathered herself with lavender lotion.

She looked in the mirror on the back of the door, examining her body from all angles. Not bad from the front, she thought. Her stomach was still as flat as when she was a young woman. Her small breasts not yet sagging. Her waist had thickened in the past 10 years, giving her figure a little boyish look.

Then she turned around to survey the back. That's when she remembered the love scene from a recent episode of her favorite sitcom. Murphy Brown got in bed, covered from head to toe with her jogging suit and insisted her younger boyfriend turn off the lights before she removed her clothes.

Maybe after a few more years at the gym I'll be ready, Rachel sighed.

Chapter 22

The email from George caught Rachel by surprise, and she was completely baffled as to how to respond.

Rachel, I'm planning to be in DC visiting some friends and hope you'll join me for dinner one night while I'm in town. Please say yes. George.

Rachel remembered how he had looked at her. And more importantly, how she had responded to the twinkle in his eye. If she hadn't gotten the call to come back home after Ben's parents' accident, who knows where that would have led, she thought.

Should she tell him about John or was she presuming too much – that he was interested in her romantically. Maybe she had read his intentions wrong.

Maybe she should accept the dinner invitation and ask if she could bring John along.

She was surprised to realize she didn't want to include John.

She wasn't surprised to feel that damned belt tighten again.

"George, how wonderful to hear from you," she wrote. "When exactly will you be in DC?"

Stalling for time, she decided not to worry about the date until she knew when he was coming. Maybe she'd be busy.

This was definitely a matter to discuss with someone wiser than she was. Susan maybe, or Georgia.

Just then the phone rang, and, as if she had mental telepathy, Susan was on the other end of the line.

"Sorry to be a pest, but I was wondering if I could get the Style section from you. There's a coupon in there I need, and Jim has already left and taken the paper with him."

"Sure. Come on over. I've just made a fresh pot of coffee."

Susan wore bib overalls and one of Jim's flannel shirts. Her work boots clomped down the hall toward the den where Rachel still sat at the computer.

"Morning, sweetie. Actually, it's almost afternoon. Where are your guys?"

"John took Ben over to the Circle with Ralph. We needed a few things from the drugstore. The paper's there beside the door."

"Thanks. You going to the hospital this afternoon?"

"Right after lunch, I think," Rachel said and then stood up to give her friend a hug.

"Susan, I've got a question for you," she said and then told her about meeting George at the farm and about his email.

"Go," Susan said without any hesitation. "A little jealousy would be good for John Turner. Make him know you've got options. I remember one time . . ."

"But, I'm too old to play high school games, Susan."

"It's not a game, Sweetie. It's serious business. Plus, you need to be sure about your feelings for John. There's nothing like spending time with another man to make you appreciate the one you truly love. Go."

"Well, maybe."

The computer tinged, signaling that she had a new email. Glancing at the screen, Rachel saw that George had already replied. Unable to resist, she opened his message.

"My god, he's coming next week."

"Tell him you'll meet him for dinner."

"Maybe lunch."

"Rachel, go to dinner with the man. I bet John would go out with his old girlfriend if she came to town."

The idea made Rachel have second thoughts about George. About John. About life.

Why had her world gotten so complicated all of the sudden, she wondered. She wasn't sure she liked it.

"What do I tell John?"

"How about the truth?"

"Which is . . ."

"You're having dinner with a friend who's in town. Period."

"You make it sound so easy."

"It is. Sit down now and tell that man you're looking forward to seeing him. Now."

Rachel hit "Reply" and typed.

Looking forward to seeing you next Friday. I'll make a dinner reservation at Mrs. Simpson's for seven and meet you there. Have a good trip.

She hit "Send" and looked up at Susan.

"Good luck, girl."

"Thanks for your advice – I guess."

"Want to help me plant daffodil bulbs?"

"Not now. I've got some more emails to answer before I leave for the hospital."

"Need any more free advice?"

"No. I think you've done enough damage. Go home."

"Love you, Sweetie. And thanks for the coupons. You need any panty hose?"

Rachel wadded up a piece of scrap paper and threw it at Susan's back as she made a hasty retreat out the door.

*   *   *   *

"Are you sure it's a good idea to take Ben to the hospital with us?" Rachel asked John as they got ready to leave. Ben ran upstairs to his room to get a toy to take to Mary. "It's so soon after the accident. I wonder . . ."

"I really don't think Ben will make a connection between Mary's hospital stay and his parents' car wreck. But thanks for your concern, Rachel. That's what I love about you, you know."

John helped Rachel with her sweater and then pulled her close.

"You looked so warm and inviting in your bed this morning. I had a tough time resisting climbing under the covers with you."

"Yeah, that old robe always has that effect on men," Rachel teased.

"You mean other men have seen you in that tempting ensemble?"

Ben came bounding down the steps, saving her from having to answer that question. He carried Pooh and looked very pleased with himself.

"What do you have there, pal?" John asked.

"I'm taking Pooh to the hospital for Mary. I think he can make her get better, don't you, Rachel?"

"I think you're a very generous boy to share Pooh is what I think, and I'm sure having him will make Mary very happy."

John shot her thumbs-up and hoisted Ben and Pooh up onto his shoulders for the walk to the hospital.

*   *   *

Mary sat up in bed eating a peanut butter and jelly sandwich when they arrived.

"My goodness, who *is* this child?" Rachel exclaimed.

Mary beamed when she saw her friends and held out her hands for Pooh. Ben plopped the bear into her lap and said very seriously, "I'm just *loaning* Pooh to you, remember. Not *giving* – *loaning* – to make you well so you can come home."

He looked a little doubtful about his decision as Mary clutched the stuffed animal to her little chest.

"Thank you, Ben. You're so sweet to share," Belle said and then turned to John. "And thank you for what you've done. The tests were able to identify some unusual strain of virus and they changed her medicine last night. As you can see, already she's one hundred percent better. They're talking about maybe letting her go home Tuesday."

"Belle, that's wonderful. We'll start to work right away getting the apartment ready for you. Nobody's been down there since John and Ben moved upstairs. It'll need airing out a little, and I'll get some food in the fridge for you."

"And I've still got a few boxes stored down there I can get out so there's room for your things."

"Thanks, but we really don't have many things to worry about," Belle said. "Are you sure you want to do this, Ms. Springer?"

"I'm sure. Are you?"

Belle bowed her head and when she looked up, Rachel saw the tears. "I just wish Granny were still there."

"She is," Ben's little voice chimed in. "She's an angel Granny – just like Mommy and Daddy. Really."

"Thanks, Ben," Belle said. "Really."

*   *   *

Rachel was on her way up the steps to the third floor when she realized she and Ralph were being followed.

Looking behind her, she was surprised to see Ben, padding up the steps in his pajamas.

"Hey there, little guy. I thought you had gone to bed."

"Can I medidate with you and Ralph?"

"Meditate? I didn't know you liked to meditate, Ben. But, shouldn't you be in bed? Tomorrow's a school day. Maybe we'd better ask your Granddad first."

"I'll go ask him," Ben squealed, hopped down the steps and disappeared into the den where John was reading.

Within a couple of minutes he was back, joining Rachel on the stairs.

"I can medidate!!! He said I can—as long as I don't bother you."

"'Okay, let's go," Rachel said and took his little hand in hers.

When she opened the door into her third floor sanctuary, Ralph ran straight to his window seat.

"Is that where Ralph medidates?"

"Yes, and here's a pillow you can sit on right next to mine," Rachel said, arranging a throw cushion next to her zafu. She draped her pale yellow cashmere meditation shawl around her shoulders like a tent and sat in the lotus position, motioning Ben to do likewise.

He crossed his little legs perfectly, sitting straight as a tree. Rachel thought how quickly children learn if we can get to them before the world complicates things too much.

"Now, you must close your eyes and sit very quietly until you hear me ring this little bell, okay? Don't move around any, if you can help it. I'll be right here beside you."

"Does Ralph close his eyes, too?"

"I don't think so. I think he stands guard so we're safe. Are you ready?"

"I'm ready."

Rachel tapped the gong three times and closed her eyes, planning to sit for five minutes – longer than she imagined the average five-year-old would be able to sit still.

The wind whistled around the eaves of the house, sometimes drowning out the sound of Ralph's snoring and Ben's soft breathing beside her. When she opened her eyes, she was surprised to see that ten minutes had passed and the child still sat cross-legged beside her, eyes closed.

Not wanting to push her luck, she hit the gong and smiled to herself as Ben's eyes flew open.

"How was it?" she asked.

"Great. I like medidating. So do Mommy and Daddy. Did you see them?"

"No, but I'm glad you did. Ready for bed now?"

"Yup. Are you going to bed, too?"

"I think I will. Tomorrow's a big day. We need to do some work downstairs to get ready for Belle and Mary."

"Can I help?"

"I hope you will. We need to make sure it's just right so they'll feel at home."

"Like us."

"Just like us, Ben."

*   *   *

Monday morning, the health club was unusually crowded when Rachel arrived at seven o'clock. She stopped by the club office to ask Marsha, the early morning coach, to explain the crowd.

"Everybody's getting ready for the holidays. Gotta work off those extra calories, you know. How about you? Enjoying your workouts?"

"Can't say I'm enjoying them, but I am proud I'm doing it."

"Maybe you'd like a class better than working solo," Marsha suggested and handed her the schedule for yoga, pilates, body sculpting and several other ways to stretch her body back in shape.

"Thanks," Rachel said and stuck the piece of paper in her pocket, knowing it would probably go straight to the shredder as soon as she got to the office. As boring as it might be, solo was her style.

As she walked across the room to the exercise bikes, she noticed Melissa working out on the treadmill beside them.

"Rachel, I didn't realize you were a member here. How long have you been coming?"

"I joined last month, but I'll admit I haven't been very regular in my attendance."

"You look great. You must have been doing something."

"Just walking. Gets to the point, though, when the parts above the waist really need some attention, too. How about you? Settling into DC all right?"

"I love it. Work's crazy, but I wouldn't change a thing. By the way, I gave somebody your name the other day about a child custody case. Walter Riley. I'm doing some estate work for him, and he's an okay guy. I think you can help him."

"Thanks. I appreciate your thinking of me," Rachel said as she positioned the seat on her bike and opened up the *Southern Living* that already lay on the bike's magazine rack.

She didn't want to be rude, but she also didn't like to talk while she exercised. Melissa got the message and put on her Ipod headset.

* * *

Rachel was surprised when she got to the office and Georgia handed her a phone message from Walter Riley. This guy must really be in a hurry, she thought. As soon as she poured herself a cup of coffee and glanced through the handful of other messages, she dialed his number.

A receptionist with a polished telephone voice, that sounded almost like a recording, answered the phone. When Rachel identified herself, she put her right through to her boss.

"Good morning, Ms. Springer. Thanks for calling back so quickly. Melissa said you would be good to work with, and we've certainly gotten off to the right start."

"How can I help you, Mr. Riley?"

"I'd rather not discuss it on the phone. When can I see you?"

Rachel glanced at her calendar and saw that the first available appointment was on Friday.

That news didn't make Mr. Riley very happy, and he asked if perhaps he could schedule an appointment after her normal office hours.

In the past, Rachel wouldn't have thought twice, but since John and Ben had come into her life, she looked forward to getting home and was reluctant to give up her private time. She stood her ground.

"I understand you're the best, so I guess I'll just have to wait," Mr. Riley said.

"Tell you what. If I have a cancellation in the meantime, I'll give you a call," Rachel said, proud of herself for not giving in.

As she hung up the phone, she noticed Georgia standing in the doorway, staring at her.

"What's happened to you?" she asked.

Rachel just smiled and opened the file in front of her.

"I've been medidating," she said and smiled.

* * *

Later that evening, Rachel stood in the basement apartment with John and Ben, surveying their work.

When she had gotten home around six, John had a pot of soup ready to be served. They ate quickly and hurried downstairs to get to work.

Susan had loaned her a pink ruffled bedspread with lacy pillow shams and some of her daughter's dolls and stuffed animals.

John moved all his boxes out of the closets and into the attic.

Rachel stopped by the market on the way home and stocked up on coffee, milk, bread, oatmeal and several cans of soup. Chocolate chip cookies filled the brightly painted ceramic Pooh Bear cookie jar, thanks to Georgia.

Ben made a "WELCOME HOME" sign and propped it up on the kitchen table. He added two stick figures to the dog and three people who appeared so often in his school art projects.

"Looks like our family is really growing," Rachel said to him.

"Think Belle and Mary will like my picture?"

"I'm sure they will," Rachel said, looking around the small nest. "I just hope she won't feel too confined down here after enjoying a childhood upstairs."

John pulled her into a big hug. "Rachel, you worry too much. You're doing a wonderful thing for Belle and Mary. Relax. Everything's perfect. She'll love it."

"Just like we do," Ben chimed in.

* * *

Rachel called the hospital early Tuesday morning and was told that Mary would be discharged around ten o'clock. John had a meeting and wasn't able to go with her, but she told him not to worry. She felt like she'd be able to handle settling everyone in by herself.

When she stepped out of the cab, she was shocked to see Belle and Mary already waiting outside the hospital's front door.

"My goodness, I've never picked someone up at a hospital and not had to wait before," she said to Belle.

"Guess they're anxious to get rid of us," Belle answered. "Most people are."

Rachel was a little taken aback by the girl's bitterness but decided the best approach might be to ignore it. "Well, I'm glad to be getting you. We had trouble getting Ben to agree to go to school this morning. He wanted to be part of your welcoming committee."

That brought a smile to Belle's face, and Mary danced Pooh up and down on her lap and sang, "Ben. Ben."

"Looks like Mary's had a complete recovery," Rachel laughed, lifting the little girl into the back seat of the cab.

"Yeah. The doctor said she should be fine now. She's supposed to finish her antibiotics and see a doctor in a couple of weeks for a follow-up. On to the next challenge."

"Maybe there won't be another challenge for a while," Rachel said, but down deep she doubted her own optimism. While life hadn't been as much of an uphill climb for her as it had been for Belle, Rachel knew some of the same fears and doubts the young woman experienced.

In fact, she thought she felt that damned belt tightening around her chest as she remembered her own current challenge – how to tell John about Friday's dinner date.

The short cab ride from the hospital to the house on O Street saved her from worrying too long about Friday.

"This it, ma'am?" the cabbie asked, interrupting her thoughts.

"It sure is," Rachel said, searching through her pockets for her money. "Welcome home, girls," she said, turning to Belle, who held Mary on her lap. She noticed a cloud pass over Belle's face and wondered if, in trying to help, she had brought the young woman to a place she wasn't ready to face.

Nonsense, she thought. Nothing happens by accident. This is part of a perfect plan.

"Here, let me help you with your things," she said to Belle, who moved silently out of the cab. Holding Mary in her arms, she waited on the sidewalk while Rachel paid the cabdriver and gathered up the two paper grocery bags of clothes.

Belle followed her up the walk to the door at the side of the house. Just as Rachel was about to unlock it, she heard Susan's cheery "Yoohoo" from across the street.

Looking up, she saw her friend run toward them in her hot pink jogging suit, carrying a bouquet of yellow helium balloons.

"Welcome, welcome, welcome. My goodness, you don't look like a little girl who's been in the hospital. Hi, Belle, I'm Susan, from across the street. And you must be Mary. My, you're a big girl. Won't we have fun!"

As Susan rattled on, Mary reached out for the sunburst of balloons.

Rachel opened the door to the apartment, thankful once again for her friend's joyful burst of energy.

Belle set Mary down and watched as the little girl tottered over to the refrigerator and opened the door.

"Looks like somebody's hungry now," Rachel laughed.

"No, Mary," Belle said, diverting her daughter's attention to Pooh again. "Thanks, Rachel. For everything," she said, indicating the full refrigerator. "I'll pay you back some day, I promise."

Rachel started to tell her that wasn't necessary but wondered if maybe that wasn't what Belle needed. Maybe her pride had been hurt by the generosity. Instead, she acknowledged the girl's offer to repay her with, "Whenever you can. No hurry."

Mary, still bent on exploring, rushed into the tiny bedroom and crowed with delight when she saw the toys piled in a corner.

"Wow, you're really spoiling us," Belle said.

"You've helped me finally get rid of some of the toys from my basement," Susan said. "And there's more when she gets bored with those. Listen, I'm going on back across the street. Come on over when you're ready to eat."

"Thanks, Susan," Rachel said. "Belle, I'm going to leave you all alone to settle in for a while. I need to call the office to check on things there, but I'll be back down in about 15 minutes, and we can go have lunch together. Sound okay to you?"

"Sounds fine. When will Ben be home?"

"John brings him home around three, but you don't need to worry about that today. Just take it easy this afternoon, and we'll talk about how you can help with Ben at supper."

Belle looked doubtful but didn't argue. She hugged Rachel and thanked her again before closing and locking the apartment door. As she walked away, Rachel heard the padlock click and the chain rattle in place.

Chapter 23

When Rachel finally walked in her office at two o'clock that afternoon, every inch of her drooped.

Georgia looked up from the letter she was typing, stopped and stared. "My god, you look awful."

"Gee, thanks."

"What's wrong? You look like you've just hiked the Appalachian Trail."

"Maybe I'm too old for all of this. Romance. Little boys. Family stuff."

"Don't be silly. You'll get used to it. Remember when you first got Ralph. This is just like training a puppy. It's all going to be worth it in the end."

"Promise?"

"I promise. Here are your phone messages. Mr. Riley called to confirm his appointment at three. Nothing else on your calendar for this afternoon but tomorrow's the deadline for answering interrogatories and request for documents in the Peterson case."

"Right. Thanks, Georgia – for everything. How are things at your house? Mike feeling better?"

"He went back to work Monday, and he's feeling great. Like nothing happened. We're so blessed."

"Yes, you are," Rachel said and patted her friend on the shoulder as she went by to her office. "Think I'll take a quick power nap before Mr. Riley arrives. Buzz me in 10 minutes, please."

"Okay. Sure you don't want 15?"

"Ten will do it, thanks," Rachel said, shut her office door, took out her earplugs from the desk drawer and lay down on the loveseat. In five minutes she dropped off to sleep like a field hand.

*   *   *

Mr. Riley looked to be about her age, if the graying hair at his temples and crows feet at the corners of his eyes weren't premature. His Armani suit, gold Rolex watch and Gucci shoes were a clear message of wealth. His briefcase was soft Italian leather and bore his monogram in gold.

His handshake was firm but not intended to intimidate. More intimate, Rachel, thought, as he held on to her hand a little longer than business handshakes required.

"Thanks for seeing me," he said, seating himself in the chair in front of her desk without being invited. He got right down to business.

"My son and daughter-in-law married five years ago," he began without a prompt. "They had a son a year later. Six months after the child was born, they started having problems and two years ago they divorced. At first, I was allowed to see my grandson, but about two months ago, Ethel announced that she is getting married again and that she wants all ties to Joseph's family severed. I miss my grandson and want to have a relationship with him. I need to know what my legal rights are and whether you can help me make sure I get them."

The thought occurred to Rachel that in all the years she had practiced law, she'd never had a client seeking grandparental rights. It seemed strange that children were being introduced into her personal and professional life at the same time. Must be some lesson to be learned, she decided.

"Mr. Riley, you've come to the right person," she said, smiling. "Just let me ask you a few questions, and we can get the ball rolling."

*   *   *

Rachel knew she'd always been a good lawyer. She had graduated from law school among the top of her class and had no doubt about her strengths in the intellectual arena she had chosen.

She also felt confident in her organizational abilities and knew that her attention to detail was an important ingredient in her success.

Her business savvy stood out among the other attorneys she knew who depended on accountants and brokers. She had learned early from her father how to make a nickel go a long way, and she kept up with her stock portfolio compulsively.

Her people skills also contributed to a busy practice. Most of her work was repeat business or referrals and rarely did she deal with a client whom she didn't like – at least by the end of their time together.

For almost 35 years, Rachel had enjoyed her work as an attorney and felt she made a valuable contribution to her world. Recently, however – in fact, ever since John and Ben entered her life – she felt a sense of even deeper importance to her mission of helping people.

Maybe this is what they call the "opening of the heart" she thought as she walked home after saying good-bye to Mr. Riley and assuring him of his rights and that they could be enforced.

Since Rachel started on the Buddhist path, her daily meditation and study of loving compassion and kindness had added another dimension to her law practice. She had been able to feel the connection between herself and her clients in a way that gave her a patience that she knew some professionals in her field didn't enjoy. Her personal benefits had grown as she incorporated her personal and professional lives – embracing the suffering of others as a way to end that suffering.

But lately, she was aware that her caring was going a little deeper.

Sometimes it frightened her. Sometimes she wondered about the wisdom of being open and vulnerable.

As she walked up to her front door and inhaled something that smelled a lot like gingerbread, she smiled to herself. The glow of lights in the living room spread over her as she got closer. She heard Ben's joyful laugh and Ralph's yapping as they rolled Ralph's favorite ball back and forth in the foyer.

Rachel opened her front door and did a *Leave It to Beaver* imitation. "Hey, honey, I'm home."

*   *   *

After dinner, the three moved into the den to play a game of Chinese Checkers.

"Hear anything from downstairs?" Rachel asked as they waited for Ben to set up his marbles.

"Ben and I checked on the girls when we got home. Everything seemed to be fine. Belle is going to start picking Ben up for me next week."

"Mary and me played with Ralph in the backyard," Ben offered. "I taught her about fetch."

"You're going to be a good teacher for her," Rachel said. "She needs a big brother, you know."

"Really? I'm a big brother?"

"Not really, but since she doesn't have one, you can do the job," Rachel said.

Ben turned serious. "Are you going to be my Mommy?"

Rachel looked to John for help. He refused to look at her. Ben jumped to her rescue, "You can, you know. My real Mommy says you know how, even if you *are* pretty old."

The ice broken, Rachel and John enjoyed a good laugh.

"I appreciate your Mommy's vote of confidence, Ben. It means a lot to me. How about I just do the best job I can at being your friend?"

Ben didn't look at all satisfied, but John managed to distract him by saying he could go first in their game of Chinese Checkers.

*   *   *

After Ben wiggled into his Star Wars pajamas, brushed his teeth, John read him a Pooh Bear story and Rachel kissed him goodnight, the two adults came back downstairs to clean up the supper dishes.

"By the way," Rachel said, feigning nonchalance, "A friend from the farm is coming into town this week, and I'll be having dinner with him Friday night." Rachel was sure John could hear her heart banging against her chest from across the room.

"*Him?*"

"Yes. George. He's the guy Nancy and her husband hired to help them on the farm. I met him when I went for the anniversary party. He's coming to visit some friends here."

John avoided looking her in the eyes and appeared to be very intent on wiping a spot off the stove. Finally, he glanced up at her. "I didn't know you were in the habit of socializing with the hired help, Rachel."

His condescending tone of voice took Rachel's breath away. She didn't know what to say.

"But, if that's the way you want to spend the evening, I guess Ben and I can find someone else to use the ticket I bought for you."

"What ticket?"

"Sesame Street is coming to the DC Armory. I thought I told you last week."

"I don't believe you did, John. I really think I would have put it on my calendar." Rachel knew she sounded more confident than she felt. "Maybe you can get another ticket and take Belle and Mary."

"Maybe," John said, folding the tea towel carefully and hanging it on the drying rack. "I think I'll go to bed and read. I hope you sleep well,

Rachel. I've got a meeting after work tomorrow, so I'll be late. I'll ask Susan to pick up Ben and keep him overnight."

"That's not necessary. Let me get him from school. I'd love to."

"I don't want to be a burden on you, Rachel. Susan offered."

"But I *want* to, John. Please let me."

John looked at her without saying a word. She held her breath and waited. Finally, she took a step toward him and reached out to touch his hand. He drew back.

"What is it, John?"

"Nothing. I just don't want to . . . don't want to ask too much of you."

"You're not asking. I offered."

Still John hesitated. "I'll think about it and let you know in the morning." He turned and started out of the kitchen. Then he stopped and without looking at her said, "Thanks for the offer."

"You're welcome. And goodnight."

When John walked out of the room without a word, Rachel felt a darkness drop over the room like the black hood over the head of a condemned man about to be hanged.

*   *   *

Without even looking, Rachel knew what the note would say the next morning.

"Rachel," John wrote, "thanks again for offering to pick up Ben after school. I think it's better to let Susan do it. John."

Rachel laid the piece of paper back down on the kitchen table and dropped into one of the chairs.

A couple of cheerios lay near the spot where Ben ate his breakfast. Seeing them there brought tears to her eyes. She was about to let them flow unchecked when the phone rang.

Rachel wondered who could be calling so early in the morning.

"Saw your light on and thought I'd check on you," Susan chirped at the other end of the line. "Are you okay?"

"I'm fine."

"John seemed a little tense this morning when he brought Ben over, and when I asked him how you were, he acted even weirder."

"I'm fine, Susan. Gotta go. I'm running late for work."

"Call if you need to talk."

"Thanks, Susan, but I don't need to talk. Bye."

After Rachel hung up the phone, she was tempted to call Susan back and let her have it with both barrels. After all, Susan had encouraged her to go to dinner with George. So much for the benefits of a little jealousy, she thought on her way upstairs to take a shower.

*   *   *

Rachel lay in bed reading the latest issue of the *New Yorker* after a very long day when she heard John's key in the front door. She held her breath as he climbed the stairs and walked down the hall toward her door. He tapped gently.

"Yes?" she answered.

"May I come in for a minute, Rachel?"

Rachel looked across the room to the mirror, but without her contacts in, she couldn't see more than a rumpled blur. She could only imagine the unbraided hair, unpowdered, uncolored face. She wore her frumpiest flannel granny nightgown. Still, she longed to see him and told him to come in.

He opened the door slowly and slid a beautifully wrapped gift box around it in front of him. When Rachel didn't respond, he poked his head around the edge – still not speaking.

"What's that?" Rachel asked, shocked by the extravagantly beribboned offering.

"Open it and find out," he answered, walking toward her and dropping the box in her lap.

Rachel let go of the covers she had pulled up under her chin so that she could pick up the box. She looked up at John, her eyes full of questions.

"Go ahead. Aren't you curious?"

"I can't ever remember being *quite* so curious. I'm not used to getting presents for no reason," she said as she carefully removed the glittery silver ribbon and babies breath. She laid them on the bedside table and then eased off the scotch tape to unwrap the handmade navy paper.

"I should have known you'd be this meticulous getting into it," John laughed. "Come on, you're driving me nuts. How can you be so patient?"

"I want the pleasure to last. It feels so good. But, why, John?"

"Stop talking and open."

Slowly, she lifted the top and peeled back the tissue paper to reveal a soft, robins egg blue cashmere shawl. She pulled it out of the box and draped it over her shoulders, hiding her calico flannel gown.

"It's beautiful, John. Thank you."

"You're beautiful, Rachel, and you don't deserve to be treated the way I treated you last night. I acted like a spoiled brat. After all you've done for Ben and me in the past few months. Making a home for us. Sharing your house."

"And heart," Rachel interrupted.

"I hope so, Rachel. Please forgive me for being such an asshole. I just . . ."

"Just what?"

"I just got scared, I guess."

She waited for him to go on and when he didn't, she gently prompted him.

"Scared of what?"

"About this guy you're having dinner with tomorrow night. Scared he'll be tall, dark and handsome and have more to offer you than I do. That you'll . . ."

"That I'll what?"

"That you'll change. Everything's been so wonderful here for us. You and Ralph. Chinese Checkers. Now Mary and Belle. It feels like a family, and I don't want to lose it," John moved away from the bed and walked over to stand at the window, looking down at the street. He spotted Jim taking the garbage out to the curb and moved back into the shadows before he was seen in Rachel's bedroom window.

"Come here, John," Rachel said, patting the side of the bed.

He turned back and did as she asked. She moved toward the middle to make room for him, struggling to find the right words.

"I know how you feel, I think. When I went up to the funeral and met your friend, Alicia, I was terrified that you wouldn't come back to DC. She was so beautiful, and she seemed so comfortable in your home."

"I didn't know you felt that way. I'm so sorry. You shouldn't have, you know. That relationship never had a chance."

"I'm not going to say 'you shouldn't' be afraid of my having dinner with George, because you're entitled to your own feelings, but I will tell you that George is just a friend and that I have no intention of giving up what I have with you and Ben. I enjoy our life together, too, you know."

"I hope so," John said and got up. At the door he turned and said, "Rachel, I love you so much."

"I love you, too, John," she said, pulling the meditation shawl tightly around her like a cocoon. "And I hope you're not still scared."

"Not right now. Goodnight," he said and blew her one last kiss.

Rachel turned off the light and rolled over to get comfortable. The door opened again and she heard John clear his throat.

"What *does* this guy look like?" he whispered.

Rachel threw the box top at him.

*   *   *

Wrapped in a cloud of blue cashmere, her bare legs peeping out from the edges, Rachel sat propped against plump pillows, sipping coffee.

John walked in with the paper and stopped several feet from the bed to look at her.

"You are glowing," he said.

"Thank you, sir. I feel fabulous. And I've had a great idea. Why don't you come with me to have dinner with George tonight. I think you guys would enjoy each other."

"I doubt that George wants me crashing his dinner date with you, Rachel."

"Nonsense. The more the merrier. I'll call him later today and tell him you'll be with me."

"Suit yourself, but if he seems reluctant at all, don't push. I'll survive a night without you."

"Are you sure?"

"I'm sure. You survived Alicia. I can make it through tonight. Now, how about some breakfast? You take your shower and by the time you get dressed, I'll have Ralph walked and the cheerios on the table."

Chapter 24

At 6:55 p.m., Rachel stepped out of the taxi in front of Mrs. Simpson's. George had "seemed reluctant" and she hadn't pushed. Still, she was determined to convey the message that she wanted a platonic relationship with him.

The host opened the door for her and greeted her by name.

"Your friend is waiting for you," he said and walked her over to her favorite candlelit table in the far corner.

George rose and walked forward to welcome her.

"You beat me here. I wanted to get here first to do you the honor. Sorry," Rachel said.

"Nothing to be sorry about. I guess I was anxious to see you," George said, opening his arms for a hug.

Rachel leaned into his embrace, but not too close, gave him a peck on the cheek and broke the hug quickly.

George looked disappointed and a little puzzled as he pulled out her chair, seated her and walked around to take his place opposite her at the small table. He studied the menu carefully, stalling for time.

Maybe this was the wrong thing to do, Rachel thought. John is scared. George is confused, and I'm caught in the middle. Damn Susan.

Rachel chose her outfit carefully earlier in the evening, making certain she didn't send a message that would further confuse the man. When John saw her coming down the stairs in a navy suit and red turtleneck power blouse, he said she looked like she was on her way to court, rather than a dinner date.

George looked up from his menu. "You look so different. Beautiful, but like a different woman than the farm girl I met," he stammered.

"Really? Well, what you see, is what you get. I *am* a city girl, through and through," Rachel rushed on, admitting to herself that the statement was a lie. If truth be known, she was both, but she didn't want to connect with George the way she had before. Presenting her big city image would surely turn him off.

"Well, what do you recommend from the menu, big city girl?"

"Let's hear what the specials are before I make a suggestion," Rachel said, beckoning for the waiter.

She ordered rack of lamb for two and a bottle of Pinot Grigio. As the waiter poured the sweet white wine into their glasses, Rachel looked across at George and realized she felt none of her initial attraction for him. How was it possible for her to change that much in such a short time? Did he feel the same way? Evidently not, she thought as he reached across the table to take her hand.

"Tell me how you've been," he asked, smiling the crooked smile that had caught her attention only a month before.

"Very busy at work," she said, launching into a long description of one of her most boring cases. "In fact, I'm afraid I have to get home fairly early tonight to work on my notes for tomorrow's meeting with the client."

"On Saturday?"

"Yes. It's a special case."

"I'm sorry to hear that, Rachel. I hoped you'd take me on a cab tour of the city tonight. Maybe join me tomorrow for a visit to a couple of galleries."

"Thanks, George, but that really won't be possible. You see . . ."

The waiter interrupted further explanation as he arrived with their dinner, and Rachel was thankful for the diversion.

They ate in silence for a few minutes. Finally, Rachel asked George about the farm. He told her that her cousins were planning a trip, leaving him alone in charge of things while they were gone.

"They must really trust you," Rachel said. "How lucky for them you came along."

"I wish you felt the same way."

Rachel was caught off guard by his directness and felt herself blushing. She cursed her body for betraying her.

"Something's changed about you, Rachel. What is it?"

In her lawyer mode, Rachel went into a defensive stance, automatically wanting to deny his observation. Before she opened her mouth, however, she decided he deserved better from her. She set down her fork and took a big gulp of wine.

"I've met someone, George. Someone special. Someone I hope to spend the rest of my life with."

George followed her cue and drained his wine glass. He looked at her silently for a few moments.

"If only I had a chance to show you my photographs," he laughed, hoping the joke would ease the tension between them.

"I'll come to the farm sometime in the spring and would love to see them then. Nancy says they're truly beautiful."

"It's a date," George said, raising his empty glass in a toast. "And here's to you and the rest of your life."

*   *   *

John sat by the dying fire when Rachel got home at about nine o'clock. He closed his book and looked up at her. She walked over to where he sat and eased down into his lap and kissed him on top of his head.

"How was your evening?" he asked.

"Fine. And yours?"

"Sesame Street was a hoot. I was able to get an extra ticket and took Mary and Belle. Ben was hardly able to contain himself." John paused for a minute and then, with a twinkle in his eye, said, "I hope George was able to contain himself after seeing you in that suit."

"Hard as it must have been for him, he did," Rachel teased him in return. "I missed you. Is Ben all settled in?"

"Finally. I had a hard time getting him to bed. Took three stories."

"You're a good man, John Turner."

"How about a nightcap?"

"I'd love a hot cup of chai. Can I fix one for you?"

"Sounds great. I'll put another log on the fire. And, Rachel . . ."

"Yes?" Rachel asked as she turned at the door to face him.

"Take off that damn suit and put on something comfortable."

Rachel smiled and slipped off her jacket.

*   *   *

The digital clock on her bedside table read 2:10 when Rachel waked from a deep sleep. Ralph barked at the window.

"What is it, boy?"

Then she heard a man's voice on the street below.

"Belle! I know you're in there, dammit. Come out here and don't think I won't come git you if you don't!"

Rachel heard John's bedroom door open. She ran out into the hall, Ralph right behind her. `"What in the world . . ."

"Go call the police," John said, pulling on a bathrobe and running down the stairs.

"What's that noise, Granddad?"

"Go back to bed, Ben. Everything's going to be all right."

"But, I'm scared," Ben whimpered.

"Come with me, Ben. We can keep each other company," Rachel said.

The little boy held tight to her hand as they went to the kitchen phone at the back of the house, away from the commotion on the street.

Rachel got through to the police quickly and reported the drunk in front of her house.

She glanced down the hall and saw John standing at the front door, watching to see that the man stayed outside and didn't try to break into Belle's apartment.

Rachel could hear movement from the basement.

"Belle," the man yelled again. "You can't hide in there forever. I'm out here, you know. I want to see Mary. Mary, it's me. It's your Daddy, Sweetie. Come to Daddy."

John opened the door to go outside.

"John, don't!" Rachel whispered loudly. "He might have a gun."

John motioned for her to get back in the kitchen and closed the door behind him.

"What's Granddad doing?"

"I don't know, but he's going to be all right," Rachel said, acting more confident than she felt. She pulled Ben up onto her lap and held him close. As he buried his head in her neck, she inhaled his little boy scent and felt a calmness envelope her.

A police siren broke the quiet that had settled outside since John went out. Blue lights bounced along the hall and into the kitchen.

"Come on, Rachel, let's go see," Ben said, hopping down and pulling at her robe.

Rachel was tempted to follow him to the front of the house but her desire to protect him overrode her curiosity.

"No, Ben. Granddad will be in shortly and tell us all about it. Let's get some milk and cookies and wait here."

The wait was even longer than she feared. Three cookies and two glasses of milk later, they heard John open and close the front door as the police cruiser pulled away.

John came into the kitchen, shaking his head.

"What happened, Granddad? Can we go look now?"

"Nothing to see, Ben. The policeman took the loudmouth to jail. We can all go back to bed."

"Was he really a bad guy?"

"Just a drunk guy."

"Did he hurt Belle and Mary?"

"No, but they might be scared, so I'm going down to their apartment and see if they want to come up here," Rachel said.

"Let me do that," John said. "You two go on back to bed, and I'll get them settled in my bed."

"Where are you going to sleep?" Ben asked eagerly.

John looked over at Rachel, hopefully, but she ducked her head. "Guess you'll have a roommate tonight, buddy. Is that okay with you?"

"Oh, boy!" Ben said and ran up the stairs to his room before Rachel could even get to the door.

John came to her and wrapped his arms around her. "Wish I could be your roommate," he whispered in her ear.

"One day, John, but not tonight."

"I know you're right, but I hate it," he said. "Think I should call downstairs or just go knock on the door?"

"She'll hear the front door and know it's you. Just go on down."

John left and Rachel climbed the stairs to check on Ben. He was wide awake and asked for the fourth story of the night.

When Rachel read the last page, and John had still not come back, she began to worry.

"Ben, you close your eyes now while I go make a phone call."

"When's Granddad coming?"

"Soon, Sweetie. Be good now and try to go back to sleep."

"But, Rachel . . ."

"Please, Ben."

The child stuck his bottom lip out, but didn't say another word. Rachel left his room and went down the hall to the upstairs extension.

John answered the apartment phone.

"Belle doesn't want to intrude," he said. "Says they've caused enough trouble. In fact, she's packing their things and wants to leave."

"Put her on the phone."

Several minutes passed before a tearful Belle said, "Hello."

"Belle, please come on up here for the rest of the night. We'll talk tomorrow."

"I can't stay here, Ms. Springer. You've been so kind, but now I'm messing up your life, too," Belle managed to get out between sobs.

"You're not messing up my life. We need you to help with Ben, starting Monday. You promised, and we're counting on you. Tonight was just one night and it's over. That man's in jail now. It's over, Belle."

"It'll never be over. He's Mary's father. He'll be back."

"We'll make sure he won't. And he definitely won't tonight because he's in jail. Come up here right now. That's an order."

Belle was silent. Rachel could here John encouraging her and Mary's little voice saying, "Please, Mommy, please."

John took the phone and said, "We're on our way up. Get the tea ready."

Ben was sound asleep when Rachel moved past his door. She closed it gently so any noise from the kitchen wouldn't disturb him.

Belle's face was red and swollen from crying, but Mary looked as excited as if she had just arrived at a slumber party.

"Me sleep with Ben," were the first words out of her mouth when her mother carried her into the kitchen.

"Ben's asleep, Honey. You and Mommy are going to sleep in the big bed in the room next to Ben's room. In the morning, you can eat breakfast together," Rachel said.

She poured a glass of warm milk for the little girl and laced Belle's chai with a little brandy to help her sleep.

After she had Mary settled, she moved to where Belle stood and opened her arms to the young woman. Reluctantly, Belle allowed herself to be embraced.

"Everything's going to work out, Belle. Trust me. Drink your tea, get a good night's rest, and we'll start legal proceedings against this man in the morning to make sure he doesn't bother you again. You've got a new life ahead of you now. Don't let tonight spook you into going back to the old one."

"We really want you here," John added. "Ben's looking forward to having you as part of his new family. He's lost so much in the past month. Please don't make him lose you, too."

At that, Belle seemed to shift from hurt child into mother mode, wanting to protect Ben from further suffering. She took a swallow of tea and tried to smile.

"We'll give it another shot," she said. "And thanks. I'm really sorry to put you through this."

"It's really not as big a deal to us as it is to you," Rachel tried to assure her. "If I don't get back to bed though, it might be a big deal tomorrow. Good night all."

She kissed John lightly on the cheek on her way out of the room and saw a sad smile cross Belle's face.

Chapter 25

Georgia sat at her desk sipping coffee and reading the paper when Rachel walked through the front door. She glanced over the top of the Style section and immediately dropped it.

"Now, what?" she asked.

Rachel sat down in the rocking chair near the front window and released her briefcase onto the floor beside her like a thousand-pound weight.

"What have I got on my calendar this morning?"

Georgia looked at the day's schedule and gave Rachel a rundown.

"Push everything from now 'til noon to tomorrow, if you can. We've got a restraining order to file."

Rachel told Georgia about the night's events, including Belle's reluctance to being helped and her desire to move back to the shelter.

"That poor girl. What do you think's going to happen now?"

"Well, we're going to make sure that same jerk doesn't come back again, first of all."

"What if there are more like him? What if . . ."

"Stop right there. We're not going to think that way. 'Be here now,' remember?"

The phone rang, stalling Georgia's response. She put the call on hold and announced that Susan was asking to speak to her "for just a sec."

"Morning, Susan," Rachel said in a tone of voice she hoped conveyed the message that she was busy.

"What in God's name was going on last night in front of your house? Jim wouldn't let me call or come over and then I slept late this morning and you were already gone when I got up and . . ."

"Susan, it's okay," Rachel stopped her. "One of the homeless men who knew Belle from the shelter got drunk and tracked her to our house. We called the police. I'm working on a restraining order now. All is well."

"But, what if . . ."

"Susan, relax. I'm taking care of it. It won't happen again."

"But the Moser's said that they saw . . ."

"Susan, I don't want to hear it. I appreciate your concern, but the best way you can help is to be calm so Mary and Belle won't feel like they're causing a problem for the neighborhood. Belle is already talking about going back to the shelter, and I don't want anybody making her think that's what anybody else wants."

"Of course not, but . . ."

"Gotta run. Talk later. Love ya," Rachel said and hung up the phone before Susan could say another word.

*   *   *

Rachel walked the restraining order through the system herself and called Belle to tell her everything had been taken care of.

"Let's go out to eat tonight to celebrate," she suggested. "Where would you like to go? Better yet, what would be fun for the children?"

As Belle hesitated, Rachel realized that the young woman's former life left her ill-equipped to suggest a place to eat other than the hotdog stand at Dupont Circle.

"Tell you what," Rachel said. "Georgia has kids. Let me ask her what she thinks. You girls just be ready to go at six. In the meantime, I'll call John and let him know the plan."

Rachel was surprised when Belle didn't argue. "Thanks, Ms. Springer. That sounds like fun. I'll go tell Mary."

The rest of the afternoon was hectic with the morning's phone calls to be returned, one of which was Mr. Riley's daughter-in-law's attorney confirming receipt of her letter.

Rachel had written a letter to the woman and received a reply on letterhead belonging to what looked like a large New York law firm.

Looked like she had a fight on her hands, she thought after she read the letter that outlined the woman's reasons to believe that her client may have sexually abused his grandson.

Rachel dialed Mr. Riley's number and asked his secretary to put her through immediately.

"Riley, here," came his no-nonsense greeting.

"Good morning, Mr. Riley. This is Rachel Springer. I've gotten a response to my letter to your daughter-in-law. I think we need to sit down and talk. When's the soonest you can come by my office?"

"Why can't we just talk now? I've got a very tight schedule the rest of this week."

Rachel counted to four before she responded. Nothing irritated her more than a client who demanded she drop everything to schedule his initial visit and then balked at making time for further appointments required to do the work.

"If you want me to help you, Mr. Riley, you need to make time. Thirty minutes should do it."

There was silence on the other end of the phone line while Mr. Riley apparently consulted his calendar.

"I can see you Thursday morning at 10," he offered reluctantly, as though he were doing her a favor.

"Make that 10:30," Rachel volleyed in return, refusing to let him take control. Clients were just like puppies. They had to be taught who was boss early in the relationship.

More silence while he weighed the chances of pushing his luck.

"Okay, but I really can't stay long, Ms. Springer. I have an eleven o'clock appointment across town."

"Cancel it," Rachel said and hung up.

*   *   *

Georgia suggested Rock-o-la Cafe for dinner. Lots of energy for the children, and the food wasn't bad either.

When Rachel arrived home at 5:45, Belle, Mary and Ben were ready to go.

"When's Granddad coming home?" Ben asked in mid-hug.

"We said be ready at six, didn't we?"

"Yeah, but . . ."

"Has Granddad called to say he'd be late?"

"No, but . . ."

"Then he'll be home in 15 minutes, we'll take a cab to the restaurant and you'll be stuffing your tummy within the hour."

At that moment, the front door opened, and John made his timely entrance.

"What did I tell you?" Rachel asked.

Ben threw himself at John, Mary toddling after him. He picked both children up, holding one in each arm. He beamed like a young man who has just been told he's become a father for the first time.

"Everybody ready to go? The cab's waiting," he said.

Belle grabbed coats, and Rachel put Ralph outside in the courtyard.

"See you later, buddy. We'll see if we can't scrounge a bone for you," Rachel said to her forlorn friend.

"Why can't Ralph go, too?" Ben wanted to know. "He goes to work with you."

"You know he'd be good, and I know he'd be good, but the restaurant owner doesn't know that," Rachel tried to explain.

Ben would have nothing to do with it. "I'll tell him," he insisted, looking like he was about to cry.

"But then other people would want to bring their dogs, too, and some of them might not be as good as Ralph. Then what?"

Ben thought a minute or two and looked up at Rachel with big, wise eyes.

"Life just isn't fair, is it?"

"No, Ben, I'm afraid it's not."

"Me go. Me go," Mary chimed in, as if to offer herself as a consolation prize. Ben brightened up and gave her a hug, but as the cab pulled away from the curb, he looked out the back window and waved sadly.

*   *   *

Mr. Riley was five minutes late for his 10:30 appointment.

Rachel was not surprised. She pretended to forget to offer him coffee and got right down to business.

"I thought it better to show you this letter in person, rather than fax it to you, Mr. Riley. Its contents are rather serious, as you will see." She passed the single-page letter across her desk for him to read, which took him half a minute.

"This is bullshit," he barked, his face red with anger. He loosened his deep maroon tie a notch and pointed his glasses at Rachel. "I want to sue the girl for defamation of character."

"Now, just a minute. Let's take one thing at a time. You hired me to represent you in a case that involves grandparental rights. Let's not muddy the waters at this point."

"Do you have any idea what this kind of trash could do to my business?" he shouted, rising from his chair and leaning across the desk toward Rachel.

"Please sit down, sir. We need to stay calm to talk about the best approach to this. Certainly, diverting our attention in another direction may not be the best way to get what you want – which is to see your grandson, right?"

"Of course, it is, but . . ."

Rachel was reminded how like children adults can be sometimes.

"Allow me to continue, if I may."

Mr. Riley sat down again.

"What do you think has made Mrs. Riley accuse you of such egregious behavior?"

"She's nuts, that's what. Probably isn't taking her medication like she's supposed to. Used to drive my son nuts, too. In fact, come to think of it, she accused him of something equally bizarre – hitting her or something like that. Said she was scared of him. Scared of my son – a man who would fall apart if he stepped on an ant."

"Did she ever file charges against you or your son in the past?"

"No. Just threats. Constantly. It was a nightmare for my son living with the bitch. Hell, I should file for custody of the child, not just visitation."

"I'm wondering if perhaps my responsive letter to her attorney should suggest some kind mediation instead of an outright demand for your rights. Would you consider doing that?"

"Absolutely not," he shouted. "Sit in a room with her? I'd rather roast in hell for eternity."

"Why don't you at least think about it for a few days. I'll fax a letter to her legal representative, telling him we've met and will get back to him by the end of the week."

Rachel stood to indicate their meeting was over and stuck out her hand to shake his.

Ignoring it, he whipped off his glasses, stuffed them in his breast pocket and left her office, slamming the door behind him.

Georgia knocked gently moments later, cracked the door and poked her head in.

"You okay?"

"We may have lost a client," Rachel said, closing the file and handing it to Georgia.

"Won't make me sad," she said.

"Me either. I suspect Mr. Riley may be guilty as charged."

*   *   *

Some days it seems as though the world is falling apart at its seams, Rachel thought.

No sooner had Georgia shut her office door and she had settled down with a file to review than the intercom rang.

"Rachel, it's Belle on line two. She sounds pretty upset."

"Thanks, I'll take it." Georgia connected the call, but Rachel could barely understand the speaker on the other end of the line.

"Slow down, Belle. What's wrong?"

"Ralph," Belle finally got out between sobs. "I can't find Ralph."

Rachel stood up and took a few breaths before she said anything.

"You kept him in the courtyard after I left for work, right?"

"Yeah, but when I went to check on him a minute ago, he was gone."

"That's impossible. How could he get out?"

"I think somebody got in," Belle wailed.

"Belle, that's absolutely ridiculous. Who would want to take Ralph?"

Belle began to sob uncontrollably.

Rachel waited a while but soon realized a phone conversation was not the way to handle this situation.

"Belle, I'm on my way home," she said and hung up.

She put her jacket on as she passed through the lobby.

"Ralph's missing. I've got to go home."

"Want me to go with you?"

"No. You stay here. But call John, if you will, and let him know what's going on. He may need to pick up Ben after school this afternoon."

Rachel was able to hail a cab the minute she stepped out onto the sidewalk. The traffic gods were with her, too, and she pulled up in front of her house in five minutes.

She was surprised when Susan opened the front door as she got out of the cab.

"I heard Belle and Mary outside calling Ralph and came over to find out what was going on," she explained.

"Thanks, Susan. Where's Belle?"

"They're in the kitchen," Susan said, leading the way into the house. All was quiet when she opened the front door, but as soon as Belle saw Rachel, she collapsed into hysterics again.

"It's Ricky. I know it's Ricky," she wailed. "He's getting even with us because of the police the other night."

"But how did he . . ."

"I told him about Ralph a long time ago. About how much you love him and about how his life was better than ours at the shelter. I'm so afraid of what he might do to him," Belle said and buried her face in her hands.

"Let's think, Belle. Where would he take Ralph? He can't take him to the shelter, so where would he go?"

Belle seemed thankful to have a focus and appeared to think about the question.

Susan gave her attention to Mary, trying to keep the child occupied so she wouldn't add to her mother's frustration.

Meanwhile, Rachel called the city animal control department to report the missing dog. Her heart raced wildly, but she tried not to let Belle see how deeply afraid she was.

An even worse feeling was guilt that she had never installed a lock on the fence. As a way to make Belle feel less responsible, she shared her own torment.

"No, don't do that to yourself, Ms. Springer. This is all my fault, and as soon as we get Ralph back, Mary and I are leaving before anything else horrible happens."

Rachel saved her energy and didn't argue. She'd do that later.

After Ralph was home.

Shortly after she finished her conversation with the animal control office – a none-too-satisfying exchange in which a harried operator took down the information but didn't offer much hope – the phone rang.

"Hello," Rachel answered, her voice strained with fear.

"Rachel? Is that you?"

"John," she said, fighting back tears.

"I didn't recognize your voice. What can I do?"

Rachel stood silently, trying to gather her composure so she could talk. "Stop everything you're doing and find Ralph. Come hold me. Tell me everything's going to be okay," was just the beginning of what she wanted to say, but she didn't.

"I think I've done everything that can be done here, John. But Belle's pretty upset, so you'd probably better pick Ben up this afternoon."

"I'll do it. And Rachel . . ."

"Yes?"

"I love you."

"Thanks. I needed to hear that."

Not "things will be okay" from a man who had lost his son and daughter-in-law so recently. "Everything's going to be okay" would have had a hollow ring, Rachel knew. "I love you" was full of truth.

She hung up the phone and fixed herself a cup of tea.

"After I drink this, let's walk down to the Circle and see if anyone has seen Ralph or heard any rumors," she said to Belle, knowing she had to do *something* and suspecting that action was what Belle needed, too.

"We could also ask around at the shelter," Belle said.

"Great idea. And Belle ..."

"Yes, ma'm?"

"I love you."

Chapter 26

Rachel, Belle and Mary went to the shelter first, but nobody had seen Ricky since early morning. The men ate breakfast at seven o'clock and by eight were out on the streets – supposedly looking for work.

They didn't have much better luck at Dupont Circle.

Deejee pointed out what should have been obvious.

"He wouldn't bring Ralph here. We all know Ralph. He's not stupid. He's just a drunk," she said.

"I'd look over round Union Station," the clerk at Eckerd's offered. "Sometimes he hangs around there."

"Wherever he is, I doubt he's got Ralph with him," a man Rachel didn't recognize said. "After all, he didn't take him cause he wanted a pet." When he saw Rachel's reaction to that death knell, he said, "Sorry, ma'm. I shouldn't oughta said that. Sorry. I'm sure the mutt's fine."

"Just shut up, Mickey. You've done enough damage," Belle barked at him.

Seeing Rachel's pain seemed to bring Belle out of her own, and she managed to take charge.

"Let's go over to Union Station. Somebody might have heard Ricky say something. He's crazy enough to have bragged about what he did."

Rachel was doubtful but agreed to get on the metro with Belle.

The car they got on was almost empty at mid-afternoon but still filled with the smells from early morning and lunchtime commuters. Cigarette smoke, cologne and stale beer intensified Rachel's headache, and she was thankful when they reached Union Station.

It was not a metro stop she frequented. In fact, she didn't think she had been there since the place reopened after major renovations.

Despite her focus on finding Ralph, Rachel looked up with awe at the statues of Roman soldiers standing high above her on ledges around the periphery of the gigantic lobby.

"Pretty, isn't it?" Belle said. "My granddaddy used to work here. In fact, he was here the day the train jumped the track and crashed through that wall over there."

Rachel looked at the girl in amazement. "Your grandfather worked here?"

"Yeah, he was a ticket agent for years. Died of a heart attack when my daddy was six years old."

Rachel was digesting that information when she suddenly saw Chelsea, the Dupont Circle regular with the hot pink porcupine quilled-hair. She headed toward her.

"Hey," the girl said, appearing glad to see Rachel. "What you doin' at the station?"

"We're looking for my dog. You remember Ralph, don't you?"

"Sure. He's lost?"

"Well, we think somebody took him."

"Not 'somebody' – Ricky Leach. You know him?" Belle asked.

"Long braided beard and gold front tooth?"

"That's him."

"Yeah, I saw him this morning."

Rachel's heart leaped at the possibility that the girl might have a clue.

"Did he say anything about taking a dog?" Belle asked while Rachel held her breath.

"Why would Ricky want a dog?"

Rachel's heart fell to the pit of her stomach.

"He *doesn't* want a dog. He wants Rachel *not* to have one."

"That mean son-of-a-bitch. I'll kill him," Chelsea said. "Wait til I get my hands on . . ."

"Now, wait a minute," Rachel stopped her. "We don't *know* he took Ralph. Let's not go killing anyone until we're sure what happened."

The girls didn't say anything, but the way they looked at each other, Rachel knew they thought she was crazy. In the world of the streets, where nothing was fair, justice sometimes sought retribution and checked the facts later.

Rachel and Belle said goodbye to Chelsea and wandered around the station asking if anyone else had talked to Ricky that morning.

Getting nowhere, they boarded the metro and headed home. The skies were dark by the time they walked up the front sidewalk to Rachel's house.

Ben met them at the door.

"Did you find Ralph? Where's Ralph?"

"No, we didn't find him," Rachel said, pulling the little boy into her arms like a tonic.

"Oh, no. Has he gone to heaven, too? Is he with Mommy and Daddy?"

"Ben, we're not sure right now," John interjected. "Let Rachel get her coat off," he said, pulling Ben away so he could offer his own hug. Rachel buried her face in his neck.

"John, I'm scared," she whispered. He patted her back and said, "I know."

*   *   *

Rachel had a hard time falling asleep that night. Finally, she got out of bed and climbed to the third floor, realizing she had forgotten to meditate.

But when she positioned herself on her zafu and wrapped her prayer shawl around her shoulders, she couldn't focus on her breath. Ralph's window seat was palpably empty.

She tried.

Within minutes of closing her eyes, she heard the door open softly. John walked to her side.

"Mind if I join you?" he asked, placing what appeared to be a brand-new-fresh out-of-the-box meditation cushion on the floor opposite her.

Rachel smiled and closed her eyes.

Before she counted to five, she felt herself relax.

*   *   *

Rachel didn't have the same luck the next morning at work. Finally, after several attempts to get answers to questions she had about several cases, Georgia suggested her boss go home.

"I can't. Home is the last place I want to be right now. Ralph's not there."

"Why not go over to the gym and work out then? I can hold the fort here."

Rachel thought about that a while and realized it might be the most productive thing she could do. She certainly wasn't getting much done at her desk.

Belle left the house with Mary when John went to work, with the intention of continuing her canvassing of the city. She was sure she'd find someone who had seen Ralph or heard Ricky talk about taking him.

Rachel wasn't so sure.

"Okay. You're right. I'll go home and get my gym clothes and be back here around one o'clock. Can I get you anything while I'm out?"

"You just focus on taking care of yourself."

"Right. I sure didn't do a very good job of taking care of Ralph."

"Rachel, don't. This has nothing to do with you. It's about a sick man. You did nothing wrong."

"The lock . . ."

"Rachel, look at me."

She did.

"This is a crazy world. You're a good woman. Let it go."

Rachel buttoned her coat, picked up her purse and walked over to Georgia's desk and kissed her on the cheek.

"Thanks, friend. You're the best."

                    *   *   *

"We need to talk about what we're doing for Christmas," John said over dessert that night.

"Yeah, Christmas!" Ben squealed.

Rachel stared at them with blank eyes.

"Ben and I want you to go to New York with us. Maybe leave here the day before Christmas Eve and come back on the 26th. I want you to meet the rest of my family. They've heard so much about you."

Rachel still couldn't bring herself to respond.

"Grandma and Grandpa live in a really cool place with an elevator and a liberry and a pool and . . ."

"You don't have to make a decision tonight. We've still got a month, but I just thought it would give us something to look forward to. Ben and I really want you to go."

"You're so sweet. Both of you. I'm sure that once Ralph gets home I can make some plans. Right now, I just feel . . . I just feel . . ."

"Scared?" Ben prompted.

"Yes, scared. Thanks, Ben."

"I know how you feel. Granddad says to think happy thoughts when I'm afraid. Have you tried that?"

"Probably not hard enough, but thanks for reminding me."

"A hug would probably help her, too," John suggested. Ben didn't need telling twice. He jumped out of his chair, ran over to Rachel and grabbed her around her waist in a huge bear hug.

"Thanks. That *did* help. Now, how about a game of Chinese Checkers?"

"Really?"

"Really."

"You guys get the board set up, and I'll clear the table," John said.

"Thanks, John – for everything."

John smiled. "You'll love Christmas in New York. Trust me."

That was part of the problem, Rachel thought. Trust.

*   *   *

Rachel woke in the middle of the night and thought she heard a sound downstairs.

Convinced it was Ralph at the back door, she jumped out of bed and flew down the stairs.

She jerked open the back door, fully expecting to see the black dog standing there, waiting to be let in.

But the back stoop was empty.

Rachel stepped down into the courtyard and walked around the periphery of her property. That's when she noticed the hole.

She walked closer and saw a freshly dug tunnel under the azalea bush next to the fence between her yard and the Moser's property next door.

Rachel dashed inside and dialed her neighbors' phone number.

Mr. Moser answered immediately.

"Mr. Moser, I'm so sorry to bother you. It's Rachel."

"Rachel. What time is it?"

Rachel could hear Mrs. Moser in the background saying, "What's wrong? Who is it calling at two o'clock in the morning?"

"Mr. Moser, you know Ralph is missing, right?"

"Did you find him?"

"No, but I think I have a clue. I just discovered the place where I think he dug under the fence and into your yard. So, I was wondering if maybe he's gotten trapped in your shed or in your basement. I hate to bother you, but do you mind if I come over and look?"

"Not at all. I was awake anyway. Come on over. I'll meet you in the backyard."

Just as Rachel hung up the phone and turned to go back outside, John walked into the kitchen.

"I think I may have found Ralph. Come on."

She grabbed his hand and pulled him out the door with her. Mr. Moser had beaten her to the gate and swung it open for her as she approached.

"Let's look in the shed first. I was working out there a couple of days ago and he may have gone in and fallen asleep."

"Please, God." Rachel whispered to herself.

But the shed was empty.

"How about the basement?" John asked.

"We can check, but if he was down there, looks like we would have heard him bark," Mr. Moser said.

The three looked in every corner, but still no dog.

"The only thing I can figure is that he may have jumped in the gardener's van, fallen asleep and gotten a ride out of town," Mr. Moser said.

"Dear, god, he could be anywhere," Rachel moaned.

"But this is better than thinking some drunk did away with him," John said.

"I'll call Pete first thing in the morning," Mr. Moser said. "I'll let you know what he says as soon as I can get hold of him."

Rachel just nodded her head.

John took her hand as they walked back home.

"I know that was hard, getting your hopes up like that and then not finding him," he said.

Rachel couldn't speak.

John closed the back door softly, trying not to wake Ben or the girls downstairs. He and Rachel tiptoed upstairs.

"How about some tea?" John asked.

Rachel shook her head and walked ahead of him into her room. She stood at the door, looking at him forlornly. John stepped inside and wrapped her in his arms.

"Go ahead and let yourself cry, Rachel. Please trust me. Trust me enough to let me see you cry. You're safe.

And so Rachel cried. She cried like she hadn't cried when her mother died. She cried the tears she never shed when her father died and when the college love affair soured.

All the tears burst through the dam that night, and John held her while she emptied herself. Finally. Completely.

And as he kissed away the last drop from her cheek, they heard Ben in the hall.

"Granddad? Granddad, Rachel's crying."

"Yes, she is, Ben. She's sad about Ralph."

"Maybe she needs somebody to sleep with."

"Maybe she does," John said.

"I'll sleep with you, Rachel," the little boy said, running around the two adults and over to the bed and burrowing under the covers. "Sometimes a family needs to stick together."

"Guess I'm all set now, John. You can go on to bed," Rachel laughed.

"Gee, thanks."

Rachel smiled and shut the door.

Chapter 27

A week passed before Ralph came home, and Rachel was sure that those were the longest seven days of her life.

Mr. Moser called Pete Spicer, the yardman, but the dog wasn't with him out in Bethesda.

"I thought it looked like somebody – or something – had been in the back of my van," he said when Mr. Moser told him the suspicion that Ralph had climbed in the vehicle and gotten a ride out of town. "Things were turned all upside down and something had eaten my meatloaf sandwich. But I never seen him. Must have jumped out somewheres along the way."

Rachel's despair accelerated a couple of notches when she heard the report of the conversation.

Georgia called the area radio stations and asked them to announce that the dog was missing. Rachel posted pictures of him and the fact that there was a $500 reward for his return on telephone poles around her neighborhood.

When he finally showed up at the office Friday around noon, he looked like he'd been to Siberia and back. His fur was dirty and matted. One ear had a piece missing and was crusted with dried blood. He limped.

Rachel was on her way to the gym when he arrived.

She backed out the office door, trying to maneuver her briefcase and gym bag and almost fell over him.

She dropped everything when she looked down and saw Ralph sitting at her feet.

When she fell to her knees, he propped both front legs on her shoulders in what could only be described as a doggy hug. He covered her face with doggy kisses.

Georgia came outside to get in on the reunion.

"My god, Ralph. You stink," she said. "Where have you been? The dump?"

"He smells wonderful. Cancel my appointments, Georgia. We're going home."

And they did.

*   *   *

That night Ben wanted to sleep with Rachel again.

"And Granddad and Ralph," he said. "Families should sleep together. Mommy and Daddy did."

"You mother and father were married," John said. "They were husband and wife. You and Rachel aren't. You have your own beds."

Ben thought about that for a while and looked at Rachel in the way only a five-year-old can look – as though he knew something far wiser than his elders.

"Do you feel better today?" he asked.

"Much better."

"Probably because you slept with me," Ben said, driving his point home.

Rachel and John looked at each other, at a loss as to how to argue with that.

"I know," Ben cried. "Let's get married. Then we can all sleep together every night. I get lonely, don't you, Granddad?"

"Yes, I do, Ben," John said, looking at Rachel. "Very lonely."

"Do you get lonely, Rachel?" Ben persisted.

"Well, I've got Ralph."

Ben appeared crestfallen and looked to his grandfather for help.

"Of course, Ralph's not the same as you and your grandfather. You're pretty special, and I love you very much. You were so good to me when Ralph ran away. I don't know what I would have done without you."

"Does that mean we can get married?"

Rachel blushed and laughed to hide her embarrassment.

"How about it, Rachel?" John jumped in, following Ben's lead. "We could get married in New York during the Christmas holiday."

When Rachel didn't answer right away, Ben grew concerned. "I think you're supposed to give her a ring, Granddad," he whispered.

John laughed at that and reached over to take Rachel's hand.

"For now, you'll have to pretend, I guess, but you shall have a ring, Rachel, and it will be the most beautiful . . ."

"Wait a minute," Ben shouted and ran from the room. They heard his feet pounding up the stairs and doors and drawers opening and closing. Finally, he burst back into the kitchen, clutching something in his fist.

"Here, Rachel, is your marriage ring," he said, handing over an orange plastic Scooby Doo ring he had gotten at a birthday party the month before.

"Ben, it's a beautiful ring, and I'll wear it forever."

"Thanks, Ben. You saved the day. No, you saved my *life*," John said.

"*Our* lives," Rachel said and reached out to touch his hand.

"Now we can sleep together, Ralph," Ben rejoiced, throwing his arms around the dog.

Ralph wagged his tail, and boy and dog headed upstairs.

Acknowledgments

Many thanks to Mercy, the little black dog who found me and opened my heart. To my husband, Jim McMillan, who keeps it open and who patiently shared me with the characters in this book.

To my grandson, Ethan Green, for posing for its cover and for inspiring the character, Ben.

To my sons, Frank and Severn Eaton, artists who chose the difficult path. May they continue to find as much joy in their journeys as I have.

To my local sangha and our sangha leaders, Kirtan Coan and Mary Martin Niepold, for showing me the value of the meditation Rachel practices.

To my friend Catherine Wandell, for enjoying this book so much that she lived parts of it.

To Lynn Felder, who gave me a chance to write a society column, which led to enough freelance work that I have been able to live the life of a writer.

To all the lawyers I've worked for in my life – and their clients – who have taught me about people and the different ways they go about solving their problems.

Most important, thanks to my mother, who read this book as an emailed serial. And to my father, who made sure she saw it every morning. It was her love of the story and constant encouragement that keep it going long enough for Ralph to come home.

Sometimes, it really does all start with a dog.

About the Author

Leigh Somerville McMillan has written the society column for the *Winston-Salem Journal* since 1998. She wrote the non-fiction story, *Long Time Coming: My Life and the Darryl Hunt Lesson.* *It All Started with a Dog* is her first novel. She lives in Winston-Salem, NC with her husband, two cats and a dog. For more information, visit www.studiomcmillan.com.

Printed in the United States
136397LV00003B/4/P